LOCKDOWN

STORIES OF CRIME, TERROR, AND HOPE DURING A PANDEMIC

LOCKDOWN

STORIES OF CRIME, TERROR, AND HOPE DURING A PANDEMIC

EDITED BY
NICK KOLAKOWSKI AND STEVE WEDDLE

The following is a work of fiction. Names, characters, places, events and incidents are either the product of the author's imagination or used in an entirely fictitious manner. Any resemblance to actual persons, living or dead, is entirely coincidental.

Copyright © 2020

Everything Is Going to Be Okay, by Gabino Iglesias
No Honor Among Thieves, by Rob Hart
Desert Shit, by Renee Asher Pickup
The Rescue, by Scott Adlerberg
Your List, by Angel Luis Colón
At the End of the Neighborhood, by Steve Weddle
The Diamond, by Gemma Amor
Misery Loves Company, by Ann Dávila Cardinal
Apocalypse Bronx, by Richie Narvaez
Personal Protection, by Terri Lynn Coop
A Kinder World Stands Before Us, by Nick Kolakowski
The Loyalty of Hungry Dogs, by S.A. Cosby
Fish Food, by Jen Conley
The Seagull & The Hog, by Johnny Shaw
Por Si Acaso, by Hector Acosta
Herd Immunity, by Eryk Pruitt
Unscathed, by Michelle Garza and Melissa Lason
Asylum, by V. Castro
Outpost, by Alex DiFrancesco
Come Away, Come Away, by Cynthia Pelayo

Cover and jacket design by 2Faced Design
Trade paperback ISBN: 978-1-951709-17-4
eISBN: 978-1-951709-18-1
Library of Congress Catalog Number: 2020937781
First Trade Paperback publication: June 2020 by Polis Books, LLC
www.PolisBooks.com
Interior designed and formatted by E.M. Tippetts Design

TABLE OF CONTENTS

EVERYTHING IS GOING TO BE OKAY

By Gabino Iglesias

Joanna coughs twice and turns over yet again. Then she coughs again. She groans. The sound and her shifting wake Pablo up. He doesn't move. With his eyes closed, he sends a prayer up his Virgencita, asking her to make the fucking cough go away. *Por favor, Madrecita santa, haz que mi mujer deje de toser.* He accepts the prayer won't work before he's even done praying.

Joanna coughs once more, wheezes, moves again. She's looking for more than a comfortable position. She's looking for something that won't come. The old springs underneath her creak loudly as she adjusts her legs under the covers. She won't go back to sleep. Pablo groans. The coughing, like a tide, came and went all night long. It was just as bad as the night before. Pablo wonders how long it'll take for her to crack a rib.

Pablo hates himself for being so pissed at her. Poor thing would love nothing more than to stop hacking up a lung, but that seems to be out of the realm of possibility. The cough is now always there, and there's apparently nothing anyone can do about it. The hospitals are packed. There is no medicine for this. They can't even afford some of the Clorox shit the orange idiot has been talking about. They're stuck, the glue of poverty holding them down and making them powerless the same way it's always done.

Pablo tilts his head to the right and stretches his neck. Thirty years of working his ass off on the deck of commercial boats has taken a toll on his body. Everything hurts. Everything's wrinkled. Everything aches. His joints and lower back push him to stay put as much as possible, but the coughing pushes him out the door and onto more boats. Everything's shut down but people still have to eat. As long as people have to eat, his ass will be on a boat, his busted fingers smelling like fish despite the gloves he wears.

The calluses on his hands sound like sandpaper when Pablo rubs his face. The skin on his arms, face, and neck is leathery enough to make wallets from it. He feels older. Then he remembers half a joke, something about sleeping in the fridge and putting a bit of WD-40 in his morning coffee to stay young. Maybe the funny part is the half he doesn't recall.

Getting out of bed quietly is easier said than done. Pablo lets his legs slip off the edge of the old mattress, finding a pool of cooler sheet along the way, and then uses his arms to push himself into a sitting position. Joanna coughs again. This time it doesn't stop. She coughs and coughs. She sits up on the bed, a hand on her chest, her eyes bloodshot. Pablo knows she's struggling to breathe. His powerlessness smacks him on the face and slices his soul in half.

The coughing subsides. Joanna stays like that for a few seconds, gasping for air. Pablo hasn't left the bed and he already feels tired. He has to do something. He needs to get Joanna some help. Medicine. One of those ventilator things everyone keeps talking about on the news.

He stands up and walks over to the chair whose sole purpose is holding his clothes. He steps into a pair of dirty jeans and fishes out a bent cigarette from a pack that will be empty before noon. He refuses to get on a boat without enough smokes, so buying a few packs goes on his mental to-do list, half of which he knows he'll forget until the boat is far from shore. The bent cigarette looks like a yellowish worm in the dimness of the room. Pablo wants to light it and suck some warm smoke into his body. That might scare away some of the aches, maybe smooth his anger a bit. But he can't light up. Joanna's cough can be triggered by smoke. She doesn't need that, so he steps out, crosses the hallway and living room in the dark, and opens the door to the front porch. Behind him, Joanna coughs again.

There's an old wooden chair that was white a few decades ago and a table with a yellow ashtray sporting the name of a beer Pablo doesn't recall ever drinking. A small radio sits next to the ashtray, looking like a black smudge in the pre-dawn darkness. Pablo walks to the apparatus and feels around for the iPod he knows is stuck in the slot in the top of the machine. His son, Roberto, gave it to him a few birthdays ago. The small rectangle weighs next to nothing and contains more music than Pablo ever owned. He scrolls using the wheel and finds some Roberto Roena. Maybe a small tribute to his son. Pablo replaces the iPod on the machine and clicks 'play.'

A percussive explosion blasts through the tiny speakers and Pablo quickly lowers the volume. No need to wake Joanna up. There's a chance she has finally fallen asleep again.

A sound in the dawn-soaked street makes Pablo look up from the iPod. A fat Mexican on a bicycle is slowly pedaling down the middle of it as if he were driving a large car. The motherfucker is probably up to no good. Only hardworking men and criminals are up at this hour, and the Mexican doesn't look like he's on his way to a business meeting. Pablo remembers a time when living in Galveston meant you could leave your door open. Now it only means you're closer to the polluted, brown water and have to put up with drunk, annoying rich kids a few times a year. While Roena sings about santos blessing him, Pablo thinks about his upcoming gig. In a day he'll be jumping aboard the Carol Sue, a fifty-one-foot white boat, to trudge through the dark waters of the Gulf of Mexico, trying to catch as much red snapper as possible. It'll be his seventh trip with Captain Joseph "Big Joe" Weiss. They'll hit some fishing spots seventy miles off the Galveston shore. It'll take them a day to get there. Then they'll spend two days fishing and one more day coming back.

All his life, leaving for four days was no big deal. Now it feels weird. Everything feels weird nowadays. The world has changed. The damn virus changes everything in a matter of weeks. Everything is closed. The stores aren't open. They are using fucking cheap toilet paper Pablo stole from the last boat he was on the previous week. Pablo wants to leave, to be in the open ocean and forget about this damn lockdown and all the people dying, but now that Joanna is sick, the trip is a pain. Pablo wants to be as far from home as possible and wants to spend every minute trying to make his wife feel better. He suffocates in her presence because the coughing won't stop and he feels guilty that he hasn't caught it, but he can't breathe when he's away because worry crushes his chest. A lot of people survive, but he guesses those people have access to hospitals. They probably have health insurance.

Pablo gets the urge to call Big Joe and tell him he's no longer available. Then he remembers he needs all the money he can get if he's going to try to get Joanna to a hospital soon, and any thoughts of politely bowing out evaporate with the last of the morning fog. Inside the house, Joanna starts coughing again. Pablo winces, takes another drag, and starts thinking about the beers he'll be having tonight at Big Joe's place with the captain and whoever else will be joining them on the water.

Big Joe's meaty, calloused paw is wrapped around a large glass full of dark, heavy beer. He's addressing Pablo and three other deckhands from the comfort of a gigantic green chair that's been stained with every possible food.

Pablo is sitting in the left corner of Big Joe's ugly beige sofa. Next to him is Nick, a quiet, short man who's somewhere in his fifties; Alex, a thirtysomething bald Cuban with a dark goatee who's always talking about golf and cars; and a pudgy young man named Steve who Pablo hasn't seen before. They'll leave from Katie's Seafood Market on Pier 19 at noon the next day. The place is closed because of the lockdown, but Big Joe has a key to the place.

"Get ready to do battle," Joe says. "I wanna come back with those coolers full of fish. Ice, bait, gut. You know the drill. Everything else can wait. We'll work long hours. Two-hour shifts, teams of two. Stay fresh and we can work around the clock. I wanna come back to this fucking place as soon as we can. The government is butchering this thing. I wanna be with my family and know most of you feel the same way." He looks at Pablo when he says this.

"Y'all know the fish ain't biting like they used to, but we need pounds to bring in the dough. My contacts sound desperate. If we don't work, people don't eat. I told everyone we'd bring back some fish and that's exactly what I plan to do. As always, I don't want any booze on my boat. Save that shit for when we come back. I don't want one of you going overboard on my watch. Take care of yourselves and each other. Watch the hooks. Hospitals are a fucking mess right now. You fuck up, that's on you. Work clean and fast and we'll be okay. Any questions?"

Big Joe stops talking and looks at them. Pablo sees the worry in the captain's eyes. Fishing in the Gulf of Mexico is a billion-dollar industry, but not much of that lands in their pockets. Folks like them catch shrimp, oysters, blue crab, and several species of finfish, but the big money happens elsewhere and ends up in hands that have never held a net or a fishing hook. Big Joe has three kids, two of them in college. They all came back for Spring Break a couple days before everything went to shit. Now they are living with Joe and taking their classes online. They're probably eating everything in the house. The captain needs money as bad as Pablo does. That's why they're going to focus on the American red snapper, the iconic Gulf fish. Its market price goes up every season, and that's a good thing. With the way things are now, their price is even higher. Everything is flying off the shelves and into refrigerators. They will sell everything they bring back at a decent price. Too bad the number of fish they catch has been going down in the last few years. If all goes according to plan this time, they'll catch ten to twelve thousand pounds of red snapper on this trip. That's about fifty thousand dollars for Big Joe. Each crewmember will be paid a couple thousand dollars, depending on how much they individually catch. Pablo plans on working overtime and packing his coolers to the gills. He knows it won't be enough, but it might be enough to get them to a hospital. Steve interrupts Pablo's thoughts.

"What do you guys do when you get bored out there? This lockdown shit has me going crazy at home. I don't wanna also go crazy on the boat." At the beginning of the meeting, Big Joe said something about having a greenhorn on the boat and smirked. Everyone knew he was talking about Steve.

Pablo looks at Steve's hands. They look like he's never seen a gaff hook. He has the loose mouth and shiny eyes of a drunk.

"You won't have time to get bored," Pablo says. Big Joe finishes his beer and taps the glass against his leg. That signals the end of the usual speech. Everyone mumbles a goodnight and suddenly Pablo finds himself standing around with Steve and a lukewarm beer. He wants to talk to Joe about maybe getting a bit extra from his next check.

Steve gets up and approaches Pablo. He starts telling a story about his father, a man who owns a used car lot in El Paso. Pablo tries to tune out. Big Joe is by the door, cracking a joke about social distancing on a boat being a trip to the can. When Joe comes back, Steve keeps talking. He's one of those men who process alcohol by flapping their gums endlessly. Joe says he's gonna check on a few emails, pulls out his phone, and walks to the kitchen, leaving Pablo with Steve.

Twenty minutes later, Steve's recounted his last six years working for his father and the fact that he swindled forty-two thousand dollars in small bills and ran away because his dad is an asshole. Steve keeps saying he refuses to sell used cars for the rest of his life. That, he says, is the life of a fucking loser. He's been living in his car and cheap motels since he ran away. He smiles as he says this, apparently proud of having stolen from his father. Pablo knows revenge is a powerful thing only made more vicious by sharing the same blood, but says nothing. Steve keeps talking.

"I don't like having the money in the car, but I can't take it to the bank because all of the banks I've seen are fucking closed. And I can't carry that shit with me, you know? I need to keep it close until the old man gives up looking for me. I'm gonna jump on some boats and make a few thousand bucks while this whole lockdown thing blows over and then use the money to open up my own business in Portland. I have some buddies up there. It's also fucking far from El Paso. Ha ha! I'm gonna open up a coffee joint specializing in exotic blends. Portland is full of hipsters, man. They're gonna flock to this place. I've been there before and Portlanders love coffee. I'm gonna be swimming in money in no time."

Pablo looks at Steve's eyes and sees the pudgy man is sauced, his words pouring from his mouth fast and slurry. He hears Joanna cough inside his skull, sees her sitting up in bed and gasping for air like a fish out of water. "Listen," Pablo says, "Katie's garage is a small place, just an old shack right on the pier. You don't want to leave your car there with the money inside. Take my garage. I'll drive you down to the pier. You can find some other place to stash it when we get back, but it'll be safe while you're gone."

Steve pats Pablo on the shoulder and thanks him before asking for his address. Pablo realizes for the hundredth time in his life that youth and stupidity are synonymous.

When Pablo's cooler has enough ice for the morning's first haul of snapper, he moves to a wooden workstation attached to the edge of the boat. His spot is beside one of the ship's six hydraulic bandits, mechanical reels that allow them to catch thousands of pounds of fish in a matter of days. It's six in the morning—only orange glowing lights from neighboring oil rigs shine in the darkness. Pablo's head is buzzing. They've been on the water all night. They're starting the trip back home in a few hours. The lack of sleep has made Joanna's cough louder in his head. He imagines coming home and finding her dead in their bed and something thick and warm grows in his throat. He can't check the news, but he reads a bit of his phone when he takes a shit.

The lockdown is getting worse. People are dying. Hospitals are getting full. New York is fucked. Pablo knows it's now or never.

Knowing they're about to start reeling in the hooked line, Big Joe switches on the boat's floodlights and, after an audible thunk, the bow of the boat is illuminated in a bright yellow glow. Pablo and Steve are working together. Big Joe said that was the only way they'd keep the greenhorn from fucking up the equipment, the boat, or himself. Pablo feels something tightening in his chest. The feeling makes him think about Joanna. He hears her coughing again. Before leaving, he sat out on the porch, smoking a cigarette and listening to Roberto Roena while wondering if his son was okay. Inside, Joanna, after giving him the kind of kiss that still made him feel things after a life spent together, was coughing again. The memory helps the tightening in his chest to subside.

"You ever eat a snapper tongue?" Steve asks Pablo, his hands struggling to unhook a fish from his line. "They don't have tongues," Pablo says dismissively. Then he thinks about Joanna again and changes his tune. "That thing coming out of their mouths when we pull them up? That ain't a tongue, man; it's their stomach. They get the bends, just like divers. The decompression blows their stomachs out through their mouths."

Steve looks at the fish in his hand, turns toward the ocean, and vomits. Pablo sees the man's silhouette against the orange-tinged sky and drops his line. In a second, he thinks about getting the car keys from Steve's rucksack half an hour earlier as the man slept through their two-hour break. That was the first move. He also took his floatation vest and placed it behind a cooler. Steve woke up and got to work without asking for it. All greenhorns do it. They forget. It's normal. Now Pablo only needs to do the damn thing. He takes two steps and grabs the buoy hook from the wall next to the cabin's entrance while looking at the door to the cabin. The others are probably sleeping. Big Joe is in the wheelhouse. The coast is clear. Pablo turns to Steve. The man is spitting into the ocean, coughing a little. The coughing is almost too much.

Pablo knows he has to put everything he can into the swing. Steve has to hit the cold water completely knocked out or he'll scream. Pablo pulls the buoy hook back and swings with all his strength. The thick metal pole hits Steve's head with a loud thunk that shoots pain down to Pablo's elbows and makes his shoulders feel like they're about to pop out.

Steve's head snaps to the side and his left arm flies up. He stays there for an endless second before exhaling a strange moan and going overboard, his legs stiff.

Pablo leans over starboard and peers into the water. Steve is facedown, bobbing in the dark water and already drifting away from the boat. His clothes will soon pull him under. Pablo will head inside and use the bathroom. He'll sit down and take a shit. Let a few minutes go by. He'll read about the lockdown while he's in there. He'll send Joanna a text saying he loves her. Then he'll come back out and scream for Big Joe. Steve is just another idiot who made a mistake. He slipped and slammed his head. He wasn't wearing his life vest. Happens all the time. Fucking greenhorns. That's why there are ads for commercial fishing accident attorneys all over Galveston. This is a dangerous job and many fishermen lose their life every year. The floor is slippery with water and blood. Lack of sleep makes them sloppy, careless. A tired greenhorn drowning is no biggie. The story is not new or weird or unique. Steve slipped and cracked his head before going overboard. Everyone has heard of stuff like that happening before. It happened while Pablo was inside taking a dump. He had to. It's nature. No one will blame him for taking a few minutes to hit the can.

Pablo replaces the buoy hook on the wall and looks to starboard again. He keeps expecting to hear a scream or to see Steve's hand grabbing the boat. Neither happens. He walks into the cabin and heads to the small bathroom. He remembers the fat Mexican on the bicycle. Maybe he was just going somewhere early. Maybe he was going back home after having sex with some chola a few blocks down. Maybe he lived nearby and was out for a ride because being locked inside drives people crazy. Everyone has a fucking story. Pablo just wants this one to be over. He wants to hold Joanna and tell her they're going to be okay. He has the money to take her to a hospital now. Yeah, everything is going to be okay.

Again, he thinks he's being jumpy. Houses make noise. Especially big, old houses with dips in the floor from where the wood has warped.

Except, usually the reason the wood groans is because someone stepped on it. This one sounded suspiciously like that spot in the kitchen, just inside the sliding glass door. That particular creak etched in his mind. He hears it a few times a day now, when his office feels too claustrophobic and he needs to take his laptop onto the back deck for some air.

Roger sits, swinging his feet onto the plush carpet. Looks at the bedside table. Considers the contents of the drawer: a black case with a fingerprint scanner on the outside. On the inside is a Rohrbaugh R9 Stealth Elite, a lovely little gun built from aircraft aluminum that weighs less than a pound when unloaded. He could have gone for something bigger, something with more stopping power, but he also never thought he'd actually have to fire a gun in his own home. If anything, it would be a visual deterrent.

Karen liked having it there. Sometimes she would bite his ear and whisper: "Take it out. Make me yours."

He pretended she wasn't talking about the gun.

Roger sighs. Listens. No more sounds from within the house. But what's the point of having it then? He opens the drawer softly, so Karen doesn't wake, takes the box out and presses his thumb to the pad. The latch clicks and he opens it. He takes out the gun and a clip, then puts the box on the floor and slides it under the bed with his heel. He steps into the bathroom to load the gun and chamber a bullet, so the harsh metal *clack* doesn't wake Karen, either.

He feels silly holding it. And anyway, who would be breaking into houses right now? The thought had crossed his mind the other day, even struck him as funny, as he considered all the industries that were going to suffer from this. Surely the field of home invasion would hit hard times, what with everyone suddenly home.

It made him think about the trip he took into his office yesterday. For years now, there's been this guy at the corner of William Street and Exchange Place, between the Thai restaurant and the vape shop. Every day, sitting with his coffee cup and his sign about… something. Roger pulls the buoy hook back and swings with all his strength. The thick metal pole hits Steve's head with a loud thunk that shoots pain down to Pablo's elbows and makes his shoulders feel like they're about to pop out.

Steve's head snaps to the side and his left arm flies up. He stays there for an endless second before exhaling a strange moan and going overboard, his legs stiff.

Pablo leans over starboard and peers into the water. Steve is facedown, bobbing in the dark water and already drifting away from the boat. His clothes will soon pull him under. Pablo will head inside and use the bathroom. He'll sit down and take a shit. Let a few minutes go by. He'll read about the lockdown while he's in there. He'll send Joanna a text saying he loves her. Then he'll come back out and scream for Big Joe. Steve is just another idiot who made a mistake. He slipped and slammed his head. He wasn't wearing his life vest. Happens all the time. Fucking greenhorns. That's why there are ads for commercial fishing accident attorneys all over Galveston. This is a dangerous job and many fishermen lose their life every year. The floor is slippery with water and blood. Lack of sleep makes them sloppy, careless. A tired greenhorn drowning is no biggie. The story is not new or weird or unique. Steve slipped and cracked his head before going overboard. Everyone has heard of stuff like that happening before. It happened while Pablo was inside taking a dump. He had to. It's nature. No one will blame him for taking a few minutes to hit the can.

Pablo replaces the buoy hook on the wall and looks to starboard again. He keeps expecting to hear a scream or to see Steve's hand grabbing the boat. Neither happens. He walks into the cabin and heads to the small bathroom. He remembers the fat Mexican on the bicycle. Maybe he was just going somewhere early. Maybe he was going back home after having sex with some chola a few blocks down. Maybe he lived nearby and was out for a ride because being locked inside drives people crazy. Everyone has a fucking story. Pablo just wants this one to be over. He wants to hold Joanna and tell her they're going to be okay. He has the money to take her to a hospital now. Yeah, everything is going to be okay.

NO HONOR AMONGST THIEVES

By Rob Hart

Five minutes ago

Something wakes Roger up.

He's not sure what it is. He just knows it was *something* that pulled him from dreamland and left him staring at the white expanse of his bedroom ceiling. Mouth sticky, bladder full, head pounding a slow and steady beat thanks to the three glasses of Lagavulin he had after dinner.

He glances at Karen. Her back is to him, her body slowly rising and falling. Just them in the house. Just them in the house for a month now, and given the state of the world, it's not like sleep has been easy—hence the Scotch—so he shrugs his awakening off to a general sense of discomfort. Like a fly buzzing around his head that he can't quite swat, so he may as well get used to it.

Try to get some rest.

But then he hears it, or maybe hears it again?

A groan from somewhere in the house.

Again, he thinks he's being jumpy. Houses make noise. Especially big, old houses with dips in the floor from where the wood has warped.

Except, usually the reason the wood groans is because someone stepped on it. This one sounded suspiciously like that spot in the kitchen, just inside the sliding glass door. That particular creak etched in his mind. He hears it a few times a day now, when his office feels too claustrophobic and he needs to take his laptop onto the back deck for some air.

Roger sits, swinging his feet onto the plush carpet. Looks at the bedside table. Considers the contents of the drawer: a black case with a fingerprint scanner on the outside. On the inside is a Rohrbaugh R9 Stealth Elite, a lovely little gun built from aircraft aluminum that weighs less than a pound when unloaded. He could have gone for something bigger, something with more stopping power, but he also never thought he'd actually have to fire a gun in his own home. If anything, it would be a visual deterrent.

Karen liked having it there. Sometimes she would bite his ear and whisper: "Take it out. Make me yours."

He pretended she wasn't talking about the gun.

Roger sighs. Listens. No more sounds from within the house. But what's the point of having it then? He opens the drawer softly, so Karen doesn't wake, takes the box out and presses his thumb to the pad. The latch clicks and he opens it. He takes out the gun and a clip, then puts the box on the floor and slides it under the bed with his heel. He steps into the bathroom to load the gun and chamber a bullet, so the harsh metal *clack* doesn't wake Karen, either.

He feels silly holding it. And anyway, who would be breaking into houses right now? The thought had crossed his mind the other day, even struck him as funny, as he considered all the industries that were going to suffer from this. Surely the field of home invasion would hit hard times, what with everyone suddenly home.

It made him think about the trip he took into his office yesterday. For years now, there's been this guy at the corner of William Street and Exchange Place, between the Thai restaurant and the vape shop. Every day, sitting with his coffee cup and his sign about… something. Roger had never bothered to read it. Another sad story in a city full of them. Every day he saw the man—bald head, heavy beard, thick military jacket even in the summer—sitting on a pile of blankets, empty coffee cup perched next to the sign.

Every day the man just sat there.

Until yesterday, when Roger needed to go into the office for files he didn't have access to electronically. Karen asked him not to go, to have someone who actually lived near the office go over and scan them, but there was a reason those files weren't on a computer. And he was curious to see the emptied-out city. As he stepped off the 2 train, coming up into the chilly, overcast day, he found the street to be completely deserted.

Except for the beggar.

It was easy enough to ignore him when the streets were filled with people. But Roger found himself almost immediately locked into prolonged, awkward eye contact. The man started to speak, and Roger turned, intent on taking the long way around to his office building, so he wouldn't actually have to pass him. But the man got up and followed. Calling after him: "C'mon man. Just help me out. I know you saw me."

The man relied on foot traffic. The shelters were currently giant petri dishes. Things must be getting tight. Which was making the man aggressive. Desperate. Roger turned the corner and ran the rest of the way to his office. When he left, he lingered in the lobby to make sure the coast was clear, before walking up to Fulton Street to get back on the 2 train.

And as he steps out of the bedroom he thinks: maybe that's this. Desperation. As the matrix of the thought knits together, he realizes his hand is shaking. He looks down at the gun, puts his finger on the outside of the trigger guard. He steps onto the runner in the hallway to muffle his steps and makes his way through the darkened house.

Telling himself, with every step, that this was the house settling, or any number of rational explanations. But still, comforted by the fact that his hand isn't empty.

That, and by the state-of-the-art security system.

It dawns on him then: if someone broke in, the alarm would have gone off.

By the time he reaches the bottom of the stairs, the tension has disappeared from his shoulders, and he feels foolish, walking around an empty house with a gun. Still, no way is he getting to sleep now. Surely another glass of Scotch will help.

Ten minutes ago

"Explain to me again how this is supposed to work," Keith says, making sure to keep his body concealed by the shadows cast by the tall hedges.

It's not that Keith doesn't believe Mauricio. He just wants to hear it one more time. Because this isn't their usual gig.

He isn't getting cold feet. Never did, never will.

He just wants to hear it again.

"This is the deal," Mauricio says, looking up and down the empty sidewalk, making sure they're alone. "I pulled the FCC filings on the security system, which is wireless, right? And the filings include the frequency range that the sensors use to communicate with the base station. And it's a common frequency, same one used by stuff like garage door openers and baby monitors, right? So this." He holds up a black plastic brick with a stubby antenna. "Handheld radio. Broadcast it over the same range, right? Except, this is five watts, whereas the sensors only have, like, a couple of milliwatts? This'll be screaming while they're trying to whisper to each other."

"Drown out the signal," Keith says, glad for an analogy he can grasp, because a lot of the time when Mauricio talks, he just hears a dull thrum. "You sure this'll work? You got the right security system? Do they all use the same range?"

"They don't, except…" Mauricio nods his head toward the house. "Guy has that little placard on his lawn, saying which brand he uses. It was on Google Street View. And I have to tell you man, I just, I wonder when these guys are going to smarten up, right? Like, stop making our job so easy?"

Our job.

He says it like this is a typical gig.

Except, again, it is not.

Their typical gig didn't involve a home in Westchester, surrounded on all sides by a mile of suburban streets, so that there were no crowds or train stations to disappear into. Worse, everyone being home means way more opportunities for nervous neighbors to clock them. Keith and Mauricio did not exactly give off "Westchester vibes."

Bradford, the guy who hired them, looked like he was born in a country club. So even sitting in a dark SUV at 3 in the morning, he'd be fine. He dropped them off a few blocks away, promising to wait at the corner of Oakwood and March.

Normally, Keith would not throw in with a trust-fund looking kid with glasses more expensive than most of Keith's wardrobe. But he handed him and Mauricio five cool—each—with a promise of another ten after the job was done.

Fifteen, each.

On top of the payday, Keith and Mauricio were welcome to take anything they came across in the house. Anything they could take that wasn't tied down. But the goal—the thing Bradford wanted more than a kid wants cake—was a file folder.

Again, not the typical target. Usually Keith went after things he could sell, drugs he could flip. How was he supposed to tell the difference with paperwork? But Bradford said the guy had only picked it up yesterday, and chances are it'd be sitting on the desk.

"This thing is so valuable you're hiring us to get it," Keith said, as Bradford drove up the Saw Mill River Parkway. "He won't have it locked up? In a filing cabinet or something?"

Bradford shrugged. "He's home all the time. Gets his groceries delivered. Just him and his wife there. What's the use of putting it away?"

It stood to reason. Still, Keith was good at finding things. Especially in the dark. A childhood of hiding at night gives you a good sense of space, an eye for details. What's important, what's not.

What's safe, what's not.

So he was optimistic. More than that, he was a little fired up. They didn't often take clients. But Bradford had tracked Keith down, to the stoop of the Bushwick brownstone where he rented a damp basement apartment that reeked of mold. And after the initial pitch, Keith laughed and told Bradford to fuck off. Sure, the money was good, but the risk didn't level things out.

"Things are different now," Bradford said.

"How so?" Keith asked.

"Because, look, this guy works for a bank, right? And what's that bank doing right now? Is it helping people with easy access to loans? Is it reaching out to businesses? Is it pitching in to help? Or are they looking out for themselves and their investors? They're like Smaug."

"Smaug?" Bradford furrowed his brow. "The dragon from *The Hobbit*? Hoarding gold."

"Okay."

Nerd.

"Doesn't matter," Bradford said. "It's time for the banks to pay their fair share. Me and some people, we're working together on this. You're going to help us take them down a peg. *Redistribute* things a bit."

Keith looked down the block, at the endless stretch of aluminum gates. The other way, and the line outside the bodega on the corner. Thought about his neighbors trading dried beans for toilet paper, waiting for salvation that a bunch of people in Washington were currently arguing over whether they deserved.

"Think about it," Bradford said. "He rides this out in the lap of luxury. Why? Because he's good at manipulating pretend numbers? Help us."

Keith was surprised to find himself nodding along. Yeah. This bank guy, in his big house, more food than he needs, more money than five families need to survive, is just there. Like he didn't have to climb a whole lot of shoulders to get there, leaving those people he climbed over scrambling for his crumbs.

Yeah, things were different now.

Mauricio clears his throat. Keith checks his watch. Just past three in the morning. The burgling hour. Too late for the insomniacs, too early for the up-and-at-'ems.

"You ready to do this?" Mauricio asks, holding up the radio.

"Yeah man," Keith tells him. "Let's go slay us a dragon."

Mauricio doesn't understand, but he doesn't care to ask.

They move quietly through the grass, sticking to the shadows, mindful of sensor lights that would force them to scurry for cover. They get to the rear of the house, next to the sliding glass door, the view from the neighbors blocked by high fences and more shadows from the back deck.

Mauricio holds up the radio, his hand tenses, and he nods.

Then Keith climbs the stairs of the deck and goes to the sliding glass door. Grabs the handle and pulls, ready to create a tiny opening so he can slide the tip of his knife in and pull up the latch—sliding glass doors always had the shittiest latches. And he nearly tumbles when the door just yanks open.

The sound of it grinding in the track makes him hold his breath. He ducks down, listening for dogs, even though the Facebook and Instagram accounts of the people who lived here didn't indicate they had any. Dog people always let you know they're dog people.

Silence. Stillness.

He laughs under his breath. "Dumbasses," he says.

Keith steps inside, feels the floor give a little and groan under his foot, but it's not so bad. He moves slower, allowing the house to meet him, and makes his way slowly toward the staircase and what looks like the office beyond.

Now

"Where the file?" Keith asks, a small, smooth gun now in his hand. And a fresh, sizzling gouge in the flesh of his left arm. The pain hasn't set in yet. The adrenaline roaring through his blood is holding it back.

Roger crab-walks away, ears ringing from the shot he managed to squeeze off before he lost the gun in the struggle. He alternates hands over his face, like that might somehow protect him from a bullet. He wonders about Karen. If she heard the shot. She must have. Even through the gauze of vodka and Ambien, she had to have heard. The neighbors must have heard. Someone.

Keith grips the gun tighter, aims it with purpose. "The file."

"What file?" Roger asks, glancing at his darkened office.

Keith rushes past him, into a room with so much mahogany it smells like a forest. Desk and cabinets and bookshelves, all of it gleaming in the dim light coming through the windows. Where the fuck is Mauricio?

Roger looks between the office and the kitchen. He could get up. Run to the knife block. But he would still be in the man's line of sight. The hallway was long. No way Roger would make it before the man managed to put a bullet in his back.

Keith goes to the desk, which is clean and neat. There's a small stack of folders next to a closed laptop and an empty rocks glass. He grabs them and goes back to the man. "This it?"

"Is what them?" Roger asks.

"The file."

"What file?"

Keith lifts the bundle of paper. Grimaces. The pain is arriving to the party, along with rationality. Is the wife calling the cops? Are they on their way? Cops around here don't have much to do but hassle kids and answer home invasion calls.

Roger doesn't understand how this guy can know about the file. How could anyone have known he picked it up? He was alone. The bum saw him, but that was just a bum. Was someone watching? His stomach flips. The whole reason the file wasn't on a computer was because of how sensitive it was. Offshore accounts. Names and dates. Good for fifteen to twenty in a federal penitentiary, for Roger and a dozen other people.

Keith's rationality starts losing out to the pain. He goes to the man and kicks him hard. The man falls onto his side and groans. "Is this the file you picked up from the office yesterday? Is this it?"

Roger nods. No sense in lying. Is it worth his life? "Yes. Yes, it is."

Keith trains the gun on him. "Swear to me."

"I swear." Keith looks around the house. It makes him think of a museum. Sparse and clean and white. Everything expensive. Like you'd be afraid of even sitting on the couch because they'd make you pay for it. Anger surged through him. Why this man? What did he do? How did he earn this? What did he contribute to the world? The anger burning in his chest is enough to slay a dragon.

Roger sees something move in the shadows behind the man. It's Karen, hoisting a crystal vase. She brings it down hard and it shatters on the man's head. He jerks and fires the gun and Roger feels like he's been punched in the chest.

The pain in Keith's arm disappears, relocated to his scalp. His head feels full of loose change, and he tries to turn to see what happened, but the ground comes up on him fast, and then his head slams into something with no give.

Karen drops the shattered remains of the vase. Help, she thinks. She needs to go get help. That's the only word in her head. Help. Followed by: Maria. Her neighbor. Go to Maria. Maria can help. Maria always helps. Karen runs into the cold night air, clutching her bathrobe tighter, bare feet slapping against the stone walkway. Help. She needs help.

The house is still.

Until there's another groan from the spot inside the sliding glass door, and Mauricio comes upon the crumpled figures. He heard the struggle and the shot, and it's been quiet long enough that he knew he needed to venture inside. He found the front door wide open, which told him he didn't have long.

The man who lived here, he's bled out from a gunshot wound to the chest. Right in the heart, it looks like. Mauricio drops to a knee next to Keith, whose eyes are glassy, neck kinked at an unnatural angle. He came down hard on the edge of a stair, his head a mess of black and red sticky stuff.

Keith was a good partner. Smart, reliable. And honest, as far as anyone can be honest in this field of work. But that didn't mean there was time to mourn. Occupational hazard. Mauricio scoops up the paperwork splayed across the floor, hoping it's what the guy who hired them was looking for. He looks around for something to grab, anything he can keep or hock for himself, but he knows he needs to get gone.

With nothing of value in his immediate field of vision, he opts for the back door.

But first he pauses and looks down at Keith. He kneels down and presses Keith's eyelids closed. He's seen it done in movies and it feels like a kind thing to do. Because at least now he looks peaceful.

"Goodnight, brethren," Mauricio says.

Then he hoofs it hard to the rendezvous point a few blocks over.

The car is there, like it's supposed to be, and Mauricio breathes a sigh of relief. He'd never been above Yonkers or below Staten Island, and he'd have no idea how to get home from someplace he couldn't see a subway line or hail a cab. He goes around to the passenger side as the kid starts the engine, then opens the door, the interior light washing the inside of the car in yellow.

Mauricio tosses the file on the seat, but before he can climb in, the car takes off, knocking him to the ground as it speeds away, swerving so that the door slams shut. Mauricio struggles to his feet and watches the car turn the corner, red taillights disappearing, and then it's just him on the quiet street.

In the distance he's sure he hears a siren.

Bradford blasts through three blocks before he drops the car to a reasonable speed, then merges onto Boston Post Road. He digs the burner phone out of the console and dials 911. When the operator picks up, he says that he heard gunshots, then saw a suspicious male at the corner of Oakwood and March. He tosses the phone out the window and digs out the second burner. His boss answers on the first ring.

"How'd it go?" he asks.

"Got the file," Bradford says.

"Damage report?"

"Well," Bradford says, drawing it out. "It wasn't clean. Two shots fired. Only one of them made it back to the car, and he looked pretty panicked. I suspect collateral damage."

"You took care of both of them, though? And there's nothing to trace them back to you?"

"Of course not. You know me better than that."

"Good, good." Bradford's boss inhales, then exhales. "You did good work tonight."

"Just remember this come quarterly bonus time, okay? And I'm not officially asking for Roger's corner office. I know Connor has seniority. But I'm just saying that I've had my eye on it."

"Connor may have seniority, but he doesn't have your… moral flexibility."

"Sure," Bradford says, laughing. "Let's call it that."

DESERT SHIT

By Renee Asher Pickup

It seemed like the easiest idea. Everyone was already wearing masks. No one was paying attention if you kept your sunglasses on and made sure to keep your distance. The cops were busy trying to ticket people who were going mask-free, not a worry in the world about a couple of girls leaning into the no-makeup look with their masks, sunglasses, and hats pulled down over their faces.

The governor told people not to move house. Again—fucking perfect. All we had to do was identify a house that wasn't occupied and didn't have an alarm, and we had a place to lay low while we waited for Kat's contact to move the merchandise. You'd be surprised what people will pay top dollar for when they can't go fuck off at Target for two hours and impulse-buy shit to make them feel like working forty hours a week provides them some meaning.

There are a total of four real grocery stores in a fifty-mile radius out here. You've got to drive another hour if you want to stock up on TP or cleaning products. And guess what everyone is scrambling for in a pandemic? Bleach. The stores couldn't keep it on the shelves. No bleach jugs, no disinfectant wipes, no Scrubbing Bubbles. The last thing they were going to do was tell people when the next shipment came in, because no one at a grocery store in the middle of the godforsaken desert gets paid enough to break up a fight between a libertarian desert rat and a trust funder from LA who just "fell in love with the vibe" after coming here to do mushrooms and see god. Kat and I worked in the stockroom, and we didn't get paid enough for anything.

The day we did it, no one we worked with even recognized us. We just walked right through the store, right to the loading bay, and heave-hoed every last pallet of bleach that came in. It wasn't until I closed up the back of a truck Kat's on-again off-again boyfriend lifted for a joyride that I realized she'd topped our haul off with a little extra.

"Seriously? Ramen and Ho-Hos?"

She laughed. "You can't get this shit anywhere right now! I've gotta eat."

We were offloading the bleach into the garage of the tiny two-bedroom that just sold to some jackwagon wanting to turn it into an Airbnb when both our phones started screeching with an emergency alert.

EMERGENCY ALERT:
San Bernardino County in full lockdown. Return home immediately. Shelter in place to include previously essential employees. Check local media for details on food delivery and restrictions.

"This is a joke, right?" Kat asked.

I unlocked my phone and went to the local radio station's news page. All county residents to shelter in place, do not go outside, do not pass go, do not collect two hundred dollars. The only "essential employees" were now first responders, cops, and medical professionals.

"Okay. Okay. It's fine. It's not immediate. People have to have to get home from wherever they are. Just call your guy and tell him to come now. No one gets anything if we leave it in this garage."

"Mike doesn't like when plans change," she said.

"Well, Mike is going to have to get with reality, Kat. It's not our fault."

She insisted we finish unloading the truck before calling. I don't know why I didn't argue. Kat and I had been stealing beer and scamming tourists for free drinks since high school. We were always getting into desert shit—joyriding with guys Kat liked, starting fires, fucking with tourists. Everyone loved to party with the chicks that could get anything, and it didn't hurt that we were always a couple shots from getting back to our old habit of feeling each other up, regardless of who was watching. That's why Kat and her boyfriend broke up so much. I'm sure if I signed up for a semi-regular threesome with meth-teeth, he'd like me fine. But I don't do dick. Not even for Kat.

This was supposed to be like stealing beer. And not even as serious. Technically, the ATF is on your ass if you steal booze. Whose job is it to regulate cleaning supplies? Isn't that the reason you hear about drug dealers taking payment in Tide?

We wanted it to be as easy as it sounded. So we pretended it was.

It took half an hour to unload the bleach. Both our phones were pinging with news alerts and texts from friends and family, asking where the hell we were. It wasn't just San Bernardino County. It was the entire state of California. I turned my notifications off. By the time Kat called her guy, he was squirrely. Told us to pull the truck into the garage, shut the fuck up, and wait. Kat tried to argue. I yelled to be heard through her phone.

The first night I was just happy Kat grabbed the case of ramen. It took twice as long to get the noodles soft just using the hottest water that would come out of the tap, but it was better than sitting in an empty house with no food. The next day, I saw the first patrol car. It was irregular enough to make me nervous. It would be a thirty-minute gap one time, a ten-minute gap the next. Then he might cruise up and down the street a few times before going somewhere else. Facebook was filled with videos from friends recording the same thing. Streets empty but for patrol cars.

At about four that afternoon, I said: "Mike's not coming."

"He'll come. He just has to figure this shit out."

Kat. Always hopeful.

"The cops are patrolling the streets. No one is getting in or out. I saw a cop stop and ID a grocery store delivery guy dropping food off at a house down the street."

She was intent on denial. Mike would figure it out. We'd get to leave. And hey, at least we had air conditioning and running water. At least we had ramen.

If Kat was intent on denial, I could be convinced to be intent on distraction. I pulled the phone charger out of my bag and cuddled up against the wall with her and watched the funniest videos we could find. She played with my hair. I played with her everything. We passed two more days like that. Ramen, animal videos, fuck, repeat.

None of the updates were updates. Just stay home. Food deliveries from local grocery stores would be supported. You can use your EBT. You can't leave the fucking house. Mike stopped responding to Kat.

I was pacing the empty living room with its brand-new terra-cotta tile while Kat rinsed off in the shower. It didn't do much, but it was better than just stewing in our own grease and oils without trying to wash it off. She came out soaking wet, letting her baggy tee-shirt soak up the excess water, and said, "We're going to run out of food."

I stopped mid-stride, felt my mouth hang open, was sure my heart stopped for a second. Kat is all bubbles and rainbows. All "let's just smoke some weed, and it'll be better by the time we sober up." All "everything's going to be okay" even when there was no fucking way something would be okay. But she's not an idiot. She'd been watching the patrols through the blinds. No amount of fucking and looking at kittens falling asleep was going to make it okay to order grocery delivery to a house we weren't supposed to be in, with a garage full of stolen shit.

I didn't have anything to say.

"I mean, you know I'm right. We're lucky we had anything. We can't get anything delivered here. We can't tell anyone where we are. We're fucked."

I tried to pull something out of my stunned silence that might make it okay and came up empty.

"We have to leave," she said.

"Kat. The cops..."

"Fuck the cops! We'll figure it out. They patrol less at night. I stayed up last night. During the day it's at least once an hour. At night it was every hour and a half at best. Plus, it'll be dark. There's an alleyway behind this place's yard they can't drive through. We can walk all the way to Park on it. That's like a half-mile from my place. We can just go in and pretend we were there the whole time."

I went to the window again. The coroner's van was in front of the house across the street, and everyone was in Hazmat suits. I watched them pull three body bags through the front door.

"Have you been ignoring the news?" I asked.

"Who cares about the news? It's all the same. Stay home or get arrested."

I turned to her. When she saw my face, the color drained from hers.

"I've been ignoring the news," I said.

Kat ran up to the window as a fourth body bag came through the front door. "People die," she said.

"Everyone in that house just came out in a body bag."

She started to smile like I was fucking with her, then looked out the window again. "Why are they wearing that shit? I thought the masks were enough?"

"They just pulled four fucking body bags out of that house, Kat," I heard the tremble in my voice and almost burst into tears.

"It's not the virus," Kat said.

I swallowed the rock in my throat, but knew if I opened my mouth it would rocket out with tears and panic.

"It can't be," she continued. "That had to be some murder-suicide shit, Annie. I don't care if they didn't have insurance or the hospital was full, one person dies, someone is going to call 911. They wouldn't just sit there while they died off one by one. No one would do that. No one would sit with the corpse of their kid or husband and not call 911. It's not possible."

I went to the wall where my phone was plugged in and slumped to the floor. Kat had a point. This was some kind of super bug, but no one just up and died from it. It had only been a few days since we were in a grocery store full of people. Only a week or two since we were drinking at the bar with our friends.

"It's just desert shit. The husband was probably methed up or going through withdrawals because he couldn't get it. That's it. Desert shit."

"Desert shit," I repeated.

I didn't take my phone off airplane mode. I didn't check my messages. I just repeated her words in my head like a mantra. Kat was right. She had to be.

I convinced her to watch the cops one more night. If it was every hour and a half again, we could go tomorrow. We still had some food. We had to be smart.

When I woke up at dawn, my back and neck were in knots from sleeping on the hard floor too many nights in a row. My hair was greasy and had a doggy stink from being wet but not washed the day before. I would have killed for a toothbrush. The cops had come by at more frequent intervals during the night. We still had food. We'd have to wait.

The house across the street was taped up with a notice on the door. I'd seen it before, stuck on places that had become a meth lab. It's too dangerous to enter once those chemicals have soaked into everything. Kat was right. Kat was always right.

Then I looked up the street to the next occupied lot, and my knees almost let out. Another van. More Hazmat suits. More body bags. I opened the blinds wider and peered further down the road. At least two more houses were marked off like busted meth labs.

I ran to my phone and pulled it off airplane mode, then went to my texts. I stopped notifications the day we stole the bleach. It was easier to pretend my mom wasn't blowing up my phone than try to come up with a lie.

The same handful of messages over and over for days:

Where are you?

Answer the phone.

Where are you?

Please answer the phone.

Annie, I love you, I don't care where you are, I don't care what you're doing, please just tell me you're safe.

Where are you?

Answer the phone!

PLEASE ANNIE, ANSWER THE PHONE

I talk to my mom once a week at most. I ignore her texts all the time. I had 127 notifications from her alone. Dozens of missed calls. My heart sped up so fast I thought I might pass out. Kat was still fast asleep, curled up on the tile in a position that was going to absolutely fuck her neck up. Waking her when I was amped up wasn't going to help, I tip-toed into the kitchen and sat on the floor with my knees pulled to my chest and opened up my news app:

Death Toll In California up 300%

Virus Mutation "Unprecedented."

Hi-Desert Medical Center Not Accepting New Patients

Vice President Hospitalized With Virus, Dead in 24 hours

POTUS Dead

Red Cross Volunteers Wiped Out in High Density Areas

I barely made it to the sink before I puked up a stomach full of noodles and fake chocolate gunk.

"Annie?"

Kat heard me retching. I turned on the garbage disposal and rinsed my mouth out, trying to think of anything I could say that wouldn't blow us both into full panic. When she came to the doorway, wiping her eyes, I spat out, "We should have been answering our calls." Then I burst into tears.

Kat's heart is so big, she can't do anything but go into mothering mode when someone else is losing their shit. She didn't ask questions, didn't start checking her phone, she just ran to me and held me while I sobbed. When I was calm enough to speak again, I stepped back, wiped my face still stinging with tears, and took a deep breath.

"My mom has been calling non-stop for two days. I have over a hundred texts from her."

Kat tilted her head, squinting at me, then pulled her phone out of the back pocket of her jeans. Her fingers swiped over the glass and she pursed her lips.

"My mom hasn't tried me since the day we got the bleach." Her chest heaved and I watched as she shook her head and tried to convince herself to stay calm. "But… that doesn't mean anything, Kat. Does it?"

"I read the news."

I let the statement hang in the air while she did the mental math. She left the kitchen without saying a word and went to the living room window, splitting the blinds less than an inch. After what felt like hours at the window, she silently went back to the wall we'd been eating, sleeping, and fucking against the last few days.

"This isn't real," she said, sitting down.

I was still standing half-in, half-out of the kitchen, trying to keep my emotions in check despite the thoughts speeding through my brain and the fact that my stomach desperately wanted to push more up and out of my mouth. "It's really bad. It's really bad everywhere. We still have food, we should stay a few more days, see what changes. Maybe they'll figure something out. Maybe the… the fucking National Guard or the goddamn Marines will deploy medical help, I don't know. But…"

I ran out of things to say. Kat nodded silently, wiped her nose on the shoulder of her shirt, shut her phone off, and laid down again.

The fifth day we were there, the electricity went out. A few hours later, the water was off, too. It was the fifteenth. People couldn't move houses, they couldn't rent Airbnbs, but that didn't mean they had to pay utilities on all the places they couldn't be. Within hours, it was so hot in the house we stripped down to our dirty underwear and bras, fanning each other with our sweaty t-shirts.

"I can't do this. We have to get out tonight," I said.

Kat nodded. "The patrols are less regular now. I think maybe too many cops…" she trailed off but we both knew she was going to say "died." Too many cops died to send them up and down every street in town. Besides, the only houses not taped up in this neighborhood were the empty ones. Even if they had enough healthy, living cops to patrol the neighborhood, why would they bother? Dead people don't spread viruses.

Then, the awful thought: Fuck, what if they do?

I fought the urge to Google whether California was burning corpses.

"We have to wait until a couple hours after sunset, 'til it's really dark. We can do what you said, creep down that dirt alley until we hit Park Road and then… then we see what the hell is happening. Maybe if the cops aren't around here, they're not around your place, either."

Before it got dark, we went into the garage and found the masks we'd cast aside when we were unloading the bleach and they made our faces sweat. I looked around, hoping the old owners had left a shovel or a hoe, anything that might work as a weapon if we ended up needing one. No dice. Kat used her teeth to break the plastic on top of the bleach pallet and then tore it away.

"These are a few gallons each. If we swing them, it'll hurt. Maybe buy us time."

"We won't need to fight anyone. Everyone is at home." Or dead.

Kat shrugged and pulled two off the pallet anyway. We went back into the dark house and sat. Then paced. Then sat. Neither of us looked out the window. There wasn't anything to see, nothing to make what we were about to do feel safer. We couldn't stay there, and that was all that mattered.

When the sun finally went down and the temperature started to drop, instead of feeling relief at the cooler air coming through the open window, the tension grew into ropes in my stomach and knotted together until it climbed up my throat and nearly choked me. I wanted to ask Kat if she was okay, but I knew she wasn't. I knew if I asked, I wouldn't be okay, either.

Finally, it was dark. I told Kat to turn her phone off and sit in the dark with me for a while so our eyes could adjust. We went out the sliding glass door in the back bedroom, each carrying a bottle of bleach and hoping we'd get to her place and laugh at how stupid it was to take a jug on a walk in a deserted neighborhood. The back fence was chain-link, and we both got over quickly, but Kat ate it on the way down and winced when she stood up and put weight on her left foot. Twisted ankle.

We talked about how important it was to stay silent as we walked through the alleyway. We couldn't afford for anyone to come looking to see who was whispering. It was dead quiet, no lights on in any of the houses for blocks. I told myself it was the nature of quarantine. Nothing to do, nowhere to go, so you pass out at eight-thirty or nine when it gets dark and you've watched enough trash TV to last you all year. Kat was still limping. If we hit the end of the alley and had to sprint, we were in trouble. There was a lone streetlamp at the end of the walkway, and I kept staring at the area it illuminated, praying not see anyone.

When we hit Park Road, I paused to study the fire station a little further down. The bay doors to the garage were open, empty. I looked around, and only saw one house with a light on.

"OK," I whispered, hoping Kat could make out what I was saying through the layers of bandana I had wrapped over my lower face before we left. "I think we're good. We just have to get out of this light."

We crossed the road as quietly as we could and ducked into a pocket of blackness on the other side. Kat led me to another dirt alley and waved me in after her. I followed her through the dark, both of us looking over our shoulders every second or third step. We got to her neighborhood and I had to keep myself from sprinting to her house. Her perfect little manufactured shithole seemed to scream at me, begging me to come inside and be safe.

We looked at each other, and, with a nod, agreed we were just going to do it. Out in the open, walking, not running. Just get to the house. We made it three steps before a stern, muffled voice said, "FREEZE."

Kat dropped her bleach bottle. I held my breath.

The man in a Hazmat suit walked closer but stopped a good ten yards away. "What the fuck do you two think you're doing? You think you're special? You think this thing won't kill you like it fucked over everybody else?"

Kat said, barely audible, "Please don't shoot."

The man came a few steps closer. "I can't hear you, honey, but I have orders to shoot people breaking quarantine on sight. I can fucking see you, can't I?"

Quieter, Kat repeated herself. She closed her eyes and held a wince.

I found the strength to speak from somewhere deep in my gut. Held up the bleach. "Sir, please. A friend left these outside for us. We needed to disinfect. That's all. We live there." I pointed to Kat's house. "Just let us go back. No one has to know."

The man didn't take the gun off of us. I couldn't see his facial expression. The flashlight he was shining at us made it impossible to see anything but his outline. His posture seemed to soften, though.

"Goddammit," he said. "Fine. I won't call this in. Just get your asses in the house. And do not fucking come out again. This isn't a joke. If I see you again, I will shoot you. And if someone else sees you? Well. You'd better hope they're as nice as I am. Go." He motioned toward where I'd pointed with his pistol. "But I'm not taking this gun off of you until I see you inside."

Kat slowly crouched down and picked up her dropped bleach bottle with a trembling hand. I noticed I was shaking, too. My breath was ragged and hot inside the folded-up bandana. We walked slowly around the man with the gun, keeping space between us, and then to Kat's house. I wanted to run so bad I could barely stand it. When I looked over my shoulder, the man still had the gun on us. I put my hand on Kat's shoulder to remind her to walk. To remind myself.

Kat tipped over a flowerpot and pulled out her spare key. When I head the lock click, my body relaxed. We got inside, locked the door, and pulled off our makeshift masks.

"Holy Christ," I said, laughing.

Kat smiled big and walked toward the bathroom. "It's my house, so I get to shower first."

When I got in the shower, I turned the water so hot it burned. I scrubbed my body with the washcloth so hard it felt like I was using steel wool. I wanted to wash the last five days off of me—the stink, the sweat, the general grease of living without soap. I wanted to wash anything that might kill me off my skin, too.

When I came out, Kat tossed me a t-shirt and pair of shorts and pulled out her weed stash. "Let's get so high we don't wake up until this is over," she said.

After two hits from her pipe I couldn't handle any more. It relaxed me, but not enough to make me think I could afford to come off high alert. The idea of being too stoned to function was tempting and terrifying in equal parts. Kat took a third hit and started coughing so hard the vein in her temple pressed out against the skin and her eyes bulged. She kept coughing.

"Holy fucking shit," she wheezed between body-racking coughs, her eyes red and wet. "Fuck. I hope I'm not sick."

"You're not sick. You're sucking down shitty weed after a week of inhaling nothing but AC air."

I believed it when I said it.

Kat turned her swamp cooler on high and we sat under the vent and stared up at it until we started to shiver.

"Come on. Come to bed. Everything is going to feel so fucking awesome after a night in a real bed."

I bet she believed that when she said it, too.

We got in under her sheets, no comforter, and she turned her back and pushed up against me. I put my arm around her waist.

"Hey, Annie?"

"Yeah."

"When this is over, I don't want to be friends anymore."

My heart stopped; I instinctively pulled her closer. "What? Why?"

"That's not what I mean. It's always been us. We've always been together. I couldn't have done all this shit with anyone else. I don't want to. I don't want to keep fucking around. I don't want to be a girl to you anymore. I want to be *your* girl."

"Ah, Kitty," I said, nuzzling her neck. "You've always been my girl."

"Is that a yes?"

"Of course it is."

She sighed what sounded like a happy sigh and wiggled her butt against me. A few minutes later her breath went slow and steady. She was asleep. I held her close against me and tried not to think about the heat coming off her skin or the rattle that came with every exhale.

I tried not to think about the article I read on my phone while she was in the shower. Symptoms can take up to a week to show in an otherwise healthy patient. Once coughing and fever are present, the virus progresses quickly. Death can occur in as little as 24-48 hours.

THE RESCUE

By Scott Adlerberg

The bureaucracy never rests, and neither do those who guard it. Here's what I mean:

The virus had been spreading and killing for three or four weeks when the commissioner gave the telework order to our agency. Everyone considered non-essential to the agency's operations would, until further notice, be doing their job from home. Since our agency is the one that collects taxes and fees for New York, you better believe that most every employee working for it is essential, but what the commissioner meant is that everyone who could conceivably work at home would do it that way. Needed for that: a personal computer, not much else. We'd be given remote access to the agency data systems we used all the time. There'd been talk over the last fortnight that telework was coming, but the actual implementation of it happened fast. We came in for business as normal Monday, and the commissioner sent out his agency-wide decree via email late that morning. Tomorrow, on Tuesday, we were not to come in, and our lives as public servants who could work with a laptop in bed, wearing pajamas, would begin.

That final afternoon was hectic. I transferred necessary files to a Zip drive, gathered papers and notes. *Is there anything I'm forgetting?* I kept thinking, because I didn't know when I'd be able to return to my office. They might lock up the municipal building until the virus danger passed. Or they might allow in commissioners and division heads and upper-echelon people like that and prevent entrance to regular staff and the midlevel managers like me. Plus, since I am in charge of fifteen people, I had to hold a meeting with those reporting to me and lay out a plan for how we would function as a unit from our homes. Nobody sounded upset to be going under lockdown, not with the virus on the upswing, ravaging the city, the death toll increasing daily, but they had their concerns about working under quarantine.

"My computer is old and slow."

"If CityTime doesn't work, can we do our timesheets manually?"

"Hope this doesn't last too long. My wife and I together all day..."

I clocked out two hours later than usual, and not until I was in my apartment, sitting on the couch having dinner, the TV on across the room, did I think about the one thing I'd left behind that I should have taken home with me—my plant. Somehow, unfathomably, I'd forgotten it. I'd overlooked it because of the day's craziness, the thousand little things I had to arrange and remember. Fuck!

Pachira aquatica, my lovely Guiana chestnut.

It stood on a corner of my desk where it could catch sun through the window. Bright green leaves, the tall braided trunk, the white pot. I had it on a tray covered by wet gravel. No one knew how long this telework situation would last—maybe weeks, perhaps months—and my little money tree required water often. The species I had comes from Brazil, the swamplands. A long lockdown would desiccate and kill it. And don't get me started on the fertilizer I use, a top-of-the-line product. If I didn't retrieve my plant soon, it would die, and I couldn't allow that to happen. The plant meant too much to me. It connected me to what I could not give up. I saw Octavia, my wife, watching me with her arched-eyebrow doubtful expression, and I said to myself I couldn't let her down.

"I won't disappoint you," I said. "I'll get the plant."

I hope she believed me.

"Stop looking at me like that."

I went back to eating, shaking my head, laughing while I chewed my food, aware of what grief can do to a person.

Whatever. We all suffer and have our relapses.

Octavia had bought me that plant, and I couldn't let it sit in my office and die.

In the morning, I phoned the head of my division, an assistant commissioner, to inquire whether we'd be allowed back into the municipal building. As non-essential employees, that is. I explained that in yesterday's rush, I'd neglected to copy a file on my computer desktop, something I had to get as soon as possible. It would help me with a project, viral outbreak or not, uncertainty in the city and world notwithstanding, I was expected to finish by deadline.

"The one you and I discussed," I said. "With the commissioner. I'm supposed to give him an update by next week."

I could hear the AC's dog barking and her daughter talking in the background. The AC would be spending the lockdown time with her family: husband, the two girls, their pet. That might not be so bad, really, if they were a family that got along and enjoyed most of their time together, and I compared it to my own circumstances.

With me, well, in my apartment, and what I'd be staring at during the quarantine period…

"How could you forget that file?" the AC asked.

"It's not like they gave us much warning."

"They didn't, no. You should get it, though, yes."

"The building's open?"

"Far as I know."

Clarity isn't a strength of bureaucracy, even to answer a simple question like is our work location accessible, but I took what she said as good enough for a go-ahead. Come what may, I'd attempt the mission to rescue the plant. But if she was wrong and the building was locked, or if it was open and the security people on the ground floor refused to let me in because I didn't have some special authorization, I'd be forced to figure out a way to break in, though my office was on the 24th floor. How would I do it? And what if I failed? I could see the news story already:

`City Worker Arrested. Tried to Enter a Government Building to Get His Plant. Said, "Smirk if you must, but we all have our companions. I merely wanted to please mine by bringing it through this crisis."`

Yeah, if I got caught, I might just say this, and the more I imagined myself saying it, the more I thought I'd elicit sympathy if I did.

"The guy wanted his plant. He's put in the time with it. Invested his emotion in it. Gonna throw him in prison for that? Now? Of all times? Fuckin' people are dying left and right, losing their jobs, don't know what the hell's to come, and locking this guy up's a priority?"

I laid out my mask and gloves, ready for the expedition.

With so few people outside, the playgrounds empty, the basketball courts chain-bolted, the delis open but quiet and somber, no one lingering at the counter to talk and joke with the person at the register, my Bed-Stuy neighborhood had an eerie feel, and when I descended into the subway, I found myself on an empty platform for the first time in my life. I could smell the disinfectant the transit authority had sprayed—another first—and listened to the loudspeaker tell me the importance of social distancing and of washing my hands regularly. No zombies or mutants or post-apocalyptic beasts shambling about, but a number of solitary individuals were in the subway car I boarded, masks on, eyes wary, seated or standing as far from the next person as they could. These were the ones without a choice but to go to their low-paying jobs, I assumed, and the thin black lady with death in her face in the best of times was there, trudging through the cars begging for money, and so was the guy repeating his line that he hadn't eaten in three days, could someone spare food or change, he'd appreciate a dime or a nickel, anything you could give him. The homeless remain homeless, I thought, and don't change their routine one iota for the lockdown, and I did my best, despite my protective dishwashing gloves, to touch no one and nothing, not the poles or the seats or the doors. The train rattled and I stood with my legs spread for balance, stomach muscles clenched. I jumped out at Chambers Street, hurrying toward the stairs.

Fresh air.

But this goddamn mask.

It felt hot and itchy and I wanted to yank it off.

Don't do that, not till you're inside, and don't touch your face.

Lower Manhattan and its grid of streets was nearly deserted, and I had no trouble keeping distant from others as I made my way to the muni building. I pushed the button, the doors swung open into the lobby, and the security crew glanced at me with their familiar disinterest. Okay then, no issues. I nodded hello and used my key card at the turnstile.

I was in.

Upstairs, after getting off the elevator, I swiped open the door to our unit's area, a long and wide space filled with workstations—desks, chairs, screens, keyboards, partitions—and walked past everyone's stuff to my office. Manager's privilege, I guess. A spacious private office within the general office, with a door I could close. I didn't need to flip the light switch; the sun was shining through the windows and all the blinds were up.

There it stood, verdant and healthy, on my desk. But why wouldn't the plant be fine? Thinking about it all last night and since waking up today had made it seem as if I hadn't seen it in ages, but it had been less than twenty-four hours since I'd been here. And I'd watered it two days ago.

The bag of fertilizer I put in my backpack. I lifted the plant in its pot. I'd resigned myself to leaving the tray with the gravel, since it was too cumbersome to carry, but I knew I could arrange something at home that would serve as a moist bedding.

On my way out, at the door to the hall, I looked back at everything. Several people in my unit had plants, and I wondered if anybody else would feel guilty for leaving theirs behind. Would anyone make a trip over for a rescue, flouting our agency's orders and risking infection? I suspected not, but then again, who among my group felt as strongly about their plants as I did about my Guiana Chestnut?

I had to put it down on the elevator floor to push the lobby button, and when I arrived at ground level, I picked it up with two hands. The subway, as I considered it, might be difficult; it'd be easier to grab a taxi.

"Sir?"

"Take care," I said.

The guy at his station, in his security guard jacket, held up his hand. The woman back there beside him, dressed in the same brown pants and jacket, the identical transparent gloves, asked me to put the plant on the counter. I saw these people every weekday and sometimes said good morning to them, but each had a hostile and remote appearance as they eyed me over their surgical masks.

"Should I sign out?"

"Yes," the guy said, his voice not unfriendly. "And do you have a slip for the plant?"

"A slip."

"You took that from your office, didn't you?"

"I did. I'm bringing it home."

"You need the slip to take anything from your office."

"What are you talking about?"

"The authorization form," the guard said. "You should know that."

Here's where I paused, observing them both. Could this guy be serious, or was this his version of city security guard humor? Bureaucracy in the time of the virus: a farce.

"I own this plant," I said. "I brought it from home and now I'm taking it back. If I don't, it will die."

"It's coming from your office," the guy's partner said. "You need your superior to sign the form."

"I'm an authorized signer. You're gonna make me go up and get the form?"

"You can't sign yourself out."

"My AC is at home. Like everyone else."

"Sorry, sir."

"I could understand with supplies," I said. "Maybe. But a plant?"

"We can't let you out."

And what would they do, from behind their island's black marble top? Neither had a weapon that I could see, and even if they did have one tucked away in there, would they pull it out and shoot at me if I bolted for the lobby exit?

"To me, this plant's important. My wife bought it for me years ago, and since she's been gone, what can I say, I feel I need to have it close to me."

"Sir, can you bring it back upstairs, please?"

"Did you hear what I said? My wife got this for me, and if I leave it here during the lockdown..."

That's when the idea came, brilliant in its simplicity.

I reached into my coat and plucked out my mask as if about to put it on, but before I lowered it over my head, I reared back as if losing control. The cough I unleashed had droplets in it, drawn from my mouth and throat, and I'd stepped forward when in the act to close the gap between me and the guards.

"I need to go," I said. "Not feeling well. I wouldn't have come out at all if not for my plant."

They were yelling as I departed, swearing at me as they wiped at their faces, and I was still laughing pretty hard when the cab I hailed from the curb pulled over so I could get in.

Octavia laughed as well when I got home. Or she would have, had she been capable of it. I knew that if I knew anything. She lay on the living room couch in her dressing gown, hands folded across her chest, long black hair parted in the middle, and I could tell she was pleased with me.

"I told you I'd keep this healthy," I said. "Authorization form my ass."

Her weak heart had claimed her—nothing to do with the pandemic—and at some point, I'd have to call someone to take her away.

The smell was starting.

But once I gave in and let her go, I would have the plant, living and fragrant.

It would be my company for the quarantine.

YOUR LIST

By Angel Luis Colón

The first thing you did was make a list.

All the things you already did—keep the routine.

All the things you wanted to do—may as well, there was time.

All the things you'd never do—a reminder that you had limits. That you would not let this make you into something that was less of you.

Life in quarantine wouldn't be easy, but you convinced yourself that you could find structure, and through that structure, you'd navigate a path over to the brighter side. It wasn't denial or a delusion that life would be easy; it was simply a way to digest the truths and work past the stress so you could survive—and maybe emerge with six-pack abs as a bonus.

And it was easy? The first two weeks were unnerving in their long silences between conference calls, but otherwise things were uneventful. You watched the world from out your window on the 10th floor of your building. Scoffed at joggers and teenagers grouping together on bikes. You made a point to recognize the people who always went without masks and wondered if you could memorize the eyes of those who did. You reminded yourself this feeling of ease wasn't meant to last forever. Two weeks was a drop in the glass. What if this went on for two months? Two years?

It wasn't pessimism; it was realism.

You bought a lot of "things." Snacks. Grocery items you never even glanced at when you could go to the supermarket. You disinfected everything the courier brought to your door—even the off-brand disinfectant wipes. You bought a treadmill. It worked great until it became a clothes hanger. You started to bake. Your sourdough starter matured the way the guy in the YouTube video said it would. You made three whole loaves of bread and ate them all within a week. Pajamas were now formal wear.

The wail of ambulance sirens, you grew used to them. You knew things would calm down. They said so. They said the curve would flatten, that staying inside and keeping away from the most at-risk would be beneficial in the long term. You clung to that belief because what else was there to believe in? And the news proved those words true. They told you the death tolls were going down. They said that tests were being made available.

Then why did it feel like the sirens were becoming a constant sound throughout the city? Why were your neighbors being carted away on stretchers, their hands scratching at their necks as they rasped indecipherable goodbyes to their loved ones or gurgled desperate pleas to remember their confused pets?

You reminded yourself to hydrate. You worked out twice a day—the abs were showing, a miracle. You traded the bread for other, healthier treats and trimmed down your grocery list. You discovered the joy of a bidet toilet seat and decided it was impossible to go back to the two-ply trash you'd been indoctrinated to believe kept your ass clean. Your work calls were easier. Your productivity was through the roof and your superiors made promises that none of this would affect their employment numbers. You were safe in the bubble and even though your doorman mentioned an entire floor below you was sick, it didn't worry you. You were doing everything right.

You were safe.

You were not safe.

Another neighbor, this time down the hall, taken in the middle of the night. Their cough like mourning in catacombs—deep, guttural—echoed well after they were gone. The sirens were ever-present. They drowned out every noise. They drowned out the clapping at night—support for those who buried more than they saved. The news remained the same. Hollow optimism. Racist dog whistles. Fingers pointing blame at foreigners or others who defied the norm. You watched looters from your window. They all looked like you. All in great shape. They took pet food and toilet paper and televisions out of the closed stores down the avenue. They reveled and hollered.

None of those looters looked like the ones on TV.

You checked your list. Your routine was airtight. The list of things that interested you, all crossed out. You were a master baker and able to do jumping push-ups without effort. The quarantine was the best thing that ever happened to you.

You ignored your desperation list. The list that contained looting. The list that mentioned suicide. All the things you knew would happen if things went too far. But it was OK. Things were not going too far. There was a light at the end of the tunnel.

Lies.

You were not safe. You would never be safe.

You knew that as soon as you heard that coughing again. This time it was through your thin walls in the bedroom. The coughs boomed. Like thunder. Like a hammer pounding against the foundations of the building. You did your best to ignore them, but maybe it was a good idea to take precautions. You sealed your bedroom windows with plastic and tape—just in case. You investigated the seams in the floor and crown molding in the room. You sealed any gaps you found with extra caulking by hand because you never invested in the stupid gun. You checked every inch of your walls for holes or other entryways for air from the other apartment.

The actions felt safe, but you didn't feel safe when you were done. You were restless. Legs constantly moving whenever you sat still. Your heartbeat audible. Was that shortness of breath? Why did you feel a tightness? How could that be possible? Was there a place you forgot to seal up in the walls and doorframes?

You didn't feel safe when that same coughing erupted near your front door. You repeated the plastic and tape routine again. This time for your door and your living room windows. Set it up so you could open the door when it was absolutely necessary and reseal quickly. You checked the entire apartment. Used your window fans to make sure you weren't suffocating yourself to death. You checked your vents—were these safe? Were you better off sealing them? It was getting warmer. Wasn't like you needed heat, and air conditioning wasn't necessary either. You were home. If you got hot, you could take a nice shower or use a cold compress to cool off.

You made a note to remember to check the carbon monoxide/smoke alarm batteries every few weeks.

Your boss asked you if everything was OK. Your hair was getting shaggy. You looked pale. You were wearing heavy metal t-shirts during important video calls. You let that sourdough starter starve. You were ordering so many more snack cakes and chips than you ever did before. That damn treadmill couldn't hold more pants and you wouldn't dare to take the trip downstairs to the laundry room, no, not after you heard the doorman sniffling the last time you called downstairs to check on a delivery. No, no, no. You decided the tub was a great place to wash your clothes anyway.

The coughing started again. You looked through your peephole whenever you heard it. Then you checked whenever you heard footsteps or the sound of someone using the trash compactor. You had to know who it was—who was infected. You waited for the EMTs to arrive any day. Another body for the meat wagon. Another siren joining the chorus out in the streets.

You started making facemasks with some of your older clothes—especially the older work clothes. You couldn't imagine going back to the office anymore. Your co-workers seemed to share the sentiment. They were looking like you—even your boss. Everyone asked each other if they were OK and everyone said they were. You figured that was great. They were all being safe. Safe, just like you were.

You didn't feel safe.

The coughing was growing louder. This time two coughs. Both deep and bellowing. Both from the same apartment. You stared at your walls when the fits started, willing them to stop. Willing the virus to go away. The thought of it didn't scare you as much as it disgusted you. You wondered what it was these idiots did to get sick. Why did they lack the common sense to self-isolate? How did they have the unmitigated gall to place the building and its residents at risk? You found yourself ready to scream, ready to stomp your feet and point at that damn wall to tell these people a thing or two about hygiene, good health, and being a considerate neighbor.

You kept checking through your peephole and imagined what they looked like. Were they Chinese? No, that was terrible and racist to assume. You stopped yourself then. You voted Democrat. You weren't like that. You were just concerned about your health and your neighbor's health. You remembered seeing the stretchers and the sirens. This wasn't about hate; you were simply concerned—deeply concerned.

It felt like weeks, but you finally caught sight of one of your neighbors on a Saturday night. Young man. Dressed very well. He was drunk. He coughed into the crook of his elbow while he was talking on his phone.

"Nah, man. They setting up speakeasies now. My boy told me about one in the Bronx. Been hitting that up."

Speakeasies? You didn't understand. Why would anyone want to go out and risk infection? Why would this idiot put the whole building in that kind of danger? The rage you felt nearly sent you out the door, but you stopped yourself. You didn't have any clean masks and your gloves were on back order. It wasn't worth the risk. Not worth getting sick over this idiot's incredibly irresponsible behavior. Instead, you stomped into your bedroom and found your notebook. You grabbed your list and made a new one.

Things to do to my neighbor if he gets me sick, you wrote.

You wrote about breaking down the wall like a blood-starving Kool-Aid Man. You wrote about crafting a makeshift flamethrower with a bottle of Lysol and a barbecue lighter. You wrote about drowning them in a shallow pool of whatever hand sanitizer you could spare. You wrote about stapling masks to their faces; if they didn't want the responsibility, then you would make them accept it.

It was cathartic and relaxing. You felt safe for the first time in weeks. Felt like there was a level of control in your sphere for the first time in mental decades even if you stayed home all day, worked, watched the news, and continued ordering kitchen utensils you'd never use—a garlic press, really?

They coughed. You added to your list.

They came in late at night. You added to your list.

You wondered if this was healthy, but after a week it didn't matter. This was as normal as working from home and as never going outside or knowing what it was like to feel obligated to bathe. Your new normal felt like home and it was worth it.

Then they went and knocked on your door.

"I'm sorry," they said with a smile, "I know we're supposed to be social distancing and all, but I can't believe I'm about to ask if you had any extra paper towels?"

You examined them from six feet away. Their skin looked clammy.

They were disheveled. Smelled like sickness the way a private practice does during flu season. That light stench of sweat and Vicks VapoRub.

They watched you. Leaned forward with an arch of their brows. "I'm sorry if this is a bad time."

"It's fine," you said, surprised at the sound of your own voice. When was the last time you spoke to someone who wasn't on a computer screen? You felt like you should be wearing a headset. "I think I can spare some. Are you sure one is enough?"

They looked confused. "Yeah, I got some coming. Why do you ask that?"

"I figured for your wife or roommate or whatever," you answered. There was more than one cough. You heard two people coughing. You weren't crazy—yet. You ducked into the kitchen and got the paper towel roll. Pinched it at the hole and held it out like someone trying to catch a saving hand as they fell off a cliff.

"Oh, uh, thanks." They took the roll. "Just me in there, though. Maybe a friend came over, I don't know."

Another wave of rage sent you reeling. 'I don't know'? How did they not know? How could they possibly be so dim? This was a pandemic—a historical and unprecedented event. The death toll was not subsiding and this chucklefuck was living free. They didn't give a damn about anything but themselves and if you had a knife right there you would have carved the message loud and clear across their throat in bold red letters: SELF-ISOLATE.

You didn't have a knife. No. Not a knife. Would have taken too long, and while you never really thought about it, you were pretty sure the sight of blood would give you a surreal level of anxiety. What you did have was the dread. The panic following. The feeling of tightness in your chest that crawled its way up into your throat like a fat tarantula. Your hands brushed along your neck. You felt as if you could squeeze it out of you, burst it like a pimple.

"You good, man?" Their voice was the finger on a trigger.

Maybe it was the anger. The pent-up emotion that isolation stacked haphazardly within you without supports or scaffolding—a tower of logs swaying sky-high in a gentle breeze—and all it took was their hot breath to send it all crashing down. Maybe it was loneliness. Maybe it was the desire to finally feel something warm in your hands. It didn't matter in the moment, not as much as it did in the aftermath, but you strangled him. You strangled him as hard as you could.

But it wasn't enough.

That treadmill. The workouts. All those things on your list that you followed like scripture for the first couple of weeks. The efforts you ignored because your spirit became a black hole to motivation; it would have been in your best interest to continue those list items. Instead, your rage gave you the ability to severely overestimate your strength and underestimate your neighbor's ability to send you tumbling backwards into your dinette. The sound of glasses crashing to the floor—all half-full—accompanied his ragged breathing as he mounted you and vented his own frustrations on your face and solar plexus.

You scratched at air. His breathing wormed through your ears. You remembered all the warnings. The social distancing. The incubation period of the virus. The virus' sustainability in airborne droplets of saliva. Once you noticed your neighbor's fists were red, you wondered if the disease was transmittable through blood.

He stood up, out of breath. A cough rising out of him that threatened to heave out his insides. You scrambled away, the glass on the floor piercing your hands and back, until you could find the wall to lean on.

"I fucking knew it," you said. "You're sick. You're fucking spreading it, you piece of shit."

Your neighbor wouldn't stop coughing. He grabbed at his chest with one hand and covered his mouth with the crook of his other arm. He swayed like a boxer trying to keep his legs just seconds before the sound of the bell. Between coughs, he gasped and tried choking out words, but they were indecipherable.

You found your strength—what little of it—again and stood up. You matched his movements. It was a sloppy drunk ballet. "I could hear you. I could hear your little fucking friend too. Going out. Playing around. Spreading this fucking disease. How many people do you think you've killed, eh? How many old ladies are coughing their fucking lungs out now? Look at you." You pointed at him mockingly. "Poor you. Keep coughing, motherfucker. Keep fucking coughing and die. We need you all to wipe yourselves out. Then we can get back to normal."

You didn't have to wonder if you meant the words anymore. It was what you felt. This quarantine made you an honest person for the first time in your life. It didn't matter anymore; you could simply be you. So you watched him cough and you reveled in it. The chant in your head, 'Die motherfucker, die,' repeated until your wish came true.

Weeks later, you remained in isolation. The death toll spiked again. The rules became sturdier and less likely to roll back. But you were ready, and you were content to live the life you now felt at ease with.

Of course, there'd been the aftermath of the bastard next door.

They came within minutes of the last dry breath. Three officers all wearing personal protective equipment from head to toe. They collected the body and put you in handcuffs. They questioned you.

"I would have killed him," you told them, "I wanted to kill him. But I didn't. I was too weak." The truth set you free, even if they wanted to lock you up. But they couldn't. This was your property and the body was at the threshold—proof that your neighbor had entered without consent—flimsy proof, but hey, a win is a win—and the police had no interest in dealing with anything else once you told them he had been coughing and coughing. With that ghost of a threat in the air, everyone wanted to be out of your apartment. They left you back to the bliss of solace.

You made a new list, though. You realized you needed to be ready in case anyone else tried to spread the disease to your safe space. You cleaned the treadmill off. You wrote up an exercise regimen. You watched hours of videos on knife handling and throwing. You decided to keep a kitchen knife within reach of your front door—knives within reach of all doors.

You were feeling good, though. You lost five pounds in two weeks. You brought your sourdough starter back to life and found some great new recipes to try over the weekend. You even landed a brand-new contract for work with minimal effort.

You sat on your couch and checked emails. You finished your mint tea—and made a mental note to order more teabags. You closed your eyes and listened to the sirens a moment, a mental break to remember what the world was like. All that death and chaos outside would be unbearable, but you knew you could make it. You had your head back and you had your new list. Everything would work out, even if you didn't feel safe. Maybe it was better to never feel safe; to embrace that the world was now at war with you and the only means to succeed in this war was to simply survive.

Or maybe you'd walk away from this a really great baker.

Then you coughed.

AT THE END OF THE NEIGHBORHOOD

By Steve Weddle

The garage door lumbered closed, and I stepped out of Nancy's new-to-us car as she stood inside the kitchen and opened the door to the house.

"Were you nice to Amber?" she asked.

"At the grocery store?"

"My new car."

Opening the trunk, I said, "You named your car 'Amber'?"

"I told you that last month when we got her."

"This car is brown."

"Fine, but her name is 'Amber,' and I was asking if you were nice to her."

I pulled two *New Yorker* magazine tote bags of groceries from Amber's trunk, walked them up the steps, then went back for an Edgar Allan Poe tote. At that point, we were down to the store's "Is plastic OK?" bags.

"We have more tote bags in the hall closet," Nancy said when she noticed I'd run out. We weren't used to buying groceries for so many people.

"I'll put them in for next time," I said, bringing out the final plastic bags, one with a frozen loaf of garlic bread pondering a tumbling escape.

Nancy pulled the loaf of bread from the bag as I got to the top of the steps and closed the door behind me. "The governor just said no trips to the stores for the next two weeks, at least."

"Groceries and pharmacies are exempt," I said, setting cans of vegetables on the counter next to the stove. Peas and carrots. Corn. Peas and carrots, again.

"In Italy and France," I started.

"We're not in Italy or France. And if we were, Bella could just drive home."

"Wouldn't that be nice," I said.

"Now, be nice," Nancy replied, and lightly smacked me in the head with a 40 oz. MegaBag! of Cap'n Crunch's Crunch Berries.

Just before the Great Pandemic Lockdown, my daughter and two of her friends—one from Italy, one from Germany—were on their college's spring break. We had picked them up from the airport to take them back to school, all three still jumping from a week in Paris. But like most colleges, theirs never reopened from spring break. Then the international flights stopped. My daughter, Annie, now had her two friends, Bella and Sofie, living here with her, me, my wife, and our teenage son, Brayden (I lost a bet with my wife, so she got to name him).

We'd finished putting the groceries away and Nancy handed me a sheet of paper.

"What's this?" I asked.

"Can you just look at it before you ask?"

So I looked at it. Grids, boxes. A calendar for the week, each with slots for two meals.

Hamburgers. Italian spaghetti. Greek spaghetti. Pizzas. Baked potato bar. Breakfast for dinner. Grilled cheese and tomato soup.

"I could only get one loaf of bread because the store had a limit," I told her. "Not sure about grilled cheese for everyone."

"Scheisse," she snarled.

I laughed. "See you're picking up some German while the kids are here."

"Learned a new one today, but I don't know what it means. Just that it makes the girls laugh."

"Well, go ahead," I said.

My wife cleared her throat, leaned in and whispered, "Steig auf diese Hoden."

Around the corner, from the breakfast room, three teenage girls burst into laughter.

"Annie, what are you making your mother say?"

She stopped laughing long enough to say, "Nothing, Dad. It's fine."

Nancy tapped me on the shoulder. "Didn't you take German in college?"

"Minored in it, actually."

"Well, Herr Fancypants?"

"I mostly got D's," I said, and the breakfast room erupted again.

When the girls went out for a run, I poured a couple fat fingers of bourbon, sat down at the kitchen table with Nancy, who had her laptop open.

"What's left for you today?" she asked, taking a sip of tea from her Shakespeare Quotes mug.

"Got the shopping taken care of, so I was thinking of taking a nap."

"If you plan it right, you can get a late morning nap and a mid-afternoon nap in," she said.

I said "cheers" and took a sip. I'd been following a Reddit group for bourbon drinkers since this pandemic started and, as long as the governor kept the liquor stores open, we were going to be fine.

Nancy had taken to connecting online with people locally, through Facebook groups and hashtag challenges and neighborhood forums.

She asked if I'd seen a Weimaraner while I was out.

"Taking your German lessons pretty seriously, aren't you?" I said.

"The Powells up on Ruddy Duck said they saw one this morning, didn't know whose it was."

"That's the big lab kind of dog?" I asked.

"Pretty much. This one was gray." She turned the laptop so I could see a sixty-pound, shiny dog easing out a turd right on John and Maria Powell's back deck.

"I'm fairly confident that dog is in violation of the covenants," I said. "Bet Maria wants to find the dog and fine him."

"She's not on the POA board anymore, actually."

I asked when that happened.

"At the meeting in February."

I took a long swig of bourbon. "So disappointed I didn't get to go to that one. Sounds fascinating."

She tapped the down arrow on her keyboard a little louder than she had to. "One of us has to take one for the team, to keep up with what's going on in the neighborhood."

"And what's that?" I asked.

She reached across the table, finished off my whiskey. "Not much at all."

Brayden walked into the kitchen, said there was a man in a mask at the door.

To be clear, it's only a couple dozen steps from the kitchen to the front door of the house, but if you're a parent, and your kid has gone off on a run and then you hear there's a masked man at the door, well, you make that couple dozen steps in about three.

Somewhere in the parental fear lobe of my brain, the three girls had been kidnapped by Lee Van Cleef and I'd have to win them back using only my ability to bench-press eighty pounds and the only weapon in the house, a tourist's pocket knife that said "Niagara Falls" in confusing cursive and hadn't been opened since the gift shop where we'd bought it a decade back.

I opened the door, ready to drop the "very certain set of skills" line from that movie with that guy whose family keeps being taken from him, but it was just Dave from over on Merganser, wearing a blue bandana and a maroon Tech baseball cap.

I nodded. "Dave."

He nodded back: "Will."

"What can I do for you?" I asked, relieved it was only Dave, but still a little disappointed I wouldn't get to run around the globe strangling bad guys on yachts.

"Y'all making out alright?" he asked.

Fine. We were going to chat each other up first? "Just fine, man. How are you and Rachel doing in all this?"

"Well as you can, I figure. Say, you got any 2-stroke oil?"

Should have figured. Dave was the kind of guy who liked the idea of getting out and doing some yard work, but never thought things through. You could pass by their house throughout the spring and summer and see half-finished projects lying there, while Dave or Rachel drove out to the hardware store to get one more bag of mulch or another can of paint for the shutters, two pale blue shutters left propped against the sawhorses while fourteen were laid out, yellow and drying in the driveway.

I said I probably did. "Want to meet me around and I'll open the garage door and we can take a look?"

He turned to walk back down the sidewalk to the side of the house. "Appreciate it," he said.

I walked back through the hallway to the kitchen, on my way to the garage.

"What did Dave want?" Nancy asked. "Stain? Paint? Thousand pounds of gravel?"

"Nice guesses. Oil for the weedeater."

I whacked the button to open the garage door, stepped between the cars, and walked around to the wall where I kept the oil and gas and antifreeze and windshield wiper fluid and so forth. I saw Dave was standing halfway down the driveway.

"Want to come grab a bottle?" I said to him.

"Social distancing," he said, and I just stood there until he said if I could just leave it in the driveway and then close the door, he'd come up and get it.

I said that was fine, found two bottles, one full and one half, and set the half-full one in the drive for him.

He said thanks, waved his hand, then stopped. "Hey, was that your kid I saw making the loop on Mallard?"

"Probably. She and her friends went out for a run a little while ago."

He nodded, said he didn't recognize the other girls.

I said no, that he probably wouldn't have. Then I closed the garage door and went back in the house.

As the garage door clattered its way down and I stepped back into the kitchen, Nancy asked how Dave and Rachel were.

"Aren't they online telling everyone how they are?" I asked, opening the refrigerator for a stout.

"He's Snape and she's Mr. Wickham."

"Their screen names?"

"No. The new 'Which Villain Are You?' quiz that's going around."

"Not sure either one of those guys was a villain," I said, "just misunderstood."

Nancy laughed. "Yeah. The world has enough 'misunderstood guys' to burn the whole place down. Any idea where the wine went, by the way?"

"We had wine?"

"Yeah," she said, opening the doors of the liquor cabinet where we usually stocked a couple bottles of wine. "A Cab Sauv from the Maipo Valley. Time to crack it open for a 'Thank God It's Friday' toast."

"But it's Tuesday," I said.

"I was making a joke, but it's Wednesday, actually."

"Pretty sure it's Tuesday."

"Computer," Nancy said, tilting her head back and aiming her voice at the ceiling as she did when she asked the lady in the tube for weather and news updates, "What day of the week is it?"

"Today is Friday," the voice said.

I said I'd be damned.

Nancy said she'd drink to that.

The girls were at the kitchen table, doing their college assignments on their laptops and watching videos on their phones. Brayden was taking the dogs for a walk through the neighborhood, and Nancy and I were in the den scrolling through nothing on our phones. The weather had been nice for a couple days, but now it had gone cold again, and I was feeling guilty for not going out when it was nice out.

We had a fire pit we never used, and I asked Nancy if she wanted to grill hot dogs out there this weekend. She said that sounded good, and we both knew we'd never manage to pull that off, but it was nice to have things to look forward to, even if they weren't real.

"We do need another meal, since we can't do the grilled cheese," she said.

"Sorry I couldn't get another loaf of bread," I said, again, for maybe the fifth time since I'd gotten back from the grocery store.

"Just so you know for next time, they limit the Wonder Bread and Sunbeam and all, but you can buy as many loaves from the bakery as you want."

"You mean I should have gotten bread from the bakery part of the store?" I asked.

"It's fine. I'll figure something out. Everyone is sharing recipes."

She brought her laptop back into the den with her, started clicking through sites. "You been on the neighborhood app recently?"

"The forum thing? No. What's the top post this month, lost dog or recommend a plumber?"

She turned the laptop to me, and something in the back of my throat popped.

"Is that?"

"Yeah," she said. "That's us. And that's the girls." She scrolled, kept reading. "The Mitchells. And the Larkins son, Mark."

I took the laptop from her, scrolled up and down. "This is a list of everyone in all of Adams Creek that's travelled internationally in the past few months." I kept scrolling. "How did someone even get this list?"

Nancy sat back on the couch, put her hands in her lap. "It doesn't matter how they got it. What's the point of it?"

"I don't know," I said, reading the post over and over again. Maybe a dozen or more names from the entire neighborhood, three of them right under our roof.

"The Mitchells were on that cruise," Nancy said. "They're always going somewhere."

"So what? Why would someone even have this list?"

"I don't know why they have it, but why have they posted it to the whole neighborhood?"

I sat back against the couch, setting the laptop as far from me as I could. "So everyone in the entire neighborhood could see who the threats were."

"Threats?"

"You know what I mean," I said, noticing she was getting more upset. A couple years back, just three doors down, a man who was renting a house from the Gilberts got tired of the Ellmanns' dog always getting loose and wandering the neighborhood, so he poisoned the dog. No one could ever prove it, but he'd moved out since then and Bob Ellmann had moved away when Abigail Ellmann went into a nursing home last year. When the poisoning happened, Nancy had gotten so upset, she shook for a week and couldn't sleep for two.

All I wanted for the rest of my life was for her to never be that upset again. Yet here we were. And I couldn't do anything.

"What threats? The girls? The Mitchells? The Larkins? What kind of threat?"

"From the virus. International travel."

"I know that's their point," she said. "But a threat? What are they even talking about?"

She'd reached the point where the basics didn't make sense, so all you can do is just repeat the same thing, over and over. I didn't know how to help her.

"Maybe we should keep the girls inside?" I offered, trying to think of some kind of solution.

"Keep them inside? You're trying to protect the neighborhood now?"

"I'm trying to protect the girls," I said.

"Jesus God," She drained her glass of wine, then reached for my bourbon and finished that off, too. She made the same spitting-up-a-hairball sound as whenever she tried hard liquor, one of the hundred moves of hers that I'd fallen in love with twenty years back in graduate school.

I asked if she'd noticed who posted the list.

"No. Who?"

"Someone from the official POA account."

"Janice."

"Brooks?" I asked, refilling my bourbon.

"Yes," Nancy said, reaching for my glass, finishing it off (hairball, again) and handing me back the empty. "Her stupid brother works for the stupid air marshals."

"Really?"

"Yes. Don't you remember at the harvest BBQ last year, she made such a big deal out of how her stupid brother could shoot a stupid dime from hundred feet?"

I said I didn't remember.

"Really? And then you said 'Well, we'll know who to call if we're ever attacked by small coins?'"

I laughed. "It does sound like something I would say."

"God. Sometimes I wonder why I married you."

I said, "No, you don't," and leaned over to kiss her forehead before I refilled my glass.

Through the front window, I saw Brayden and the dogs coming up the drive in a hurry.

I went to the door, let them inside.

"Did you hear?" he asked. "Did you hear the sirens?"

We said we hadn't.

"What sirens?" his mother asked.

"On Gadwall," he said. "The fire. The whole house is on fire. Looked like one of the cars, too. Man oh man." He took the leashes off the dogs, who raced to fight over the water bowl.

"Which house?" I asked.

"Where you turn the corner. Right across from where they have those soccer nets in the front yard, you know?"

The soccer nets belonged to the Wallaces, the twin girls who played travel ball, though no one was playing much of anything now.

And the house across the street, the house on fire.

Nancy and I said it at the same time. The Mitchells.

"Where are the girls?" I asked.

"Basement," Nancy said.

We went on full lockdown that night, no leaving the house for neighborhood runs or dog walks or taking the trash to the curb. Open the back door to let the dogs out. Open the front door for packages. That was it. For three days, that was it. That was all I could take.

"I'm taking the dogs out for a walk," I said.

Nancy said like hell I was, but I was already gone, down the driveway and away from the Mitchells' house, away from Dave and Rachel, away from the cul-de-sacs and loops, towards the entrance to the neighborhood. I wanted the newspaper and a Milky Way bar and, more than that, I wanted to get out.

Jeff usually worked days at the gas station, and he could tell me what was going on. Everyone would stop there at some point, either going in or out of the neighborhood. Even if most people were trying to lock down, I knew Jeff would have heard something. And he was fine with my small dogs poking their heads into his store, if that's what I needed. A fifteen-minute walk to the store, grab the paper and a snack and some intel, and I'd be back home in time for another drink before this one wore off, I thought.

Turns out, I was wrong.

I nodded along the way at the county's prosecuting attorney and his son, who were riding their bikes up and down the wrong side of the road. They nodded back, keeping their hands on the handlebars at all times.

I passed a middle-aged woman with her phone on her arm, running at a walker's pace and singing softly to herself. I couldn't make out the song, but she nodded and I nodded as the dogs stretched their leashes.

When I crested the hill and saw the entrance to the neighborhood, I stopped in the middle of the road. Two SUVs, one red and one black, were blocking the entrance. A couple people were standing there, while a couple more were sitting in lawn chairs next to the Adams Creek sign.

I had a joke planned for when I got back. I'd tell Nancy our property values just went up and she'd ask why and I'd make a joke about how we were living in a gated community now.

Instead, when I got close to the house, I saw two men walking from our yard to the Thompsons' next door. The dogs and I picked up the pace, took the shorter route through the yard instead of the drive.

I had to unlock the deadbolt and the doorknob lock to get in. I let the leashes drop as the dogs dragged them across the hardwood to the water bowls.

I called my wife's name three times before she answered.

"We're in the basement," she said.

They all were.

"Let's talk upstairs," she said, leaving the four kids in the basement watching one of the Harry Potter movies.

She closed the basement door behind her when we reached the kitchen.

"Who was here?" I asked.

"The POA."

"The what? The Property Owners' Association? What?" I seemed to be floating out of my body at that point, seeing myself speak like a moron.

"I didn't know either of them. They had a list of everyone in the house."

"What did they want?"

"Our temperatures."

"Our what?"

"They had those scanners," she said. "Like in the Chinese cities. They scanned our foreheads for fever."

"They what?"

"We all passed." Nancy, hands shaking, took three tries to put a pod in the Keurig, hit the button.

"You let them scan the kids?"

She turned quickly and I stepped back. "You're goddamn right I did and don't you ever question me like that again."

"What?"

"They had guns, Will. What the hell was I supposed to do?"

"Guns?"

"Pistols. On their hips. Holsters. They had guns, Will. They had guns."

I reached my arms around her as she pulled her arms up between us and sobbed.

"I'm sorry," I said. "I'm sorry I went out."

I held her so tight I thought I'd pressed us into one person, so tight until I heard a trickle dripping on the floor and I thought I'd squeezed the pee out of us both.

"Scheisse," she said, turning back to the counter. "I forgot the goddamn cup."

We were laughing, standing in the pool of coffee when Brayden came up from the basement. "You know," he said, staring at us and the floor, "they make very comfortable adult diapers these days. We can have them shipped to your nursing home if you want."

"Help your mother clean up," I said, taking that opportunity to head to the den, turning off the desk lamp and staring out the front window.

The next morning, I found a man who would deliver to me, or close to me. No one was delivering anything through the roadblock at the end of the neighborhood.

That afternoon, we turned off the first-floor lights, and Nancy and the kids went to the basement. I took what cash we had from the fireproof box in the cabinet, then put on a low hat and a bandana and walked through the woods behind the house.

Down the ridge, crossing Adams Creek itself, then up the ridge to the church that backs up the woods behind our section of the neighborhood. For a second I worried that I'd show up and it would be Sunday morning, but people don't go to church buildings and days have no meaning now. I came around the sheds behind the church to see the man in the Jeep, one leg dangling out the side, listening to a jazz piano tune I couldn't place.

"Mr. Hawkins?" I asked.

"You Will?"

I said I was.

"Had me worried with that bandana on. Thought I was going to have to use this myself," he said, pulling the shotgun from behind him.

I was paying the man $800 for a sawed-off 20-gauge I could probably get arrested for possessing if times were normal.

He and I made a little small talk, and I walked back through the woods with the shotgun and two boxes of shells.

I crossed through the woods and it kept getting darker as I went. I made it to the creek, then worked my way up the hill, but managed to put myself about seven or eight houses too deep into the subdivision, so I walked the tree-line, trying to place myself.

Lost in my own locked-down neighborhood. What a way to spend an evening.

I was only about a dozen feet deep into the woods, walking along the backs of the lots, when I saw the fire pit of the next house, Dave and Rachel sitting in Adirondack chairs.

I hit a patch of twigs and Dave stood and turned. "Who's there?" he asked, unsheathing a fixed-blade knife from behind his back.

"Just me. Just me. It's Will," I said, stepping out into the twilight, the fire's glow.

"Jesus, you scared us," he said, sitting back down, flicking his knife five inches deep into the ground at his feet, then reaching over and taking Rachel's hand. "What are you doing back there?"

I showed him the shotgun. "Just doing some squirrel hunting. You know, since they won't let us go to the grocery store."

"Like hell you are," he said. "What are you really doing back there?"

I said "squirrel hunting" again and he let it drop.

"You can sit with us if you want," Rachel said.

"Thanks, but I need to get back home." I turned to step back into the woods.

"How much longer you think this is going to last?" Dave asked me.

I lifted the shotgun, laid it across my shoulder. "Not much longer," I said.

THE DIAMOND

By Gemma Amor

It was while we were in lockdown that we found the diamond.

The size of a man's thumbnail, it was a deep, bloody crimson in color. According to the internet, this was because of a defect that meant light passed through the diamond's deformed internal structure in an odd way, bending and exhibiting as red. We still had the internet, then. We'd been in lockdown only four weeks, and the world still functioned, to a certain extent. We had food, electricity, Wi-Fi, cellphones. We had each other. At that point in time, we considered this a good thing.

The diamond changed that.

There are some people who just can't quit each other. Even though it hurts, even though it makes them both miserable, they just can't sever that tie.

That was Lou and I. It wasn't a question of love; we had plenty of that. But sometimes, love isn't enough. No matter how hard we tried, we couldn't seem to make a relationship stick. And boy, did we try. Each encounter did more damage, each attempt to make it work only served to make us more tired, more stressed, more miserable. We had an idea in our heads of how we thought we should be: Lou and Mike, in it for the long haul. This idea dominated everything, led us to ignore all the red flags that told us we were not compatible. Eventually, desperate for a solution, we did what all idiots in love do: we moved in together, or rather, Lou moved into the house I rented with my friends, all of whom were men: Pete, Tom, Chris and Adam. The lads were not pleased to welcome a female into the house, but I didn't care. I wanted her with me, despite everything. I wanted to make it work. I just couldn't let her go.

But it was no use. Over time, we became a sad, ragged duet, singing an off-key song of regret.

We admitted defeat three days before Pete came home from his trip to Europe. We'd had a good run: two years, this time around. It hurt, but we agreed it was for the best. We would break up, and Lou would move out. I would stay where I was, renting with the lads.

That was the plan, anyway.

The plan went to shit when the contagion started.

Pete returned from his ill-timed Euro trip with a sore throat and a stomachache, and went rapidly downhill from there. We didn't take his symptoms very seriously at first. We jeered as he took himself off to bed with a fever, chills, a headache, and a tight chest. In those early days, you see, we hadn't been warned about the virus. We hadn't been told what to look out for, and so Pete's symptoms didn't present as anything too intimidating.

Within days, however, he became a textbook case. And when his test results came back positive, our lives changed forever.

We were told to stay indoors, to 'self-isolate' or else risk infecting others. We did as we were told, begrudgingly. We found quarantine hard. We missed the pub, the gym, working, sports, and decent coffee.

I missed my freedom, and space to think away from Lou. Chris missed his boyfriend. The others missed Tinder and chasing skirt. We stopped caring about clothes and slobbed about in our underwear. We watched a *lot* of porn, and after day five, stopped using cutlery: Using a knife and fork felt so unnecessary, somehow, like an affectation of an era gone by, like wearing a top hat and tails to dinner.

Our resentment died when we realized the scale of the catastrophe taking place outside our comfortable walls. The contagion was voracious. Within two weeks it had gone global. People died by the thousands. The country closed down. Schools, bars, restaurants, shops, cinemas... everything shut, overnight.

It was shocking because we lived in the center of a large city. Seeing the commerce and bustle grind to a halt within the space of a few hours was brutal. The streets we could see from our windows stopped funneling cars and became wide, empty promenades upon which the occasional lonely ghost wandered. The population was allowed one walk per day, exercise acceptable as long as everyone kept a strict six feet apart from each other. Policemen patrolled in cars with Orwellian diligence, watching, always watching, ready to enforce the rules.

And we stayed indoors, stewing in each other's company like ripe fruit stewing in the harsh sun.

We could hear Pete coughing through the walls of his bedroom at night, a dry, hacking cough that went on and on and ruined everyone's sleep. We became paranoid, disinfecting every surface in the house with bleach and wipes and washing our hands dozens, if not hundreds of times a day. Time passed. Our anxieties progressed. We tried to be kind to Pete, tried to make sure he stayed hydrated and fed, but his room stank like sickness, and we found it hard to stay in there long with him.

We drew up a roster, took it in turns to share 'Pete Duty,' to take him food and water, and wipe down the toilet, shower and sink after he'd used it. He was too weak to clean up after himself. Pete stared at us with listless, red-rimmed eyes for the few moments of every day we allowed ourselves exposure to him. We could tell he was hurt by our ostracization. Eventually, I felt so guilty that I moved the TV in my room to his, so he could distract himself in a way that didn't involve staring at the ceiling for twelve hours a day in-between coughing fits. I showered for a full forty minutes after I'd done this, convinced I was covered in deadly germs.

Lou, who hadn't moved out before the pandemic hit, was not impressed by my generosity. But Lou was rarely impressed by anything I did anymore, and as the days wore on, she became more and more vocal about it.

I didn't blame her, not at first. We had been trapped in an odd limbo state. No longer in a relationship, but still living together in the most intense fashion, we had to talk to each other every day, share a bed in a small room, maintain our separation amidst our isolation. She stopped smiling, and I missed it. When we first met, she would smile all the time. I was blown away by that smile, which always started small and then grew slowly, as if she was constantly on the verge of some profound realization.

Unable to socialize with her own friends, she found mine poor company. Our banter seemed harsh and childish to her. She started to roll her eyes every time one of us opened our mouths to say even the most innocuous of things. The lads grew frustrated with her in equal measure, although most of them tried to disguise it for my sake, knowing that her behavior was not my fault, and also knowing that I still cared deeply for her. Most of them, except for Tom, who did little to hide his distaste whenever Lou spoke.

It all came to a head the day we found the diamond.

We were sitting around in the living room in silence. I was trying to read a book, Chris was sketching in his pad, and everyone else stared at their phones, mindlessly thumbing back and forth through social media feeds. There was a heavy, bored silence amongst us that Lou broke with an enormous sigh.

"Someone burned the kid's playground down in St. Paul's," she said miserably, gaze locked on her screen. She was beginning to get phone-jowls from staring at the thing so much, and I didn't like it. I could see a glassy-eyed fragility to her that hadn't been there at the beginning of quarantine. I realized, with a sinking heart, that depression was setting in, starting to eat her up. I had no idea what to do about it, and this frustrated me more than anything, because it made me feel futile, defunct.

She continued, her voice low and loaded: "Four garages, three warehouses and the children's playground at St. Paul's community center were set alight last night by arsonists, according to this."

Nobody replied, because there wasn't much to say in response to this cheerful update.

She carried on, like a dog with a bone, not reading the room at all: "Oh, and the corner shop on Broadway was looted, too. They took everything that wasn't nailed down, apparently."

The quiet in the room deepened as we tried to steel ourselves against her doom-merchantry.

"Looks like there won't be much of the world left when we get out of quarantine," she said, looking up from her phone to see if anyone was listening.

I weakly tried to offer some encouragement.

"I know it's hard, Lou," I said, as gently as I knew how. "But we have to try and stay positive. We can't let it get to us. It'll be over at some point. We just have to wait it out."

Lou's melancholy turned to anger, lightning quick.

"I don't *want* to wait it out any longer, Mike! I want to go *outside*! I want to see my friends! Hug them!"

I tried again, not wanting this to escalate any further, especially not in front of the lads. "I'm your friend. You can hug me."

She snorted. "You'll never be my friend, not really. You've been inside me too many times. Kind of precludes friendship, don't you think?"

I snapped my mouth shut, because that stung. Then, I tried again. I don't know why, but I always felt like there was something salvageable between us, even when she was being like this.

"If you say so. But you can't wallow in it, Lou. You need something to do. Something to take your mind off of everything. You're thinking too much."

"Thinking too much?! There are ninety-three thousand cases of the virus confirmed in the country today!"

"But only a hundred sixty-seven of those are based here, Lou." I knew the statistics; I kept an eye on the rolling data like the rest of us did. "And only twenty-seven deaths so far. It's the lowest in the country."

"And one of those twenty-seven could easily be one of us! I have asthma, you're immunocompromised, and Pete is half-dead already. Haven't you fucking heard him coughing every night?"

She was working herself up to a panic attack. What she needed now was calm reassurance, and a distraction.

What she got instead was Tom.

"Put a sock in it, Lou," he said, stretching and yawning. "I'm tired of how fucking miserable you are all the time."

There was a shocked moment of silence as Lou processed what had just been said. The rest of us froze, blinking in disbelief.

"What did you say?" She replied, face white.

I put my book down and got ready to intervene.

Tom took a deep breath. A fighting breath.

"I *said:* put a fucking sock in it, you miserable cow," he repeated, looking relieved as he spoke the words, as if he'd been biting his tongue for a long, long time.

"Hey!" I felt anger rise up inside me and tried to swallow it down. I could not afford to lose my cool, not cooped up like this. Tom was a friend, and he was stressed and worried like the rest of us. Lou was not at fault, but I knew how grating her moods could be.

"Don't speak to her like that," I said, as calmly as I knew how.

"Or what?" Tom stood up. He topped me by five or six inches. I'd never appreciated how freakishly tall he was until he squared up to me in that small room.

Friends, I told myself. *We're all friends here.*

"Or nothing, Tom," I said, refusing to be drawn. I clenched my fists, regardless.

He erupted.

"Oh, come off it, mate, she's a fucking nightmare! We all think so! All she does is mope around criticizing everything and everyone and crying when we get annoyed at her. Why you didn't dump her properly years ago, I'll never understand. She makes you look like a right fucking doormat, sometimes. And let's not even get started on the eggs!"

I swallowed again, my anger still rising. "Eggs?" I muttered. "What eggs?"

Tom swiped a hand in the direction of the kitchen. "Who do you think finished all the fucking eggs off this morning? *She* did. Fuck knows when our next food delivery will arrive, or even if they *have* any eggs. She knows I'm on a high-protein diet! She didn't even ask me!"

"They're communal eggs," Lou hissed, eyes ablaze.

"That's enough!" I said, my anger building, building. I refused to fight over eggs. It was fucking ridiculous, so I tried to keep a lid on my temper, but both Tom and Lou were making it difficult.

Tom had the bit between his teeth now, and wouldn't be silenced.

"She should lay off them anyway, if you ask me. Getting a bit chubby." He blew out his cheeks to mimic Lou's weight gain.

My mouth dropped open. Had he really just said that? Had he really just fucking *said* that??

"I fucking *hate* you!" Lou shrieked, throwing her phone at Tom. He ducked and it slammed into the wall behind him, knocking a picture free of its hook.

This sent Tom into an apoplexy. "How is that fucking helpful?" He roared, picking up the phone and throwing it back at Lou with all the force he could muster. "How, you psychotic bitch?"

The device glanced off her cheek, and she hissed in surprise and pain. I saw a small welt reddening there. Not a big injury, but enough to hurt.

All the fight went out of Lou, and she sank her head between her knees, sobbing.

I snapped.

"Not another fucking word, Tom!" I yelled. It killed me to see Lou, *my* Lou, in such a state. I had a fleeting memory of the night we'd first met, her smile, the glint in her eyes. She'd ridden me like a rodeo horse that night, her on top and me underneath looking up at her as she shuddered her way through what I thought, at the time, was the sexiest thing I'd ever seen in my life.

She didn't look so sexy now. Greasy hair stuck to her face, snot and tears pasted across her cheeks, lips raw from worry, and a long red weal on her cheekbone. She looked twenty years older than her age, and my heart ached for her.

"I miss women," she whispered then, to nobody in particular. "I just want to talk to someone sympathetic. I just want a hug."

"Boo hoo, cry me a fucking river!" Tom yelled, and Chris and Adam got to their feet, too.

"Pack it in, Tom," Adam said. Tom was perhaps closer to him than anyone, and usually deferred to him.

"Apologize," I demanded, my voice like ice.

"You're being an arsehole, Tom. Sort it out," Chris said, also cold.

Tom looked at the three of us, his chest heaving, then at Lou, who sat like a limp rag on the couch.

He relented.

"Fine," he said. "I'm sorry, Louise. You just get on my nerves, that's all."

As apologies went, it was a shitty one. Lou leapt up as if someone had placed a rocket under her.

"You're a piece of shit, Tom Ward," she snapped. "Always have been, always will be!"

She stormed out of the room, kicking at the skirting board by the door as she went. A section of the board, already loose, clattered wearily to the floor in defeat.

"Great," Tom muttered, crouching down to pick it up and hammer it back in place with his fists.

"That was your fault," Chris said, shaking his head. "That was totally uncalled-for."

I said nothing. I didn't trust myself yet. I wanted to go after Lou, but also knew that the best thing for her was some space so she could cool down. So I stayed with the others, trying to get ahold of myself, watching as Tom grabbed the skirting board and then paused in the act of refitting it, frowning at the hole in the wall behind the board.

"Huh. There's something... in the wall down here," he said, grunting as he got onto his knees. He shoved his face closer to the hole, arse sticking up in the air like he was praying.

"What? What sort of thing?" Chris asked.

"I don't know," Tom said, and I was amazed at how quickly he'd moved on from the argument, as if it hadn't happened at all. As if removing Lou from the room had reset the mood, somehow.

"Let me see," Adam said, going over to where Tom was inspecting the wall. He also got to his knees, shoving Tom out of the way for a better view. He extricated his phone from his back pocket and turned the flashlight app on, shining the bright little beam into the hole for better visibility.

"Fuck me, you're right!" Adam said. He put his hand into the wall, and it disappeared up to his wrist.

"I think there is something," he said, pulling his arm out, "But I can't reach it, not with these big old guns in the way." He flexed his arms, and his gym-bred biceps popped. He grinned a shit-eating grin and winked at me. "Needs a skinny fucker like Mike to reach in there."

I glared, still raw about the argument that everyone seemed so keen to forget. Adam smiled back, and I could see what he was trying to do: move us all on with a welcome distraction.

"Fine," I said, at last. Then, I dropped to my knees and pushed my arm into the hole in the wall.

To begin with, I couldn't feel anything except for rough masonry, so I pushed further until I found myself cheek-to-paintwork, my arm gone right up to the shoulder.

"Christ," Tom said, peering at me. "How big is the fucking cavity between these walls?"

"Shouldn't really be a cavity at all," Chris said. "This is a Victorian house, cavity walls weren't that common back then."

Adam yawned to show how uninteresting he found this. "Hurry up, Mike," he said. "Before Chris bores me to death."

I stretched further, gritting my teeth, and, finally, the very tips of my fingers brushed against something. Something cold, metallic, shaped like a loop. A handle of some sort? I used my last tiny bit of momentum to strain further forward, curling the tips of my fingers over the handle like a grab-claw, and then slowly pulling the thing out of the cavity in the wall.

A hush descended the object emerged into the light of day.

It was a box.

It was made of tin, like an old biscuit tin with handles at each end. There was a metal clasp on the front, with a padlock that was small and red with rust.

Adam went to fetch our toolbox. When he came back, he looked worried.

"Pete sounds pretty bad," he said, and we could all hear him, then, coughing through the walls. He did sound bad. He sounded like he couldn't catch his breath.

"Maybe we should call the doctor again," Chris said.

Tom shrugged. "They said it would take a while for him to get better." He rooted around in the toolbox for some pliers, disinterested in Pete's plight. For the second time that day, I felt an intense flash of dislike. Tom had always been selfish, but quarantine was bringing out the worst in him.

I held onto the box, frowning at Tom but speaking to Adam. "I'll call them again in a bit," I said, and Adam nodded.

Tom, armed with some pliers with a sharp cutting edge on the inside of the jaws, set to work on the padlock while I held the box steady. It didn't take much to snip through the slim shackle of the lock, which fell to the floor with a clatter.

Tom nodded in satisfaction, and Adam rubbed his hands together. "Hope it's vintage porn," he said, grinning like a teenager. "It's got to be, else why would it have been stuffed way back in the wall so far? Bring on the Victorian muff!"

With clumsy fingers, I undid the clasp. The lid squeaked up.

We all peered in.

Inside the box was another box, like an engagement ring box. It was made of velvet, with an ornate catch on the top.

I carefully opened the catch.

And revealed a beautifully-cut blood-red stone, the size of my thumbnail, sitting on a bed of white satin.

"Well, fuck me," Chris said, whistling. As I stared at the thing, my heart thumping in my ears, I realized I couldn't have put it better myself. I shivered. It was as if someone were standing behind me, breathing on the back of my neck. My arms came up in gooseflesh, and I shuddered again.

And the diamond watched me from its pristine bed.

The jewel sent us into a frenzy of internet activity.

"It has to be worth something," Tom said, snatching the jewel and holding it up to the window so that the light shone through it. Inside the stone, tiny flaws hung suspended, like motes of dust in a bloody sunbeam.

I held my hand out for it, feeling twitchy, and Tom reluctantly gave it back. "Let's keep it safe in the box, shall we?" I said, snapping the catch shut over the gemstone as quickly as I could. I felt uncomfortable letting it out of my control, and realized I'd been holding my breath as Tom had played with it. Once it was back in its case, I met Tom's eyes.

I saw something ugly there.

Whatever it was, it was gone in seconds, smoothed over with practiced ease.

Watch him, I told myself, lowering my gaze. *He'll steal it without a second thought.*

I blinked, surprised. Where had that thought come from?

I set the gem box on our dining table, and we all stood around it. Then, we pulled out our phones and started searching for information on red jewels.

I was so engrossed, I didn't hear Lou coming into the room behind me.

"What are you all doing?" She said, voice thick and phlegmy from crying.

We all jumped, startled.

"Christ, Lou, what's wrong with you? A bit of warning next time!" I said, more harshly than I intended to.

She came and stood next to me, frowning. "What's that?" She reached for the box.

"Hey, hands off!" I yelped, moving to block her. The others all did the same, forming a protective ring around the jewel.

Lou reared back, looking hurt. "What? What is it?"

I shook my head. *Why is she always interfering?* The thought surprised me. It was as if a meaner, sharper version of me was starting to take over my internal dialogue. Feeling like a horrible person, I forced myself to climb down a little.

I opened the box and showed her the red stone sitting inside.

"What is *that*?" She breathed, eyes wide.

"We found it. We're trying to figure out if it's worth anything."

For the first time in weeks, Lou smiled.

"I think it's a red diamond," she said, unable to stop looking at it.

"How can you possibly know that?" I asked. I didn't like the way

Lou was looking at our discovery. Her knowing about it implied some sort of shared ownership, and it already felt as if too many of us had a claim on it.

Tom snorted in derision, but I saw him type *'red diamond'* into the search engine on his phone.

"I used to be a mineral and gemstone nerd when I was a kid," Lou continued, and I could tell she was itching to reach out and touch it. "It's like a normal diamond, only the red color is due to a rare occurrence in the atomic structure."

I raised my eyebrows. So did Chris and Adam. Tom peered into the screen of his phone as if he was about to fall headlong into the device.

In the background, we heard Pete coughing again. This time, it sounded far worse than we'd ever heard him sound before. I was pretty sure I could hear him groaning, too, only for some reason, it didn't bother me like it should have.

"Shall we go to him?" Adam said, dreamily, and the others yawned.

"Nah," Chris said. "He'll live." Tom nodded in agreement.

Lou didn't even appear to have heard us. She just stared at the red diamond. "We have to try and figure out if it's real," she murmured, and it was an echo of a thought I'd had myself not long before she'd come into the room. Figure out whether or not the diamond was a fake, and then decide what I was going to do with it.

You mean 'we,' my internal voice said. *What 'we' are going to do with it.*

The thought made me feel ill. And jealous.

According to the internet, there are a number of ways to tell whether or not a diamond is real.

"Number one," Adam intoned, reading aloud from an article he'd found. "Place the diamond in front of your mouth and fog it up with your breath. A real diamond won't allow condensation to stick to the surface."

I winced as Chris reached out and gripped the diamond. Every time someone else touched the thing, it was like a punch in the stomach. I kept my arms to myself with difficulty, desperate to snatch the jewel back.

Get a grip, Mike, I said, silently. *Don't give anything away.*

We watched as Chris breathed on the diamond, and I tried not to think about the virus, about any germs Chris had sticking to something so beautiful.

His breath made the surface of the gemstone opaque for a split second; then it cleared. No moisture remained.

"Next test?" Tom snapped. I noticed he was shifting from foot to foot, as if warming up, getting ready to run. I studied his face as covertly as I could. The fucker was planning, I could see he was. He was turning things over in his mind, mapping out escape routes.

Over my dead body, I thought, and my eyes went back to the red stone.

"Number two. Drop it in a glass of water," Adam said. "Real diamonds sink because of their density."

Lou went to fetch a glass, and we heard the kitchen tap run. She came back, eyes fixed on the jewelry box before she'd even come fully into the room.

We dropped the diamond into the glass. It sank to the bottom. Lou let out a small gasp of satisfaction, lifting the glass to her face. For a split second, I thought she might swallow the water down, diamond and all, in one gulp. Her hands trembled slightly around the tumbler.

I retrieved it quickly, upending the glass and pouring water everywhere in my haste to put the diamond back in its box. I heard Adam and Chris exhale behind me.

"Now what?" Tom said, shifting on the spot again. A powerful urge was growing in me. It was the urge to punch Tom square in the mouth.

I shook my head, feeling drunk.

What is the matter with me?

It was then that we heard Pete, calling for us.

"Help!"

It was a weak rasp, but we heard it as we stood there.

"Help... me!" Followed by a series of wet, thick choking noises.

We roused slowly, as if waking from a deep and bitter sleep. We looked at each other.

"You go check on him," Tom said to me, reaching out for the jewelry box. "I'll look after this."

"In your dreams!" I hissed, holding it away from him.

Adam intervened. "We'll all go together," he said, more calmly than he felt, if the sweat pouring down his temples was anything to go by. "I'll hold onto it, for now. It's my turn anyway."

"Since when do we take turns?" Chris said.

"Since now," Adam said, and he took the box from me, gently but firmly. As he did so, I felt an overwhelming wave of sadness and loss wash over me, as if my heart had been broken from the inside out and was now swimming around inside my veins, little sharp splinters working their way into my extremities.

"Just for a little while," he said, patting my shoulder. I flinched, not wanting to be touched by him. At that moment, I hated him.

He had something that belonged to me.

Before anyone could argue further, he turned and made his way to Pete's room. Silently, we all followed. Not because we were worried about Pete.

We followed so that we didn't lose sight of the diamond.

Pete was dead by the time we got to him.

From what we knew of the virus, it mutated as it jumped from person to person. Pete's particular variation had manifested suddenly as a series of large nodules sprouting out of his skin, clustering tightly around his neck and mouth, which is why his strangled coughs and gasps for air had sounded so peculiar at the end. As he lay there, frozen in what must have been his final seizure, head back, eyes wide, mouth open even wider, I could see a large clump of fleshy red nodules blocking his airway, filling his mouth, forcing his jaws open. They must have grown rapidly and all at once, choking him as he lay there in a fevered, already-weakened state.

"He was fine when I last checked on him," Chris said in a faraway voice.

Tom made a bored noise deep in his throat.

We closed the door. None of us felt sad, or shocked, or anything really.

We all just wanted to get back to the diamond.

Adam still held the gem box. Clumped together outside Pete's room, we watched him like a hawk in case he made a run for it.

But something felt off.

I did a swift headcount to double-check. Me, Adam, Chris, Tom…

No Lou.

With a sinking feeling, I realized that she had seen her opportunity. My instinct told me she was about to take it.

Instinct was right.

A tiny movement at the edge of my vision: my bedroom door, opening just a crack. An eye peered out, and then the door yanked open, and Lou ran at us, full speed on light, bare feet.

While we'd been preoccupied with Pete, Lou had crept into the kitchen and armed herself with a long, sharp kitchen knife. Her face as she held the knife high above her head was like nothing I'd ever seen before: twisted, frenzied, wild, completely disconnected from anything human.

With a crazed roar, she launched herself at Adam, who clutched the gem box close to his chest and only registered her presence at the very last moment. He had little time to defend himself with his free arm before she brought the knife down on his face. I heard a wet slice and smack, and a faint crunch: Adam's nose breaking under the impact. He fell backwards, the knife deeply embedded below his right eye, and a part of me thought, distantly, that we should be helping him. I thought this—but did nothing. Neither did the others.

Lou's momentum sent Adam crashing over. The box flew from his hands, hit the wall, dropped, and broke open. The diamond shot out of the box, bounced, and rolled across the floor. I dove for it, terrified that it would disappear down a crack in the floorboards. So did Tom and Chris.

I was aware, while this was happening, that Lou was stabbing Adam over and over again, grunting with effort as she did so. Blood sprayed into the air and decorated the corridor with artistic streaks of arterial bloom. She must not have realized that Adam no longer had the diamond.

"Give it to me!" She shrieked with each thrust of the knife. "Give it to *me*!"

Tom, the biggest and fastest of us, got to the diamond first. I felt true anguish flood my body as his hand closed around it. Then he was on his feet, pushing past us, jumping over the bloody mess that was Adam and kicking at Lou as he ran past her, headed for his own room. His door slammed. We heard furniture drag across the floor. He had barricaded himself in.

Silence descended.

With the diamond out of sight, I thought we might feel its pull a little less, but if anything, the desire to seize it grew stronger with the knowledge that it was now in Tom's control. I realized suddenly that I was drenched in sweat—not from fear or adrenaline, but sheer longing.

Lou got to her knees, coated from head to toe in Adam's blood. There was no doubt that Adam was dead, and Old Mike, the version of me that had existed before the diamond, would have been out of his mind with distress. He might have been terrified at what Lou had done, he might have wondered blindly if she was about to attack him, next.

New Mike simply looked at Chris and said, as if speaking through a mouth full of cotton-wool: "Should we call the police?"

Chris stared down at the red ruin that was Adam, and shook his head. "No. They will find out about the diamond. They'll try and take it from us."

I nodded in agreement.

"So what now?" Lou said, pointing at Tom's bedroom door. "He's blocked the entrance."

I shrugged, feeling my hate for Tom swell into a massive ball of resolve and determination. He had something that belonged to me, and for that, he would pay.

We decided to work together, the common goal of reaching Tom uniting us briefly in murderous collusion. We returned to the living room and lifted the coffee table. It was solid oak, heavy and durable, and would make a perfect battering ram.

We broke Tom's door down.

It splintered, the thin paneling disintegrating under our assault, and the chest of drawers that he had dragged in front of it fell backward, crashing to the floor. We kept going, forcing the door open just wide enough that we could push our way in, and…

We found Tom on his bed, oblivious to our dramatic entrance.

He sat cross-legged, turning the diamond over and over between his fingers, letting the light from his window catch and play with the stone, and his eyes were so wide, his pupils so massive, that he looked drugged. He breathed in shallow, short bursts, sweat pouring down his face, which was drenched in a red shade of ecstasy. As he rocked back and forth, he made a high-pitched keening noise in the back of his throat, like the drone of a mosquito, only more intense.

He didn't call out or protest once as we held him down against the sheets and strangled the life out of him.

As the diamond fell from Tom's lifeless fingers, Chris went for it. He tumbled off the edge of Tom's bed and lay there on his back, legs still up over the side of the mattress, cradling the diamond to his chest, sobbing.

Lou climbed off Tom's body, crossed his room, and picked up a 20kg kettlebell that Tom kept by the bed so he could train between gym sessions. She lifted it as if it weighed no more than a marble, walked to where Chris lay crooning over the diamond in victory, and dropped it on his head.

With a heavy crunch, the weight smashed downwards and settled. What remained of Chris's head spread outwards, misshapen and messy, like an empty eggshell smashed flat by the palm of a hand.

The diamond found its way to Lou.

Trembling, her mouth pulled wide with delight, she backed up toward the room's old sash window. Holding the red diamond to the sunlight, she gazed at the little flaws within, her eyes brimming with tears.

And I knew then, as I looked at her, a beam of sunshine playing with strands of her chestnut hair, hair I had loved to pull, just a little, never enough to hurt, but just enough to tease and excite, I knew then, as the years we had shared flashed past in a blur of love and pain, that I would have to kill her. I reasoned with myself that it wasn't really Lou I would kill. She had changed, like I had. Anything that was once Old Lou had been replaced by the diamond, and she was now hard and cold and bloody and filled with little flaws, just like it was.

She said something, but I hardly heard the words.

All I could think about was the diamond. It filled my brain like a rising tide.

I took a step forward.

The street outside my house is almost empty. The hour is late, and people no longer fill the city with their drunken revels at night. People stay at home, as they have been told to do, and for this I am glad.

Because I cannot kill everyone in this city, no matter how much I want to.

The body of a woman lies in the driveway of the house, arms and legs spread wide as if she is floating on her back in a pond. She is surrounded by splinters and shards of glass, glass from a sash window. I loved the woman once, but now she is dead, because I pushed her through that window, using her split second of surprise to wrest the red diamond from her grip before she fell. She looks almost peaceful, now, if you ignore the brain matter smeared on the gravel and her shattered limbs bent at awkward angles.

In my hand, a perfect, blood-red stone digs into my palm, drawing blood. It sings to me, and I stumble along the road, going where I do not know, but the whys and wherefores no longer matter, do they? Not in a world redesigned from the ground-up by sickness. Not in a world where we have all become ghosts, floating along like smoke on a breeze.

None of it matters anymore.

There is only red.

MISERY LOVES COMPANY

By Ann Dávila Cardinal

"How do you think Anna feels about all this work-from-home stuff?" Katie and I just finished our daily video check-in, and this is something that's been on my mind for days. Truth be told, I've been doing *way* too much thinking of late, since there isn't much else to do when the workday ends.

"Anna? You mean the ghost?" Katie raises her eyebrows, but she clearly isn't surprised by my question. With her electric blue hair and encyclopedic knowledge of horror films, she just… gets me.

"Yeah. I mean, do you think she's happy we're gone? Relieved to have College Hall all to herself?"

She snorts. "Wouldn't you be? I mean, she's always been kinda cranky about sharing the space with us."

"True." But I still wonder.

All of us who work in College Hall have had experiences with Anna: doors locking from the inside, pictures flying off walls, window shades just rolling up. But it took an intern to discover the true story behind the haunting. Rather fascinating, really: 1800s love triangle,

Anna shot on the college grounds by a woman she'd known her whole life. Shockingly scandalous in those days. In any days, really. But since the lockdown I've found myself thinking: What do ghosts do if there's no one to haunt?

We log off and I attempt to go back to working on the incoming applications. But it really *is* a crime that the flagship building of Vermont College of Fine Arts is sitting empty since the pandemic. I mean, sure, I'm grateful that my admissions job is something I can do from home, but I love my office: the plants, my books, the massive clown painting Matt gave me. I miss going somewhere every day, especially since I'm living alone out here in the middle of nowhere. I glance out the window at the raindrops peppering the surface of Lake Elmore, the clouds hanging around the mountain like a shroud. The seasonal residents of the houses around me are weeks away from arriving, and it's just too… quiet. I start to get the out-of-body feeling that precedes an anxiety attack and consider downing an Ativan.

But I have five phone calls to make, students aren't going to recruit themselves, so I throw myself into the work, anxiety attack averted with the talk of writing, life, and graduate school. As I hang up from the last call, I realize that the weekly all-staff meeting is starting. I rush to put on my headphones and log on to the video meeting platform. I smile as the faces of my friends and colleagues appear on screen. God, I miss them. Ten years I've worked on that campus. These people are more like family than co-workers.

As Leslie, our president, begins to speak, her face takes center screen and the others scroll in and out along the sidebar. She talks of her faith that we will weather this crisis, and she's so damn convincing, I want to believe her. But I'm a glass-is-half-empty-and-we're-all going-to-die-of-thirst kind of gal. When I see my friend Matt, our academic dean, I can't help it: I wave like a five-year-old. As an extrovert, these last five weeks have been an eternity for me, only seeing other people in pixelated versions on my ancient laptop, hearing their tinny voices with background noises of partners and children and, well… life.

At first, I enjoyed this insight into my colleagues through the settings of their homes, but now it just leaves me melancholy.

As the president is wrapping up her updates about moving the summer residencies online, I notice a new face appear in the sidebar among the familiar ones. A young woman, couldn't be more than twenty, with her hair up in a formal chignon. Who *is* that? We're a small college, how could I not know someone? As the meeting continues, I find myself staring at her whenever she comes up in the rotation, then looking for her to appear again onscreen.

The meeting wraps up, and each person says goodbye as their pictures wink out. I scroll through them, trying to see her one last time, but no luck. I'm just about to click out when I hear:

"Looks like it's just you and me, Ann! How you holdin' up?" Matt asks in his slight North Carolina drawl.

I smile. "Oh, you know. Hanging in there." Okay, so I lie to my friends, but it's not like he could do anything about it. "This is some weird-ass shit, no?"

He chuckled. "You can say that again." His wife Tammy walks by behind him and stops when she realizes it's me on the screen.

She smiles, her neat blonde bob swinging as she speaks. "Hi, honey! Hope we can bike again sometime soon!"

Tammy is about the fittest human I know and is so patient with me and my asthmatic lungs. "I sure as hell hope so!"

Tammy waves and moves off-screen, and Matt and I are saying our goodbyes when I remember. "Wait! Matt, did we hire someone new?"

He tilts his head to the side. "Someone new?"

"Yeah, a young woman. Blondish, updo..."

He gives me that teasing big brother smile, his thick, black designer-style glasses rising with his cheeks. "Are you seeing things, amiga?"

"No! Seriously, there was a woman in the meeting I've never seen before."

His expression turns slightly serious, perhaps even the dreaded 'concerned' look I hate so much. He forces a small smile. "Not that I know of." Then his phone starts to ring. "I have to get this; Leslie wants to check in."

"No worries! I'll talk to you later."

His image blinks off, and I close my laptop for the day. But all through dinner, my bath, even as I lie in bed trying to fall asleep, I can't get the image of the mystery woman out of my mind.

I make the mistake of starting the next day by watching the news. I prefer to watch it rather than read it online, as the voices keep a sort of company, but Lord it's depressing. Everything is shuttered pretty much worldwide; only essential services are allowed to keep operating in the hopes of stopping the spread of the viral pandemic. When I hear the statistic that someone is dying of the virus in New York City every five minutes, I realize I no longer have any interest in the oatmeal in front of me. I dump it, grab my coffee and phone, and head upstairs to my home office. It's a dark and rainy morning, but that seems apt, somehow.

At the last minute I grab a baseball cap from my bedroom since I haven't been bothering with the excessive grooming routine I used to do when I went into an actual office, and I tuck my unruly mop of hair underneath. No makeup, barely bathed, leggings, and slippers. The latest in pandemic office fashion.

I check my schedule. A nine o'clock marketing meeting. Oh good, it's always nice to see Alastair. Our marketing director is a British charmer who used to work in publishing, and we share a taste for speculative lit and a similarly bizarre sense of humor. I put on my headset and log on to Google Hangouts. One by one, my three colleagues enter, their images shifting like Tetris blocks as the next one joins.

Alastair begins the meeting. Even boring inquiry numbers sound interesting in his accent, and the hour flies by.

As the meeting winds down, I can't let Alastair get away without some teasing. "Alastair, did you dress to match your walls today?"

"Oh, do I match?" He pulls his shirt away from his chest to look at it, and snorts. "Totally an accident, I'm afraid. What with the schools being closed, I'm lucky I'm even dressed!" To punctuate his point, his daughter lets out a blood-curdling shriek from the other room.

The rest of us laugh, and Katie and Karen log off to join other meetings. Just as I'm about to do the same, I see a figure appear behind Alastair. It looks like a person, but featureless, like a shadow.

"Alastair, who's tha—"

At the same time Alastair says, "Well, I better get downstairs, my wife has had a lot to deal with—"

The figure looms over him, spreading over his face and shoulders like black oil, running in his eyes, into his nose, then I hear the beginnings of a scream… petrified, I peer closer, putting my face right up to the screen… was that a woman's face? She looks familiar…

Then his screen goes dark, replaced by an ominous red circle with an "A" in the center.

What the hell just happened?

I grab my phone and call Katie.

She answers on the first ring. "Miss me already?"

"Katie, someone was in Alastair's room at the end of that meeting, and I heard him scream!"

"I'm sure it was his daughter. You heard her yelling."

"No! It wasn't a child," I add before she can say it, "And it wasn't his wife!" I feel a chill on the back of my neck. "Katie, I'm worried about him." I hate that my voice breaks, but I feel anxiety tightening around my throat.

"Well, why don't you call him? I'm sure it's fine. With the kids home, everyone's house is a bit of a circus."

I sigh. "You're probably right," I offer, though I don't really believe it. I can't shake this dark feeling, like the oily shadow from behind Alastair has leaked through the screen and onto me.

"Call him if it will make you feel better."

I thank her, hang up, and dial Alastair's cell. I get his voicemail.

I can't seem to concentrate on my enrollment reports, and I dial him every five minutes, to no avail.

At five o'clock, I decide Katie's right, I'm probably getting worked up over nothing. I head downstairs, imagining a weekend of excessive and nurturing carbohydrates and a streaming binge of a season of *Lucifer*.

As I head upstairs after breakfast on Monday morning, I wonder how it's come to this. How the transitions of my days are marked only by the walking up and down of these same stairs, of only seeing other humans in boxes on a screen. Of the daily dread of the crushing silence that comes at night.

Why haven't I ever gotten married again?

Oh right, because my douchebag fiancé, the only man I've ever loved, took off a month before the wedding.

I sigh and pad across the hardwood floors to my tiny office. The rain has stopped today, at least, but the sky is still dark and foreboding. It's technically spring, according to the calendar, but in Vermont the trees are still bare, reaching to the sky with their bony fingers, and occasional piles of snow make their last stand across the property. I know, I should be grateful I have a nice house to live in and a cupboard full of food, but these last few weeks have only made me realize just how isolated I am. If I hadn't inherited the house from my mother, I would move to downtown Montpelier where there were people around, bars and coffee shops, and… life. Whenever those bars and shops actually open back up, that is.

The morning is quiet, the only sound the music from the pandemic playlist my co-worker Chiyomi turned me onto, so I'm really looking forward to the afternoon admissions meeting. All the other admissions counselors have pets, and I always ask them to hold their big-pawed puppy or furry orange cat up to the screen so I can get my fill. Social distancing is ideal for those of us who are allergic, but I do love the furry creatures. As we go through the updates, Alastair's name comes up, and with a jolt of guilt, I remember Friday's meeting.

"Has anyone heard from Alastair? He missed the music composition meeting this morning," Sarah asks, and a coldness spreads across the surface of my skin. "It's just not like him."

There's a chorus of "no" from the others, and I wrap the headphone cord around and around my finger as I struggle with whether or not I should share my concerns. I know they love me and my *quirky* personality, but since I came clean about my anxiety struggles, I always worry that people are going to think I'm losing it. But with all that's going on in the world right now, who wouldn't? I look down and see my finger is all white above the tightly wound cord.

I decide not to say anything, but as the sun makes its descent, I can't stop the dark thoughts from coming. Katie and I have a six o'clock informational video conference with some prospective students, so I decide to take a short lie-down and try to clear my head.

The call is lively (children's writers always are), and since this is our first one of these done online instead of by phone, I can't help but be pleased. It's so magical to watch the sense of community bleed into people even over the internet: I swear the college is infectious. One by one they reluctantly log off, until it's just me and Katie to do what we refer to as our post-mortem.

"Well, that certainly couldn't have gone better!" Katie's smile is big, her energy high. How does she pull that off at seven o'clock at night?

"It *was* good," I offer, forcing a bit of brightness into the last word. Truth was, the minute the last person winked off, I felt kind of… bereft. Like sitting in the tub as the bath water drains out.

"You okay, Ann?"

I look up at Katie's face staring at me through the screen. I've almost forgotten we were still on, and I sit up straighter and smile. I can rally with the best of 'em. "Yeah, yeah. I'm fine, just tired, is all."

She stares a bit more, then says, "Okay…" But she's just too damn perceptive to really believe me.

I had to sell it or she was going to start to get *concerned*. I laugh: "Really, I'm fine! Nothing a bowl of ice cream and an episode of *The Witcher* couldn't cure!"

She seems convinced. "Well, I'm going to go have some of my tofu bourguignon. It smells really delicious!"

I had to laugh. Katie was always making vegetarian meals out of seriously meaty dishes. It's as if someone dared her that they couldn't taste as good. "Okay, then. I'll leave you to it."

"I'll see you tomorrow morning. Don't forget we're presenting to the senior staff about our enrollment first thing."

"How could I forget?" I put off disconnecting. I always dreaded the last work of the day because of the nothingness that followed.

As I hover my cursor over "end meeting," I see something moving behind Katie, blocking the view of her bedroom behind her. Couldn't be her cat, could it? No, too big. "Katie, what—"

"Well, then, I'll—"

The room lights up all at once and there's a high-pitched screeching sound through the speakers, so loud I have to pull off my headset. The last thing I see is Katie's eyes, huge and glassy, her mouth open in a silent scream, and in the split second before the screen goes black, there's a woman's face.

It was her! The woman from the all-staff meeting! She was behind Alastair, too!

I jump up, knocking my chair backwards. Now I'm certain I wasn't imagining it. Hands shaking, I grab my iPhone and dial 911.

"911, what's your emergency?"

"Yes, my friend, there was someone in her house… a woman, I think… I'm afraid she's hurt!" Am I making any sense at all? My mind is skittering. "And she lives alone," I add in a small voice. Truth is, I worry about a scenario like this all the time. All alone and in trouble with no one to know. I swallow deeply.

"Okay, miss, where does your friend live?"

I give her Katie's address in Montpelier, and the woman says she will have an officer do a wellness check. I thank her and hang up. Then I pace the room.

Should I drive there and check on her myself? I look out the window. The rain is coming down sideways, hammering the roof like a tommy gun.

No. I'm such a nervous driver anyway, especially under these conditions. My heart is pounding inside my chest as if it wants out. I have to do something! It's that woman in the all staff meeting who's the key to this. I just know it! But who the hell is she?

Then I remember: the all staff meetings are recorded for people who are unable to attend. I hammer away at my keyboard and pull up the archived meetings. I find last week's and download it. My head is buzzing. Once it's downloaded, I fast-forward through the minutes, scanning the pictures on the side as they shift. But they are all familiar faces. Did I really just imagine her? Then an image flashes in and out, and I freeze. I rewind a bit and press pause. The blue eyes stare right back at me, burning holes in the screen. She's smirking.

"There you are!" My voice is loud in the quiet house.

I take a screen shot and edit it down to just the face. I do reverse image search on Google, and a series of blonde heads appear on the screen: actresses, social media profiles, none of them her. I go to the second page. Then the third. Halfway down the fourth page, I stop, my fingers freezing on the mouse.

It's her. In a news clipping. I bring the article up and scan it.

Wait. There has to be some mistake.

It's old. Like, really old: 1897 old!

The most sensational murder in Central Vermont history.

Then I notice the name: Anna Wheeler.

"Hold on a minute! The Anna? VCFA's Anna?" I ask of the photograph accompanying the article. It was the same face, only... sweeter, more innocent. I keep reading. It was the story I knew about her. Love triangle. Murdered right on campus.

I sit back and stare at the screen.

Holy shit! Was Anna the one who was hurting my colleagues? I search more, trying to get more pictures, more details. I explore ancestry sites, and local history blogs. The hours tick by as I scan each page, hoping for more clues, something more about her.

I blink awake and sit up, my hand going to my sore neck, the indentation of the laptop keys embossed into my face. And then I remember.

Anna!

Wait… Katie!

I check my phone and find a voicemail from the Montpelier police that they went by her house. Nobody was home, but they were going to check on her again this morning. I notice the time and realize the meeting we're supposed to be presenting in is about to start. Maybe Katie will be there, and all will be okay. I shakily log in and put my headset on. I click to join the meeting, and find only two faces waiting: Leslie and Matt.

"Good morning, Ann." Leslie says in her bright voice, but I can tell something's bothering her.

"Um, hi." I wave awkwardly and realize I must look like hell. I run a hand through my short hair. I have to say something. "Where's Katie?"

"We were going to ask you the same thing," Matt says, and I get a feeling there was serious conversation going on before I logged on.

Wait, senior staff has nine people on it. "Where's everyone else?"

Leslie presses her lips together. "We're not sure, but we're hoping they aren't… ill."

Oh God. The virus. Jesus.

"Well, since we're missing so many people, I think it best we reschedule, don't you, Matt?" Leslie looks into the camera, and I can tell I'm not the only one who's anxious.

"Yes, I think that would be best."

I'm not going to ramble in front of the President. Matt is different, though, so I say: "Wait! Matt! Can I talk to you a minute?"

Leslie waves and logs off.

"Sure! What's up?" Matt asks.

"I'm worried about Katie... and Alastair. I was in video meetings with them and I... saw... something, and then they were gone."

"Something? Like what? A person?"

"Yes... I mean, no." Oh man, he really is going to think I'm losing it. But I have to tell someone. "Truth is, I think I know who... or what, it is."

His voice gets really quiet. "What? Ann, what's going on?"

And then the words just spill and pick up speed. "Matt, I think it's that woman in the all-staff meeting I told you about, remember?"

"Okay..."

"Last night I pulled up the recorded meeting, and I was able to get a screenshot of her and I did a search." As I talk, my fingers are rushing over the trackpad to share my screen with him. There. The photograph of Anna in our meeting pulls up, next to the news clipping about the murder. Matt pulls his glasses onto his forehead and peers closer. I watch his hazel eyes widen as he reads the clipping on the screen, then compares the photographs.

"Are you telling me you think Anna the ghost was in our all staff meeting?"

OK, so I laugh hysterically at that, even though there is nothing at all funny about it. I just can't help it. Hearing it out loud from one of the more grounded humans I know really emphasizes the absurdity of the idea. As I catch my breath, I notice Matt isn't laughing.

Wait. Does he believe me?

He pulls his glasses back down. "I'm wondering if this is a practical joke from some disgruntled employee, there was—"

"Matt! No one has heard from Alastair or Katie! And where the hell are the rest of the senior staff?" Yes, I'm screaming now, but I don't care. I have to get someone to believe me. I take a deep breath and look straight at the screen. "Matt, I think something is happening to the staff. Something bad."

I can see him tapping away on his phone, then putting it to his ear, then tapping again. "What are you doing?"

"I'm trying to call Katie. Alastair..." Tap, tap, tap. "Anybody!" He puts his phone down, then sinks into his chair. "And you think it's

Anna?"

I watch him. Is he making fun of me? He always says he thinks I'm "hilarious," but the only thing I see in his eyes is fear.

I just nod.

He looks off, quiet for so long I wonder if he's just going to dismiss it, leaving me to think my wild thoughts by myself as I usually do. Then he takes a deep breath, straightens his shoulders, and says, "What can we do? It's not as if anyone is going to believe us."

Us.

Two letters, that's all. But they carry so much weight… and hope. "I don't know, but I've been thinking about what she wants."

"Anna?"

"Yes. I mean, hundreds of years College Hall is bustling, then suddenly, bam! No one."

"True. But why kill people?"

"I think she's pissed."

He throws his hands up in the air. "Well, she certainly isn't happy. But what does she want?"

I start thinking out loud, imagining myself as Anna. "Well, we might have irritated her, but we were company. I mean, I hate being here all by myself, so I can relate! But if you read between the lines of that article, she had her life all lined up, fiancé, school… and then, bam!"

"You keep saying 'bam.'"

"Yeah, but this time it's to represent an actual shot so it makes sense. Matt, I think she feels jilted. Abandoned. Lonely."

He stops for a moment. "Makes sense."

A warmth spreads outward from my chest. Finally, someone thinks I make sense. "I think you need to go talk to her."

"Me? Why me?"

"Well, 'cause you live a block from campus! I'd have to drive in, and—" I glance at my watch, "the weekly all staff meeting starts in half an hour, and I don't think we have that much time."

"Why do you care about the staff meeting at a time like this?"

"Because think about it! Every remaining staff member will be on that call? Matt! They could all be in danger!"

He breathes out loudly. "Jesus."

Tammy's voice comes from upstairs: "Matt? Everything okay?"

He narrows his eyes, then yells back, "Yeah, honey. I just need to walk over to College Hall for a minute to…get a file!"

I look at him, tears threatening. "Thank you, Matt."

He waves it away and starts to stand up, but then stops and waggles his index finger at me. "If I get eaten, or worse, in trouble with Leslie, I'm totally blaming you!"

I laugh and start to thank him again when he winks off.

I sink in my chair as if my bones have melted at once.

I'm already logged on to the meeting and waiting when three o'clock comes. Matt hasn't called me, but I'm hoping he's found some answers. I stare at my solitary image on the screen, the bright orange paint of my office deceivingly cheery behind me.

3:03

3:09

What the hell? Why is nobody here yet? I pull up Gmail on my phone to see if there was a cancellation message I missed. Nothing.

3:11

Not even Leslie? She's running the meeting, and she's not the kind of person to be late for anything.

3:14

My heart is galloping now, and I text Matt.

What's going on?

I stare at the screen, then type:

Nobody's logging on to the all staff meeting & I'm freaking out!

Nothing.

My breath starts to come in shallow and fast. Did Anna kill everyone? And did I just send Matt to his death? I search through my contacts and find Tammy's cell number.

"Hey, Ann!"

I'm so taken aback by the cheeriness of her voice, I can't say anything for a minute.

She asks: "Everything all right?"

"Um… yeah, yeah, sorry. I was just trying to reach Matt… is he around?"

"No, he went to the college for a file, but he hasn't come back yet. Did you try texting him?"

I need to get off the phone. I'm pretty much incapable of holding a "normal" conversation at this point. "Yeah, I guess he's busy… no worries. I… gotta go, thanks T!"

"Wait! Is everyth—"

I tap 'end' and text Matt again. Nothing.

I stare at my phone and feel my chest tightening, the air leaving my lungs in gulps. Ten minutes pass. Fifteen.

Then three ellipses appear, indicating that he's typing.

I let out a long breath.

Thank GOD. He's alive.

Can you get here right away?

I type back: *What? Why?*

I'll tell you when you get here. Just come to College Hall.

I shove the phone into my back pocket, grab my bag and my coat, and head to the car as if in a trance. What the hell am I doing? And what did Matt find? But my heart is racing in anticipation of leaving the house. Of driving somewhere other than the supermarket or the drugstore. Of walking into College Hall again.

I drive down Route 12 without even seeing the surroundings, intensely focused on just getting there. Though I have taken this route twice a day for ten years, I haven't been on it for the full five weeks of lockdown. Normally I would be admiring the budding trees, the waterfalls from the melting snow. But all I can do is drive and stare straight ahead.

Montpelier is silent, the streets empty, stores closed. Not a surprise given the governor's shelter in place order. I make my way up the hill to campus, the building coming into sight, its 1826 architecture looming and intimidating. It's so weird to see no one on the green. There's usually a couple of people throwing a ball to their dog, or kids playing around the fountain. It's like I have the college all to myself.

I pull my car into the empty parking lot, turn off the engine, close my eyes and breathe deep. An entire lifetime of being afraid, afraid of silly things. Flying on airplanes, clowns, sports mascots. But here's something *actually* scary.

Isn't it?

This isn't all in my mind, is it?

I pull a hair tie off my stick shift, complete with stray blond hairs stuck in the elastic, and pull my hair into a messy bun at the back of my head. I'm about to get out when my phone buzzes in my pocket. I see a new message from Matt:

Come up to the tower. I want to show you something.

I look up at the dark building through the car window. How did he know I was here? I get out and start walking, while simultaneously wondering what the fuck I'm doing. But I can't seem to get myself to turn around. As I walk up the concrete steps, I realize it's like this is inevitable. The glass doors are unlocked, and I walk into the cold, dark lobby, the stairs leading up into darkness in front of me. I take my time, relishing the smell of the empty building, the aging wood and dusty carpets. When I reach the fourth floor, I stop and look around. The narrow door that leads to the tower is open.

I'm out of breath from the stairs, but it's not just that. There's also a current of excitement in the air. My shoes make no sound on the faded wall-to-wall carpeting, but I can feel my pulse behind my face. I stop just shy of the open door.

"Matt?" My voice echoes in the empty hallway.

"Yeah, I'm up here! C'mon up!"

His voice sounds so normal. Even cheery. Maybe everything is okay? I feel a mixed cocktail of relief and fear. I start up the rickety stairs. The ancient wood is covered with thousands of fly carcasses that crunch beneath my shoes. It's a clean sound, and there's something vaguely… comforting about it. I round the last turn in the winding staircase, arriving at the top, the glass bell tower surrounded by darkening sky. Matt stands there, looking out over the surrounding hills, next to a woman in period dress. I give a sharp intake of breath.

They turn around and look at me, smiling.

"Hey, Ann!" Matt says. "Thanks for coming!"

Such a polite Southerner, even standing next to a dead woman.

"You were right. She just wanted some company." He indicates the woman next to him.

The edges of Anna's lips spread apart, but it's just a bit off, a caricature of a smile.

I turn and address her directly. "So… you're not going to kill anyone else?"

She shakes her head, and I can see flashes of skull beneath her hair, empty sockets behind her face, hear the rattling of what sounds like bones. I want to take a step backwards, but I can't seem to make my legs move.

"That's… great. Matt, maybe we should go—"

"Go?" Matt smiles as if I've said the silliest thing imaginable.

"Well, yes… I—"

Matt brushes by me and goes down one step. He turns to Anna. "I told you she was a better choice."

He turns to me then, and I look deep into his eyes. It's so weird to actually talk to a person close-up, face-to-face after all these long weeks of solitude, but as I gaze at him, I realize I don't know who this is. This is not my friend. I look back at Anna, and whisper, "What did you do to him?"

The creature next to me continues in Matt's voice, "I told her, you'd be better company. You're just hilarious!" It smiles, adds "bless your heart," and then heads down the stairs.

"Wait! Matt! I'm—"

Anna is suddenly in front of me, blocking the staircase, and I hear the door slam, feel the tower shake with the force.

And then there's the unmistakable sound of a lock clicking into place.

APOCALYPSE BRONX

By Richie Narvaez

They were almost old pros at it by now, this second one. The daughter, Anibel, knew to ration her time on Wi-Fi or else she'd get the yell. Martin Estevez, the father, and his boy did gigantic jigsaw puzzles, which seemed only a little less complex than the first time they'd done them in 2020. Martin and his wife, Nellie, seamlessly took turns parenting and zoning out. She usually took the day shift, he the night. Unless he was on duty—which was a lot more lately. Nellie had learned to be understanding.

But three months into #quarantine2022, anxiety still hung over everything they did. It was a rare night off for Martin, so he and the boy did the cooking. They stretched the last of their eggs, made pancakes for dinner, enough to last a few days. Pancakes held up well, made good snacking heated in the toaster oven. After dinner, the family splayed around the living room, ready to turn in—a routine familiar from the first round of covid, when they had started going to sleep as early as farmers. Anibel texted, the boy softly snored and farted against his father's leg on the floor, and Nellie scrolled through pictures of stuff that was no longer available. It wouldn't be unusual for all of them to fall asleep right where they were, in sight of each other.

There was a knock on the door.

"You order anything?" Martin said to his wife.

"Yeah, right," she said, not moving from her MePad.

He peeped through the door. Beau from the precinct. For a moment, Martin worried he was getting brought in on his night off, that his rare moment of peace with his family was being ripped away. But Beau was in civvies and, of course, his N95+.

Martin slid on his N95+ and opened the door. Beau motioned him outside, away from the door, to the side of the house.

Martin stepped out, closed the door behind him. "It's almost curfew."

Beau ignored this. "Our boy woke up."

"Shit."

"Yeah. Came out of it couple hours ago."

"Still at Flushing?"

"No, family had to come get him, what with all the covids needing beds. They took him home. To the Bronx."

"Fuck. Of all places."

"Yeah. Back home for you."

Outside it was cold and damp. For Martin, it was weird not to have any walls around him. Bayside was a primo neighborhood, quiet, tree-lined streets, a neighborhood his parents would have killed to live in, but he'd barely had a chance to appreciate it in the past two years. He couldn't remember when he'd walked any farther than the garbage can. Everything they needed was delivered by Amazon now, a habit they'd developed during #covid2020, a habit the government encouraged.

"You gotta do it," Beau said. "That was the deal."

"I mean, I guess. But how? Bridge is locked down by state cops. My badge won't do any good."

"If you don't do it, when this thing is over, all our lives won't be worth shit."

"Like the way we're living now is?"

Martin could see Beau was smirking, even with the mask on.

"Big fucking deal," Beau said. "It'll disappear just like the last one."

Martin shook his head. "That one never really went away and they say this one is going to be much, much worse."

"Ah, don't listen to them schmucks. They don't know what the fuck they're talking about."

Martin nodded, looking down. He didn't want Beau to see he was smirking now.

"Listen, it's easy," Beau said. "Take the river."

"The river? You see a boat parked in this driveway?"

"I see two cars and a lovely house, bigger than mine, and I know how you got 'em."

"You got a nice house out of it, too, Beau."

"Not a Tudor." Beau cocked his head. "You said you'd do it when he came out of it. That was the deal. Take the river. It's your best bet."

"Christ. How? Swim across?"

"Miller says there's a guy in College Point, does night drops."

Martin rocked in place. He felt the night air on his face. So weird.

Beau sensed Martin's hesitation. "Gotta be tonight," he said. "Before our boy starts talking in full sentences."

"Shit." Martin shook my head. "What the hell am I supposed to tell my wife?"

In order to avoid curfew cops, some he might even know, Martin had jogged four miles over, in a black hoodie, sweatpants, and sneakers, keeping to as many dark spots on the streets as he could. Now he stood, sweating into his mask in a parking lot in front of an out-of-business Dollar Tree. All the parking-lot lights—and cameras—had been knocked out. It was pitch black except for the phone held up to his face.

The man holding the phone wore thick blue gloves and a ventilator that had been converted from a snorkeling mask. Made him look like a fish.

"Miller sent me," Martin said, trying not to show that he needed to catch his breath. He guessed his home-gym setup wasn't really working. He handed over three hundred-dollar bills in a sandwich baggie.

"Yeah. You can call me 'Chief'—" The man said, lowering the phone and switching off the flashlight app.

The lot exploded in light. A parked SUV came alive, shining its high beams at them. Its sirens chirped. The PA system commanded: "Stay where you are."

Martin froze. He didn't dare reach for the gun in his underarm holster.

Chief didn't budge. "Who is that now?" he yelled at the SUV. "I'm paid up for the month."

"Down on the ground. Down on the ground." A cop climbed out of the truck, weapon drawn. Martin knew that, if this guy was like the rest of the force, they'd be very hesitant to shoot. As soon as this pandemic hit, the survivalists bought up every single round of spare ammo, leaving nothing for the cops. The man's partner emerged from the other side. Martin recognized him. Castellari. Must have transferred to Narcotics.

Shots then, from behind Martin. The lights on top of the truck split into fragments. Martin heard one—maybe both?—of the narcs cry out in pain. Was Castellari hit?

"All aboard, asshole," Chief said, grabbing his arm. Martin brushed him off.

"Or stay the fuck here." Chief shrugged and ran, the flash app of his phone still on.

Martin hesitated, said, "Fuck," then ran, following Chief's bobbing phone flashlight.

They scampered down a narrow alley behind the store, came to a hole in a fence, and beyond it the top of a ladder. Whoever had done the shooting was already scrambling down.

"Go go go," Chief said.

Martin knew there was something at the bottom of the ladder. But he was sightless in the darkness. Then he heard it: a boat knocking against the broken, corrugated wall.

More shots rang out. Martin climbed quickly and, as soon as he felt a surface underneath him, jumped into the boat. Legs shaky on the rocking surface, he looked back up. There was a light—followed by Chief falling right on him.

They dropped into the boat. The phone went out. They were in complete darkness again.

A voice called out: "Stop!"

Martin looked up as Castellari fired into the boat, hitting Chief's body. Blood spilled on Martin's face. This was too much, too insane. He wanted to yell, to surrender. He opened his mouth when a single shot rang out from the boat.

Castellari fell back onto the dock.

Someone in the darkness laughed.

The boat's engine suddenly grumbled and Chief's body, which was halfway out of the boat, slid into the water.

"Stay low," said the voice, followed by a giggle. He sounded high. "There might be more cops. Though I doubt it. They can't be spared."

The boat sped into the East River. Martin huddled against something squishy that he quickly realized were bales of marijuana.

"Hi, I'm Lance," the man said.

"Where?"

"Here at the stern. The back. I guess you can't see either way." Lance laughed to himself, still sounding high.

As Martin's eyes adjusted to the darkness, he realized he could see all of Lance's face. "Where's your mask?"

"Why do I need a mask if everyone else got one?" Again, the laugh.

Martin didn't say anything.

"I see you got one of those nicer masks," Lance said. A rifle with a night vision scope sat against his thigh. "Looks new. You get that from a hospital? Or from a cop. That's the type they give to all the cops now."

Martin wanted to give him the finger but didn't. He didn't want to antagonize this guy who had a rifle and was driving the boat. He had to get to the Bronx, no matter what.

"I figure you're not a cop. Not after all that. You wouldn't let a couple of your own be taken down in front of you, would you? Who knows? The world's gone to hell. I'm not even going to charge you for this ferry ride. That's how crazy this is. Keep your hands inside the vehicle at all times."

Lance started singing the *Gilligan's Island* theme. He knew every goddamn word.

Martin looked up to the dark, cloud-filled sky and wished that he had the smallest belief in prayer. Not just for him to survive the night and get back to his family. But also for Lance to shut up.

It had started to rain when they realized there was a hole in the boat.

Nellie could always tell when he was bullshitting. She had not been happy when he left.

Martin was too tired, not just from the stomach full of pancakes and the endless worry of quarantine, but also from years of waiting for this day. He told her everything.

"That's how we got this house," she said, "that mysterious thirty-five grand."

"Yeah."

"'My uncle died,' you told me. I should've known. I knew I'd never heard of Uncle Carlos."

"I'm so sorry I lied to you, baby. There's no excuse—"

She shook her head. "No, no, you do have one. You had no choice. I know what a boy's club the police are. A bunch of bullies. And you as an intelligent man of color, what else could you do? They'd never let you rise. You were caught in a trap."

"I could have said no."

"Baby, this is the way America works. This is the way it's always worked. You can't move up the ladder without going along with the rot, the rot that's always been part of the country. Play along and, congratulations, here's your corner Tudor with a wraparound front yard."

"Nellie!" Martin's chest was tight. He wanted to make everything right, needed to fix this. "I won't do it. That's all there is to it. I'll… I'll talk to the DA."

"Nope. Nope. No, you won't." She shook her head, looking at their sleeping children in the dim light of the living room. "You still don't have a choice, Martin, don't you see that? You're going all the way up to the Bronx and you're going to do what you have to do. Not just for your family, but for every person of color trying to make their way up. You're going to get your hands even dirtier than they are now, and I know that's going hurt a man like you."

"But, baby—"

"But we've come this far, we're not losing the ground we gained. Look at your son. That boy is the light of your life. And our daughter is a year away from college, we have the money that our parents never had—*never*—to send her to a good one. So you're going. And you're coming back to us. Alive."

Before he left, she made sure he wore a thick sweater and thick socks, along with his thicker raincoat. "It's always colder on the water," she said.

Through the light rain and far in the distance, to the right—was that port or starboard?—Martin saw the dimmed lights of Connecticut. Directly ahead was the Boogie Down Bronx. It wouldn't be much farther. If they didn't sink.

The bilge pump wasn't doing such a good job. Martin's sweatpants were soaked. Lance told him to grab the bucket in the front hold. Martin found it and could tell it had been used as a toilet.

"C'mon," said Lance. "I drive the boat. You bail."

Martin started bailing buckets of stanky water out of the boat.

Lance lit a spliff. "Shit, we were supposed to make ten stops tonight.

Now this."

"You don't seem very broken up over Chief," Martin said.

"My brother-in-law? Better off without him. We got beach up ahead. You're doing a shit job. This boat won't make it unless I patch that hole. Fuck."

"How far off-course are we?"

"I'm not a fucking GPS. It's not like Brooklyn or Manhattan, anyway, not ringed with guards and searchlights. It's just the Bronx. Nobody cares about the Bronx."

They smelled the bonfire before they saw it.

"Looks like someone's partying," Lance said.

Martin followed where he was pointing—a large fire on the beach that was winning against the light rain. He could see figures gathered around the inferno. What time was it anyway? Did these people not care about the curfew? Were the local cops going to shut this gathering down? On a beach, no less.

Then he smelled it.

"That's not driftwood," he said.

"Could be barbecue," Lance said. "I'm hungry."

No, Martin thought. He remembered responding to a domestic disturbance, back when they had time to do that sort of thing. The husband was known for verbally and physically intimidating the family. Neighbors had worried for years, the investigation revealed later. The bodies were found in the backyard in circle of charred flesh and ash. The horrible smell stayed on him for months.

And Martin was smelling it again now.

"Seriously, guy, we shouldn't stop here," Martin said. "Let's go down aways."

"Fuck is wrong with you?" Lance said. "Looks like a fun crowd and maybe I can get some new customers."

Lance beached the boat and splashed into the shallow water.

Martin saw the people at the bonfire, a hundred yards away, react. He got out, grabbed Lance by the collar. “Get back in the boat, now.”

For this, Martin got the butt of the rifle in his gut and, as he bent over in pain, the butt again in his face.

He leapfrogged, grabbed Lance’s slippery-wet calves, brought him down to the sand.

Lance cursed, bringing up the rifle. Martin stood up and reached for his weapon, but Lance swept his legs out from under him and he fell back, hitting his head on the boat.

“You there!” a voice called.

“Hey all!” Lance said, bringing up the rifle. There was a shot, but not from Lance. He hit the ground, and Martin, his face jagged with pain, sunk into blackness.

When he awoke a few minutes later, he was surrounded.

They all stood at least twelve feet away.

First thing he noticed: None of them had masks on. Something else was strange about them. Gray hair. White hair. Wrinkles. They were old—in their sixties, seventies, eighties, maybe even older. He hadn’t seen so many old people gather together since before the first virus. Politicians, sure, but not regular people.

A white-haired woman in jeans spoke up: “What are you doing here? This is a private community.”

“This’s the Bronx,” Martin mumbled, trying to get to his knees. He wasn’t quite sure what part of the Bronx it was. But all these faces seemed familiar, related somehow to all the people he had grown up with. His own face hurt bad—he wondered if his jaw had been broken. Lance’s body remained where it had fallen, but his rifle was gone.

“This is the New Vista Living Facility,” the woman said. “We’re in charge now. The caregivers, the nurses, the doctors, they made the choice or they were forced to leave by their families. They left us here in the first pandemic. Some came back when things started to return to normal. But when this second wave came, with people dying in the thousands the first week, well, we knew we were on our own."

"Those bodies," he said, gritting teeth through the pain. "What are you doing with those bodies?"

"Taking care of our dead. That was just for today. We set a fire every night, young man."

Martin got to his feet, wobbly.

"It's a good thing you have your mask on. Your friend was not so lucky. We can't have his kind around here. And what you brought in that boat, ah, thank you for that. We're keeping it."

"It raises risks of dying of the virus," Martin said.

"We're well aware of that."

One of the men beside him raised a hunting rifle in his direction.

The woman said, "You're going to have to come with us until we decide what we're going to do with you."

The call came in about a suspicious individual flashing money. Martin was still pretty new on the force. He had been paired with Beau, an experienced and decorated officer.

"This is it," Beau said. "Let's go get him."

Miller and Kilgore were first at the scene, Beau and Martin showed up a hot minute later. The individual, a very tall, heavyset African American male, was being disrespectful to the officers. He carried a large leather briefcase; when asked if it was his, he would only respond with answers like, "Why do I have to answer that?" "What business is it of yours?" and "Tell me what I did wrong. Just tell me."

Miller put his hand up to calm the individual down, and the individual definitely made an aggressive move. Didn't he? What happened at that point was hard for Martin to think about clearly.

The individual and Miller were suddenly grappling. Kilgore tapped on Martin's shoulder and then tapped his own nose, which was the signal for them to shut off their body cams.

It was a late afternoon, an empty street in a poor neighborhood. Which meant no smartphones, no street surveillance.

Beau and the other two had wrestled the individual to the ground. Beau was kicking him. Martin stood to the side. He kept yelling at the individual to stop resisting, stop resisting. Stop. Please. Stop.

And then the individual was still.

"You motherfuckers killed him!"

They all turned. There was a kid, Hispanic, late teens, and he was running.

Miller yelled at Martin: "Get him!"

But Martin didn't move, couldn't move.

Miller and Beau were on their feet and after him.

Martin stared down at the suspect. Spilling out of the briefcase were bricks of cash.

They found out later the suspect had liquidated stocks, was going to retire early. He was officially listed as missing.

The kid reached an overpass before Miller and Beau finally stopped him with ten rounds. He fell over the rail into traffic. There was no way he should have survived that.

But he did.

The hospital boys played along, said nothing about the bullets. Easy stuff. Reporters didn't ask any tough questions anymore, only talked about the weather, repeated what the president said, and hawked whatever new movie or TV show was coming out.

In Beau's man cave, Kilgore put a fat envelope in Martin's hand and held it there. "If you had done your job," she said, "that kid would never have been a problem."

Martin said nothing.

"We talked. We decided. If that kid ever wakes up, he's yours and yours alone to take care of."

Martin said nothing. He took the envelope.

The New Vista retirees made him walk twelve feet ahead.

They talked as they walked.

"Josephina, there's no point in bringing him closer to the houses," the one with the rifle said to the woman in jeans. "He could be infected."

"Take care of him by the fire," a tiny, ancient woman in a sweater offered. "Save the trouble of dragging him."

Josephina stopped, and they all stopped with her. "What's your name, young man?"

Martin turned. The tiny woman said, "Don't ask him his name, that just makes it harder."

"Martin," he said. He could see all their faces better now, lit by the horrible bonfire. He saw fear in their eyes, but also curiosity. He gritted his teeth, saying, "I show you something?"

"Watch out. He's got that holster," said another of the retirees.

"And Ronaldo has the draw on him," Josephina said. "Go ahead, young man."

Martin reached into his pocket and pulled out his badge.

"Fuck that," the tiny woman said.

Ronaldo said, "Oh, Christ, was the other guy a cop, too?"

"Quiet!" Josephina said, holding up a hand to silence them. "Martin, you may not see the writing on the wall, but we do. That badge means nothing because the law means nothing, not anymore. Not that it ever meant much of anything in this part of town, where the cops like you could do as they pleased. Where the government never bothered to take care of its citizens. You understand what I'm talking about?"

He was ashamed to say that he did. "S'you got your own laws?" he asked. Each word was a stabbing pain to speak. "Made your own town with you as the sheriff?"

She smiled. "You got jokes. No, it's not like that. Perhaps that would be, if any of us were younger, if any of us expected to last that long. Take a look. There are thirty of us here left. Two months ago, there were four hundred. We just want to be left alone. We're not afraid of death at all, Martin. If anything, we're afraid of letting the outside world in again. We want to appreciate and enjoy the time we have left. Without the hypocrisy, tyranny, and disease of the world as it is outside these walls. That's why I'm not so sure we can let you go. What's going to stop you from bringing a bunch of pigs back here to get us on the evening news?"

"I won't," he said.

"And we should believe you—why?"

Martin scratched his head. "Let me show you something." He took out a picture of his family, Nellie and the kids. "Girl's name is Anibel. She's sixteen."

"Pretty name," one of them said.

"And my son is Martin, Jr."

"Good-looking boy."

"Thanks," Martin said. "I gotta go back to them."

They were silent for just a minute.

"It'd be a pain to tie him up," one of them said. "Just let him go."

"Yeah, let him go," said another.

"So nice to see a new face."

"I coulda use him for a sex slave," said the tiny old woman.

Josephina pointed up the beach. "The exit is that way. Feel free to take a golf cart."

Martin unfolded the street map he had printed out. It was around five in the morning and the sun was just struggling to rise. His destination was only four miles away. In the cart, that took about forty minutes. After thirty minutes, it ran out of battery power. He pushed the dead cart up to a hydrant and walked the rest of the way. He found the building easily. These kinds of housing developments, the kind that he had grown up in, the kind he had fled, always had back doors for basement access. The lock was flimsy and he got inside easily.

He took the stairs up seven floors. It was hot as hell in the mask, which filled with the stink of his dry breath and the blood in his mouth.

Sean Enríquez had lived on his own in Queens, where he'd had the bad luck to witness three cops beating a suspect to death and a fourth cop who stood there doing nothing.

Martin peeked out of the stairwell on the seventh floor. People lined the dimly-lit hallway, neighbors and family, in masks and six feet apart. There was praying. There was crying. At the far end there was movement, the familiar jockeying that happened now when anybody moved, that effort to keep distance. He soon saw why.

They were bringing a body out.

Martin stepped into the hallway and stopped six feet from the nearest person.

"Not the virus?" he asked an older man who noticed him.

"Nah. He didn't have a chance to get better from the coma. They should never have sent him home."

People scattered or squeezed themselves against the wall as the bier came through.

As it passed Martin, Sean's right hand fell from sheet, bare and open.

Martin had a momentary urge to reach out and touch the stray hand. If it weren't for the virus, he would have. To ask for supplication.

Instead, he watched them wheel the body away. Then he took the stairs and left.

Martin flashed his badge to get on the subway without having to show Essential Worker papers. Trains were running on limited service, so it took an hour for one to arrive. Because of the delay, the train became surprisingly packed, with no room for six feet of distance. It looked like all working-class people, sullen and sleepy behind their masks.

After two transfers, he got off at his subway stop by noon. He walked through his neighborhood again, feeling the sun on his face. He took in the grand trees, the overflowing flower-filled fronts. He couldn't smell any of it.

He was surprised to find a corner bodega was open. It had been so long since he'd been to one—he went in. The boy liked apples. Maybe there'd be some for him and other surprises for the family.

Inside, the woman behind the counter smiled behind her mask. The refrigerated section was empty and turned off. Large signs said, "Six Feet Apart" and "Sorry, No Toilet Paper." The shelves were mostly empty, except for canned goods and dust-covered spices. By the front counter there was still some produce, wilted lettuce, a lone cucumber, but no apples.

He pointed to a bunch of yellow-orange things he didn't recognize, which looked like they had thorns on them. "What is this?"

"Prickly pear," the woman behind the counter said.

The boy might like it, he thought. He bought some and when he got home, he sat on his doorstep and took off his mask. He took one of the fruits out and realized he had no idea how to eat it. With his wounded jaw, he wondered if he even could.

PERSONAL PROTECTION

By Terri Lynn Coop

I handed my wife a mug reading *Will Trade Medical Advice for Tacos* and said: "I don't see why you have to go in today."

She added two more sugars before she drank deep. "Josh, you know I'm essential."

"So am I. However, I have twenty-four glorious hours off. I wanted to spend them with my girl. You're even more essential to me."

"I promise you it'll only be eight today. I have to cover a gap in the ER. When I became chief resident, we knew that was part of the deal."

Instead of reaching across the kitchen island to refill her coffee, I walked around and took her in my arms. Her hair smelled like lemons this week. It reminded me how, even with our connections, everything was hit-and-miss after more than a year of the creaking supply chain.

"Okay, eight hours, and then you're out. We're celebrating tonight."

"What's tonight?"

"Doctor Delgado, I cannot believe you are so remiss. Tonight marks fifty days until the end of your fellowship from hell, or in hell, as I prefer to think of it."

She stiffened, and I was afraid I'd gone too far. I hated her job. County was consistently one of the hardest-hit hospitals in the country. In a macabre twist, she'd catapulted from the resident pool into a prestigious fellowship when her two competitors died during the first outbreak. It gave her the chance to work under one of her heroes, and even though we'd had the worst argument of our marriage, there was no way I was going to deny her that chance. It didn't keep my heart out of my throat every time she went on shift, especially in the ER.

She kissed my cheek, and the tension melted. "Uh, talking about hell, how about those hundred-hour rotations you've been on? We haven't had five minutes to ourselves in forever." With those words, she added some bodily friction that I felt down to my toes.

"I have five minutes now."

She tugged the drawstring of my old scrub pants, and they puddled around my feet. "I was hoping you'd say that."

Even with the never-ending sirens, the city view from our balcony worked its magic on me. Okay, I was already in a pretty damn good mood. Everything from her velvet touch to her diamond-sharp brain to her parents' bank account reminded me just how far above my weight class I'd punched when Dr. Eliana Delgado had decided I was worth her time and attention. My life was on a golden trajectory until UNSPEC hit the scene.

I popped a day-off morning beer. The virus that had recently ticked its body count to over two million worldwide had cute names, official names, and imaginative names, but those on the front lines still used that first label. When the victims started choking ambulances, hospitals, and morgues, harried doctors had charted "*idiopathic organ failure resulting from unspecified infection*" as the cause of death. As the pace picked up, the chart code became a scribbled *UNSPEC*. It stuck with the people who understood what it represented.

The intercom interrupted my reverie. Tossing back the rest of my beer, I called to the voice-activated system, "Corrine, what's up?" We'd had to change the name after Eliana's nephew kept triggering it, including an accidental order for two cases of creamed corn.

The honey-smooth computerized voice replied, "There's a package downstairs from DGI. Shall I sanitize and send it up touchless?"

"Yes."

I grabbed another beer and wondered what El's dad was sending this week. With our job classifications, we ate better than most, but the boxes of questionable-market goods were always a treat. I barely had time to guess before a soft tone told me the package was in the bin outside our door. Not for the first time did I marvel at weathering the pandemic in this well-feathered nest. Apartments were a lot easier to get in the cities these days, but this wedding gift from the in-laws was a palace by any definition.

After pulling on gloves out of habit, I slit the tape and quality seals. Peeking inside, I shouted: "Holy shit, baking supplies. And chocolate. Thanks, Dad."

That's when my plan came together. I was going to bake brownies and take them to the hospital. I wasn't being totally altruistic. I wanted to make sure Eliana didn't get talked into overtime.

"What's the point of having a travel pass if I don't use it? Corrine, I need Nana's brownie recipe."

I clipped my gold-banded ID to the pocket of my "outside" jacket. With my mask and wraparound sunglasses, I couldn't count on being recognized. At the hospital, the guard waved me to the VIP entrance. After stepping in front of the infrared thermometer, I waited for the beep to let me exit the "welcome chamber." All the government and public service buildings had them now, and we avoided the real name: Lucite Man-Traps. If you had a fever, the doors stayed locked, and you were escorted, under guard, to a screening facility. Even after my hundreds of passages, I still held my breath until the light flashed green.

My job class rated me a small locker. I swapped my outside mask and glasses for inside ones and grabbed a pair of shoe covers. Personal protective gear, the sacred PPE, was in chronic short supply, so anything that helped keep the outside out was a help.

I was greeted with smiles as I headed toward the ER. I kept opening the plastic bin and showing the individually wrapped baked goods. I planned on leaving them in the cleanroom reserved for staff breaks.

"Where's Dr. El?" I asked an intern, wearing a gray trash bag duct-taped over his lab coat as a gown, who pointed toward Room 5. Before I could thank him, the klaxon sounded, along with a red strobe light. The message was simple: An ambulance with a body fluids trauma patient was on the way, and all non-essential personnel needed to get their asses out of the hall. Then someone shouted something over the intercom that sent my heart into my throat: "Five."

"No," was all I said as I ignored the order and sprinted toward my wife's trauma room, the brownie container against my chest like a shield.

"CLEAR." The outer bay doors closed and the inner opened with a hiss as the negative pressure of the isolated HVAC system equalized. I knew the ambulance techs, even through their masks and goggles. From their expressions, I could tell this was a bad one. As UNSPEC took its toll on law enforcement, the streets had taken to policing themselves. A limp arm covered in tattoos sagged off the gurney and confirmed my suspicions.

Fucking banger. Probably a dealer.

I wanted to enter the trauma room but knew even I couldn't breach that protocol. Instead, I pressed myself against the hallway window. My wife's rank and seniority rated her a stained cotton gown and gloves. I knew her mask was a week old, and the wrap-around safety glasses were barely adequate for painting, much less front-line medicine. I also knew she was a professional. Her team worked mostly on hand signals at this point. A nurse pulled back the red-sodden field dressing, revealing multiple wounds.

Looks like an AR. If it was an AK, he wouldn't still be breathing. Even with the beer in my system, my mind clicked into mission mode. Evaluate, isolate, remediate.

There was another sound over the beeping equipment and rapid-fire exchanges of the medical team. A deep booming cough erupted from the victim, leaving bloody foam on his lips.

Shit. He's hot. Baby, step back. Let him go. He's gorked.

I wanted to beat on the glass but clutched the brownies tighter, willing her to stop. Instead, the woman I loved beyond all reason took a fresh dressing and leaned her weight into the oozing hamburger that was his chest and belly.

Blood gouted from his mouth and wounds, driven from his lungs and arteries by her pressure and the beating of his diseased and dying heart. The red wave splashed across her face, covering the edges of her mask, and dripped from around and under her glasses.

It was her scream that got me moving. I lowered one shoulder and burst through the door like I had through defensive lines back in school. I hooked one arm around her waist and threw her under the emergency shower. Her tattered mask was soaked through, and his contaminated blood was pink on her teeth. Desperate, I bent her over and jammed my fingers down her throat until she retched and brought up the remnants of her lunch. I'd do anything to cleanse her body of his foulness.

It took two security guards to pry my hands loose. Her face was wet and clean, and the blood and vomit on her gown had smeared into a weird watercolor.

"Get them both to exposure rooms, now!" Dr. Rollins was her mentor. His voice wasn't angry in my ears. It was the voice of experience. He'd take care of El. He always had. She'd be okay.

She has to be okay.

As they dragged me across the hall to one of the storage closets they'd converted into tiny exam and evaluation rooms, I got a last look at the soon-to-be corpse on the table. One of his tattoos caught my eye. The bright green double-X identified him as a Westside Twenty. I knew the crew. My brain automatically cataloged their territory. If the little bastard had been shot a couple of blocks farther out, they'd have taken him to Bayshore instead of County.

"Can I see her?" I asked.

Dr. Rollins didn't answer as he dropped the thermometer probe cover into the can to be sterilized and made notes in my file.

"Can I—"

"I heard you the first time. The answer is no."

I started to speak, but he waved me silent and picked up a swab that looked more like something a drum majorette would twirl in a parade.

"You know the drill. Lean back."

When I didn't move, he put his palm on my forehead and pushed. He wasn't slow or gentle as he extracted a sample of mucus from deep in my sinuses. It came back tinged with blood. I wondered who it belonged to. After dropping the swab into a tube, he tapped the glass to release the reagent. It swirled cloudy, but I knew that was meaningless. The initial result wouldn't come back for at least twelve hours. If it was negative, I was in the clear. If it turned blue, I was presumptive positive, and they'd send it to the lab for full analysis.

After he sealed the vial, he made more notes.

"So, this is your sixth exposure and test since we went to the combined rapid reactant and PCR protocol. All negative. Very unusual. Has the state health department contacted you about being in an immunity trial?"

"Yes, they have. In fact, I let them poke me full of holes the last time we had this discussion. I have no clue what the vampires are doing with the gallon they took. They were less gentle than you."

That got me a grim smile. In the last year, the healing arts had gotten a lot less artful. In the increasingly desperate search for a vaccine, two groups could be counted on to be hounded by the researchers: Those who had recovered and those who refused to get sick. I seemed to be in the latter category.

"Doc, can I ask you a question?"

"Possibly."

"How many times has Eliana been tested?" Funny, it was something we'd never discussed. We didn't talk about UNSPEC. It stole enough of our lives without inviting it into our home.

"Like all staff, as you well know, the monthly—"

It was my turn to interrupt him. "I don't mean the spit tests. We both know those are almost worthless after the last mutation. I don't even know why we still do them. You know the test I'm talking about." I gestured toward the vial.

"HIPAA prevents me from telling you that."

"Yeah, like anyone still follows that. Please. We both know that the fever police take people all the time based on all sorts of confidential information."

That was a nasty little secret in the medical and emergency response community. Anyone who disclosed a potential exposure, had a fever or even a deep cough, ran the risk of being detained incommunicado with a swab up their nose. Public health didn't care where the information came from.

He stalled by clicking and stowing his pen and closing my file. When he met my eyes, he knew I wouldn't stop asking.

"This is only her second PCR test. She's been amazing at avoiding exposures. Her protocols have always been impeccable. So, there's no track record. We have to wait. We've also taken tissue samples from the body as a control and for research."

"Can I take her home now? We'll call in tomorrow."

"No."

That single word chilled me through. "You've admitted her?"

"Yes."

Success in my job requires complete control of my expressions and my body. Knowing when to relax and when to intimidate was critical. It was time to intimidate. It didn't take much. I translated and projected my tension and rage into my posture and tone.

"Why?"

It worked. I detected the dilation of his pupils as he looked for an escape. Seeing none, he leaned back and said, "Josh, you were there. Her exposure was catastrophic. One of the worst we've ever seen. You helped. You helped a lot. However, you also spread that man's blood everywhere. The entire team is in isolation, including the two guards who pulled you off her. We're steam-cleaning the room and hall. We're closed to trauma for another twelve hours because of your stunt and the, um, condition of the victim. Honestly, he should have never been brought in. I don't know what the EMTs were thinking."

Even though *grab and go* was still the stated mission of the ambulance corps, the reality was that a brutal triage had become the norm. The floridly ill and severely injured were usually slow-coded and allowed to die *in situ.* It was to protect hospitals and doctors. It was to protect Eliana.

"What about me?"

"You're going home pending the outcome of your test. We've already notified your boss. You're relieved of duty until you're cleared."

"Why can I leave and she can't?"

This time, I got the look that had terrified a generation of med students. It was my turn to back down from the heat of his glare.

"Don't be dense. Triage. We don't have the space. You didn't get any blood in your face and you have a low-risk testing profile. We have to prioritize."

The meaning between the lines was obvious. Eliana was more important than me. The funny thing is that I agreed with him.

I had more questions, but he waved me off. "Go home. Don't call until tomorrow. We'll call you if we need anything. Go."

Our balcony hadn't changed. The perfect southern exposure was still perfect and the sunset was still gentle and muted over the downtown skyline. As for me, I'd changed to bourbon and finished off the plate of brownies I was saving for after dinner. Our dinner. The dinner when I was going to tell her my news. The news about my job offer. The one that could be the first step to getting out of the city. There was no running from UNSPEC, but there were places where its footprint was less intrusive and insidious.

My in-laws were riding out the semi-permanent quarantine in a fifteen-room cabin on a lake about three hours upstate. Ten acres, including a hundred yards of private shoreline, kept the town and the neighbors at a genteel distance. They'd made it very clear that we were welcome any time. At Christmas, I'd told her father about my concerns and goals. He'd agreed, and we'd both worked our contacts. The result was the letter in my pocket. All we needed to do was wait out the last fifty days of the fellowship she refused to abandon. With her credentials, every practice in the area would fall over each other in a bidding war to get her on staff. I just needed to give her an excuse to leave County.

Fifty days was now reduced to twenty-four hours. Our future. My future. I downed my bourbon, poured another, and picked up my phone to make the call before I was too drunk to be coherent.

"Hi, Dad. We need to talk."

Running out of bourbon took care of the hangover problem. I swiped through the unanswered calls and texts on my phone. I'd convinced her parents to stay away and that there was nothing they could do. My boss was sympathetic but hinting about how I needed to come back to work. They were short-handed, and every hour without me was an hour of overtime and potential exposure for one of my colleagues.

There was only one call I was going to return, but I had to get ready first. I read through the well-creased job offer one more time before wadding it up and throwing it over the balcony. I wasn't going to be the new Sheriff in a charming town right out of a movie set. That dream was gone. It was time to face reality.

I wasn't a police officer. I didn't keep the peace and help old ladies cross the street.

I was the fever police.

According to the media, I was a heavily-armed door-kicking storm trooper who hauled parents away from their screaming children to the fever camp north of the city. Whether or not they returned wasn't my problem. There was truth to the stories.

Those people had a fever.

They'd been a problem to be solved.

They were UNSPEC.

And now I had a new problem to solve. I'd lied to my department about staying home during my quarantine and done my recon. I knew where the nest was. Blending in as another homeless type on the street, I'd watched the green-tattooed filth coming and going from their clubhouse. Many of them were coughing. They were UNSPEC.

I checked the load on my service weapon and stashed three more mags in my jacket pocket. I added my drop piece, a beat-up Sig Sauer, to the other pocket. My old sawed-off was bulky in its underarm sling, but nobody looked too closely at anyone on the street. Not anymore.

It was time to make the call. I punched the number from memory.

"Dr. Rollins."

"One moment, please."

"Josh, how are you doing? I'm worried about you."

"Doc, you don't have to worry about me. I want to talk to you about Eliana."

His silence told me there was no change.

Finally, he asked: "What can I do for you?"

"You have my permission to take her off the vent. Let her go."

I hung up before he could answer. It was a formality. She and I had already signed all the protocols about exposure-related treatment, including when to end it. Her position still demanded that the niceties be observed. She'd crashed before the swab had a chance to turn blue.

The PCR confirmed what we already knew. Forty-eight hours later, we passed the point of no return, even though they still pretended to consult with me.

I closed that door in my heart and turned to the immediate problem. The problem I had the skills to solve. I put my black-banded badge next to our wedding picture. Most officers didn't even wear the ribbons anymore. Our constant state of mourning was assumed. I kept the frayed reminder of all that I'd lost. I added my wedding ring. I didn't want Eliana to be part of what was coming.

It was open season on UNSPEC and there was no bag limit.

A KINDER WORLD STANDS BEFORE US

By Nick Kolakowski

Under ordinary circumstances, the offseason life is the slow life, and hopefully you've saved up enough money from the summer to see you through seven months of long nights and quiet days. I hadn't. An unexpected medical bill in July, plus a big-bill car repair, meant I faced a harsh winter unless Jimbo's needed another chef to work the line—and fat chance of that, given the emptiness of its dining room after Labor Day.

So imagine my surprise when Dennis Smith, Jimbo's owner, called me on a cold morning in early October with a fat job offer: Five hundred dollars a week to flip burgers and fry potatoes for the few year-rounders who still drifted through his dining room every night.

"If you stick around, job's good until April," he said. "If Larry Johnson's healed up, I gotta let you go then, unless something opens up on the line, in which case—"

I interrupted him. "Wait, what happened to Larry? He sick?" For the past month, the news had buzzed constantly about the virus creeping its way through the big cities. Way out here on the sandy fingertip of Long Island, we could delude ourselves that it would never reach us, but I supposed it was inevitable that a few year-rounders would come down with that deadly cough. If Jimbo's was an infection zone, I wanted no part of it.

"Nah," Dennis laughed. "At least, not in the way you're thinking. You know Larry's got a drug problem, yeah?"

"Worst-kept secret in town."

"Let's just say that Larry made some very bad mistakes over the weekend with crystal meth. Crashed the mayor's car with—get this—an actual motherfucking *gibbon* riding along with him, then set himself on fire. Anyway, too long a story to tell here. Champ, you want the job or not?"

"Absolutely." What choice did I have? A long time ago, I might have waved off an offer to slap cheese on burgers and steam clams. I had trained in the world's best kitchens. The food critic at *The New York Times*—that miserable prick—had once called my bucatini pomodoro with black winter truffles the finest pasta he'd eaten this side of Rome. But that was a long time ago.

"Good," Dennis said. "Because we got more customers than we can deal with."

I had no idea what he meant by that. During the offseason, the town's population is maybe two hundred souls, and most of them—like me—prefer to spend those cold, gray months locked in their homes, drunk as hell and watching a bright screen. Although some of the summer people will drop by for the weekend, or a bit longer if their spouses have booted them out of their beautiful apartments in Manhattan or Los Angeles or London, those folks rarely drift into a place like Jimbo's, which offers fried seafood and burgers instead of Royal Ossetra caviar and duck foie gras.

But the following afternoon, I maneuvered my smog-farting junker into the restaurant's parking lot only to find it full of Ferraris, Bentleys, BMWs, Teslas, and Mercedes sedans. I squeezed my wheels into a narrow slot beside the dumpsters in back, then headed inside to prep for the dinner rush. Dennis hadn't lied about the crush: Through the swinging doors that connected the kitchen with the dining room,

I spied every table filled with banking executives, real-estate guys, minor celebrities, and even an ultra-famous country-music star whose albums I'd bought obsessively since childhood.

The kitchen was a storm of steam and clashing metal, four cooks and a dishwasher trying to maneuver in a tight and dripping-hot space. José, the junior chef temporarily elevated to the top slot after Larry's bad weekend, never stopped slicing huge piles of vegetables as he yelled over the din of the radio pounding out Mexican hip-hop. "Full house for lunch," he told me. "Full house, dinner, too. Thank God your skinny ass is here."

"Why aren't they at Beautiful Dirt? Or Manifest Destiny?" I asked as I slipped on Larry's white chef's jacket, conveniently left on a peg beside the door. Those two luxury restaurants, located a half-mile up the town's main drag, served citrus-cured trout, scallion mousse atop charcoal-grilled wagyu, and other hundred-dollar entrees. Their executive chefs both hated my guts—just one reason why my shadow had never darkened their doorways.

"Dude, all those places are still closed," called out Beau, Larry's brother, who worked the dessert station and was busy squeezing chocolate sauce over a colorful array of ice-cream scoops in tiny blue bowls. "Everything's closed but us and the grocery. And the liquor store."

Spreading my knife roll on the counter, I drew my Victorinox Fibrox eight-inch chef's knife, which was my favorite: lightweight, well-sharpened, impressively sturdy. I had no idea how well this kitchen was stocked, and what we were running low on, but I figured that I could improvise a fine clam chowder if I had to. I felt the familiar adrenaline rush that marked the start of a shift, an old friend that kicked my heart into higher gear.

"All these rich pricks flooded into town at once," Beau added, lowering his voice in case the doors opened at that moment. "What do they know that we don't?"

As it turned out, those rich pricks knew quite a bit.

Eight days later, the President declared that the entire northeast, from Maine to Delaware, was under "strict quarantine." From what we saw on the news, the U.S. Army locked down the bridges, tunnels, highway exits, even the ports. The virus had infected millions—and the lack of testing made it impossible to tell how fast it was advancing.

By that time, hundreds of the ultra-rich had flooded into our tiny corner of the world. They brought their kids, friends, entourages, mistresses, masseuses, chefs, and nannies. They came in luxury SUVs followed by trucks loaded with enough food to feed an army. When the police shut down the bridges that connected us to the rest of Long Island, they began arriving by yacht and private plane and helicopter.

Along the beach, their huge compounds burst with light and music. When they ran low on supplies, they stripped the local grocery stores of everything but bread—too many carbs.

They also brought the virus with them, and the nearest hospital only had three ICU beds and two ventilators. Dennis shifted Jimbo's from dine-in to takeout-only, and still the cars jammed the parking lot at all hours. We worked until our hands ached and our knees quaked, and then we slept in our cars for a few hours before doing it all again. The overtime pay was beautiful, and none of us wanted to question whether the almighty dollar would be good for anything other than toilet paper by the end of the year. The trucks arrived with fresh supplies, despite the bridge closures, and we did our best to avoid interacting with the customers—we knew that the bandanas we always wore over our faces would do little good to block the virus.

Bernita, who had worked Jimbo's register since approximately the dawn of time, snapped on a pair of surgical gloves and a gas mask in order to hand out the food. She was six feet of muscle, her corded forearms inked with elaborate tattoos, and nobody—not the year-rounders, not the billionaires—ever talked back to her.

When it wasn't blaring José's favorite rappers, the radio reported the rising casualty counts, the piles of dead in every hospital on Earth. We did our best to ignore it. The scientists would find a cure, right?

How could things not return to normal?

When the supply trucks stopped arriving, Dennis had to shut Jimbo's down. The kitchen crew split up the supplies left in storage and scattered to the winds. Following that final lights-out, I found myself sitting on the nearby beach with Beau, swapping a joint back and forth. I had no family, and Beau had an ex-wife and two kids in Boston, well beyond the military checkpoints.

"No planes," I said, nodding at the stars overhead. "That's weird."

"Maybe it'd be weirder if there was anything flying." He snapped his fingers for the joint, which I passed over. "We're through the looking-glass now."

I settled back on the cool sand, wishing that the rumbling of waves would soothe the anxiety that had both hands around my throat. "It's all collapsing," I said.

"Not all collapsing." When Beau dragged on the joint, its cherry flared bright against the darkness. "For example: You can't trust anything you hear these days, but I heard the cartels down in Mexico are establishing order. The Mexican government can't do it, so these drug dealers are setting up their own little kingdoms, complete with hospitals, virus checks, trash pickup. Some lady who's like the big queen of the cartels, she's running it all."

"Who'd you hear that from?"

"It was on Twitter, before Twitter stopped working." He chuckled, his gold front tooth flashing in the moonlight. "Tweeted its last Tweet."

"Well, I wouldn't disbelieve it," I said, taking the joint back. "Time like this, you want a little fortress to hide in. Like the Medieval days."

"Maybe all those knights in shining armor were onto something. You know what else I heard?"

"Is it scary?"

"Yes."

"Go on, just tell me."

"This little fucker of a virus, it's mutating. Different symptoms every week. And not just like, this person over here's coughing, but this person over there's bleeding from the eyes. I heard it's doing weird shit, like turning people into zombies. Or making them switch genders."

"I think we've been hitting this weed a little too hard."

"I'm seeing things clearly, man. Two hundred years ago, people didn't even know what a germ was. A hundred years ago, you could've said 'splitting the atom' to someone, and they would've stared at you like an idiot. We think we know everything, but the truth is, we don't know anything."

I mimed tossing the joint into the surf. "No, seriously, we're done here."

Growling a warning, he snatched the weed away from me. "I just want you to keep an open mind. Society's toast—this version of it, at least. No more rules apply."

"Uh-oh."

"What's that?"

"You have an idea, don't you?"

"I have tons of ideas. This one's better than most. What if I told you there was a way that we could live in safety and security for as long as it took for things to un-fuck themselves? Hell, not just safety and security: Downright luxury?"

"Oh God."

"What?"

"You want to break into one of the mansions."

Beau greeted the statement with silence. He knew that I knew his brother well; that before he and Larry worked kitchens across New York and New England, they had done time for armed robbery. The family that preys together, sticks together. Because Larry liked to tell stories about Beau's exploits, I knew all about Beau banging it out with the Russian mob in Boston, and the time he blew up a banker's car in a Rhode Island parking lot to make a point.

That's what I've always loved about the culinary industry: It will take anyone in.

When Beau finally spoke again, the words had a razor's edge: "Not just any mansion. We're going to take Oleg Abramov's bullshit palace. I know for a fact he's not there, because nobody's seen him around. Come on, let's take a look at it. You got anything better to do?"

Confronted with a tone like that, I did not. Rising, I pinched my bandana over my face as I followed Beau along the dunes. We left the town beach behind, following the island's curve toward the more secluded areas where the richest folk lived. Many of their mansions were more than a century old, enormous piles of shingles and gray wood, with wraparound porches and pools.

Oleg Abramov's mansion was a different beast: Three stories of concrete and glass bursting from the marshland like a cyberpunk tumor. As we ascended the dunes to the west of it, I could see the sliver of moon reflected in the Olympic-size infinity pool in the backyard, a stone's throw away from the helicopter pad. There were no cars in the gravel driveway, but the first-floor windows were lit.

"I thought you said there was nobody home," I said.

"That's weird. Let's get closer." He began to descend toward the house, and I placed a hand on his shoulder.

"Might be a bad idea," I said.

"Oh, come on." He snorted. "You don't believe the stories, do you?"

"About the landmines? No. But he could have sensors, alarms, something like that."

"Like the cops care anymore." Yet he paused. Was he having second thoughts? Then he hissed: "Left."

I spun in that direction. In the gap between the dunes, a man crouched, lanky, his bony forearms draped over his knees. His long, thick hair hid his face.

"Hello?" I said, wondering how much this stranger had heard.

"Oleg's not home, if that's who you're looking for." The man's voice was absurdly high, almost childlike. "I heard he got sick and died on his yacht, but who knows? We're in a post-information age."

"Who are you?" Beau asked.

One of the pale hands rose, parting the hair like a curtain. I recognized the long face beneath, with its pointed jaw and absurdly sharp cheekbones. "You're that guy," I said.

The man smiled. "If I'm the guy you mean, I'm the guy."

"Who's this guy?" Beau asked, confused.

"Adam Vandermeer," I said.

"Who?"

Beau was evidently not someone who read *Forbes* or *Fast Company* on a regular basis. "He invented that startup, what's it, Gigstreet?" I said. "Worth ten billion or something before it collapsed? Sorry."

Standing on cracking knees, Adam shrugged in an offhand way, as if an imploding company was the same as losing a quarter in the street. "No offense taken. We did collapse. A real learning experience. We managed to architect an intuitive interface, but we really failed to envisioneer a new e-commerce paradigm."

"The fuck?" Beau said.

Adam cocked his head. "I know you," he told me.

"I'm sure you don't."

He snapped his fingers. "No, no, no, I do. Before Gigstreet, I had that other startup, Slicky, we were going to revolutionize food delivery? You and I met. You were the chef at that food truck Danny Gomez was running. We tried to make a deal with him."

I had no memory of that. Then again, by the time Danny assigned me that truck, which slung overpriced ramen to hungry drunks on the Lower East Side, I was out of my mind on a nonstop diet of pills, cocaine, and whiskey. Not at rock-bottom but hurtling toward it at terminal velocity.

"Oh yeah," I said. "Didn't work out, did it?"

"You tried to set my scooter on fire." Adam frowned. "Then you called me a capitalist pig."

"I was working through some stuff," I said. "What are you doing here, Adam?"

"Same thing as I suspect you're doing." As he whisked his hair from his face again, his smile clicked effortlessly into place. "Taking refuge in Oleg's beautiful house. Unlike you, I brought a hundred people with me."

Over the roar of the surf, I heard (or imagined I heard) the roar of engines, and I pictured twenty cars snaking their way down the shore's narrow lanes, stuffed with angel-headed hipsters fleeing the collapse of civilization. They had their yoga mats and Apple laptops and small, genetically engineered dogs, and they were going to take refuge from the virus at the edge of the continent. It was such an absurd vision—like something I might have experienced during my coke days—that I had to press a knuckle against my lips to keep from bursting into laughter.

"If you're amenable," he said, "come stay with us. Cook. We're going to have lots of food. Your friends, too, if they're culinarily inclined."

The night had reduced his eyes to black holes. He extended a hand to shake, and I took it. After all, what did I have to lose?

As it turned out, quite a bit.

People by the dozens—maybe hundreds—poured into Oleg's mansion. Rail-thin tech kids with custom eyeglasses and ironic t-shirts bumped elbows with investment-banker types still wearing their tailored suits. Sleek young women occupied the heated pool, which steamed in the deepening cold; old Japanese men in silk robes filled Oleg's walnut-paneled den; and on the roof, a massive drum circle of beautiful stoners tried and failed to keep a cohesive beat. The house pulsed like a heart, booming with noise, hazy with smoke.

Over the fireplace in the great room, someone had scrawled, in giant red letters, the final words of the U.S. President right before he died at the podium and transmission from the White House cut out for good:

ASSUME ALL INFECTED.
ASSUME ALL CONTACT HOSTILE.
THE BIGGEST APOCALYPSE. THE BEST.

Adam ruled over the scene like a king. He spent mornings surfing, afternoons by the pool, and nights perched in an enormous leather chair before the fireplace, nodding his head to the music pounding from Oleg's million-dollar speaker system.

I cooked, alongside Beau and José and Bernita, all of them pulled into this absurd hurricane because we had nowhere else to go. Oleg's mansion featured a kitchen that could have serviced a large restaurant, and we made full use of the massive stoves and ovens, the walk-in fridge and universe of tools. It was tiring and frantic and fun, in a way that reminded me of my first days in a restaurant kitchen, chopping and frying and flipping as an endless stream of tickets poured in.

I tried not to think of the virus jumping through the crowded rooms. The music was loud enough to drown out any coughing, anyway.

It took us a week to strip out the fridge and pantry. As our supplies dwindled to nothing, I cornered Adam by the litter-strewn pool. "We're running low on food," I told him. "You got some way we can order more?"

"Sure," he said. "I built an app for that."

It was hard to tell if he was kidding.

"Sorry." He shook his head. "Long night. Our Japanese friends left. My investors, in another life. We couldn't see terms on what's happening here."

Couldn't see terms? An apocalypse was no place for startup buzzwords. "We just need food," I said, and turned for the house without looking back.

That afternoon, I found José and Bernita in the upstairs bedroom we had requisitioned for ourselves. They were watching something on a smartphone, which sent a burst of absurd joy through me. I was under the impression that all of the streaming networks had shut down, along with their datacenters. Heck, we barely had cell coverage anymore.

But then, as I circled the room, I saw their screen: A coffin before the altar of an empty church. A tiny icon in the corner of the screen stated '27,' which I assumed was the number of virtual mourners tuned into this sad funeral.

"I'm sorry," I told them.

José wiped his eye. "It is okay, chief. It was their turn."

"Funerals, they're all like this now," Bernita said angrily as she shut off the phone and tossed it on the bed. "That was Jerry Simpson, you remember him?"

I did: Jerry Simpson delivered Jimbo's beer and wine every week. I barely knew him as a person, but his death nonetheless sent a deep pang of sadness through me, less for him than for everything we had lost. The world had done me wrong, and I had done some wrong in return, but I still missed so much about it: Drive-through burgers and dumb action movies and clean air free of pathogens.

"Where's Beau?" I asked.

"Running an errand for Adam." Bernita rolled her eyes. "Some shady shit, as you might expect."

I headed downstairs again, curious about what could qualify as 'shady shit' in these circumstances—and found, in our kitchen, something astounding: Piles upon piles of fresh meat, short loins and strip steaks and center cuts and chunks for stew, sleekly red and smelling so rich it made my eyes water. Or maybe it was tears, because I was remembering what it was like to walk into the kitchen at El Bull, the Michelin two-star restaurant where I spent some years early in my career, with its refrigerator full of the finest cuts of meat anywhere in the world.

Standing by the sink, his arms crossed over a bloody apron, his gold tooth catching the light, Beau said: "Beautiful sight, ain't it? You can thank Adam later. Let's cook."

We grilled and fried all that beautiful meat as fast as we could. It was boar, Beau said, lean and muscular, and although I would have preferred some nicely marbled cuts, we made do. The music shuddered the air and the beautiful people screamed throughout the house. I kept trying to listen for coughs, kept expecting to feel that traitorous tickle in the back of my own throat, but everyone seemed miraculously clear of disease. Maybe Adam had checked all of his guests with a temperature gun before they arrived, or maybe it was luck.

Yet a few days later, the house's energy began to fade: The screams less shrill, the crowds of folks on the couches and beaches thinning out. When the electrical grid finally died, the house drew its power from the solar panels on the roof, and the light it delivered was weak and flickering. Beau and Adam would disappear for hours and return with more supplies—crates of soda and pasta and sauces and rice, along with more meat. I never asked where they were going, but I assumed they were raiding the other houses.

I wondered what happened to the people who lived in those houses.

Beau started acting a little strange. Well, stranger than usual. He had always fashioned himself as the pirate of the back burners, the ex-con who could whip up a mean creme brûlée. At Jimbo's, he liked to pull all kinds of stunts, like pinning a busboy's splayed hand to a cutting board and jabbing a knife between the fingers, faster and faster, missing flesh by a quarter-inch or less, until the busboy screamed.

You know, friendly stunts like that.

He had never juggled grenades, though, which he was doing now, standing by the edge of the pool, toying with four little bundles of death while the few girls in the water shrieked and splashed. They weren't having fun.

"Just in time, bro," Beau said, and, before I could reply, tossed a grenade in my direction.

My fear spiking, I grabbed it. If Beau had pulled the pin, I would try to toss it into the empty yard to my left. Fortunately, he wasn't quite that insane; the pin still rattled against the grenade's body. "Not funny," I said. "Where'd you get this fucking thing, anyway?"

"Safe room, one of the other mansions." He resumed juggling the other three grenades. "The guy had a whole arsenal. Not much ammo, so we only brought back the explosives."

"Why?"

"For fun. Why else?"

"Ask a lunatic a question, get a lunatic answer." A few weeks ago, I wouldn't have dared to question Beau's sanity out loud, but I was out of fucks to give. "I'm going to warm up the grills, start cooking." Nearly everyone was down at the beach, and I knew they would return hungry in an hour or two.

Beau spun on his heel and chucked the grenades into the pool, one after the other. He left the pins in, but that didn't stop the girls from screaming bloody murder. None of it appeared to amuse Beau at all. Approaching me, he slammed a hand on my shoulder. "I've done some heavy shit," he said, sounding tired.

I touched his wrist, about to separate his hand from my skin, but thought better of it. "I know," I said. "Your brother told me."

"Ah, my bro." He sighed. "You know, he always liked you. I went looking for him, you know, one of those times I was out. He wasn't at the hospital anymore."

I imagined burial pits in the deep woods, filled to the brim with dead hospital patients, their eyes and noses crusted with dried blood and mucus. Or maybe Larry had managed to escape—he was that kind of unkillable crazy. "I don't know," I said.

"I got to hope we'll see him again." He glanced at the patio, where Adam lay on the cold concrete, towels wrapped around his head. We were fifty yards away, but Beau's voice dropped to a whisper: "Word to the wise, kemosabe. Don't piss Adam off."

And then Beau was gone.

He must have left in the middle of the night, taking his stuff with him. His mattress was bare, his prized liquor—ripped from the sweaty hands of the music producer who had turned the garage into his weed-smoggy palace—gone from its locked cabinet. He had left the grenades in a duffel bag beneath the bathroom sink.

That wasn't the only shock: When I returned to the chef's bedroom, I found Bernita and José dressed in black outdoor gear, stuffing extra clothes and supplies into a pair of backpacks. Bernita's cheeks were bloodless, her forehead beaded with sweat.

"Where are you going?" I asked, my voice sharp with real fear.

Bernita tried to speak, coughed, and shook her head. José put a comforting hand on her lower back. "We have to go," he said, not quite meeting my eyes. "You should come with us."

"Where are you going?" I repeated.

"Somewhere else," Bernita rasped. "Anywhere else."

José's eyes vibrated with terror. She was sick. Maybe him, too. I knew they had become a couple—there was no way I could have lived at such close quarters and not known it—but I had no idea she was coughing.

It was tempting to take them up on the offer, but then I read the silent plea in José's expression: Don't come with us. Let us take care of ourselves. A trip to the nearest forest, or a deserted stretch of beach, to finish everything in the soft grasp of nature.

"I'm okay," I told them. "I have to cook."

They left, and I never saw them again. Late at night, when I can't sleep and the minutes flow slowly into hours, I hope against hope they made it.

Later that afternoon, when I went down to prep the food, it was snowing outside. It fell across the gray sky like television static. It piled on the yellow grass and transformed into gusts of steam when it hit the pool. The guests—we were down to fifteen, maybe—gathered before the fireplace to hear a spindly boy with a mohawk, the former CEO of a social network, explain the culture of toxic privilege. The last of the kombucha was served.

In the kitchen, the walk-in fridge was empty, but I found a dripping pile of meat waiting for me on the main island. Adam sat on a nearby stool, tapping at his dead phone as if it would miraculously snap back to life. He had lost so much weight that he looked like a living skeleton.

"More supplies for you," he said. "I'm sorry Beau left, but I'm so happy you've decided to stick around for our little East Coast Burning Man."

When he laughed, it sounded like the wind rattling through dead branches.

"Happy to be here," I said, hoping that nothing in my tone telegraphed the dread I felt. "Where'd you source this meat?"

He shrugged. "Another house."

"Got it." I washed my hands, set the oven to pre-heat, drew my favorite blade, and went to work. It must have been the same boar as before, lean and tough. I wondered if the house managers in the surrounding mansions all sourced their meat from the same purveyor—

My knife hit something sharp that wasn't bone. Withdrawing the blade, I widened the cut with my thumb. Something gleamed yellowish in the weak light.

A gold tooth.

I should have known from the beginning, of course, but now's a good time as any to admit that I had fallen off the wagon in a serious way once we arrived at Oleg's mansion. Not that I was ever much on the wagon to begin with. Or maybe I knew all along, but just couldn't admit it to myself. Not until I was slicing into prime Beau, at least.

How many people had Beau and Adam killed to serve their hungry masses? And when the time came, where had Adam finished off Beau? Oleg's mansion had a lot of rooms—too many places where someone with a hacksaw and some plastic sheeting could prepare farm-fresh meat.

With numb fingers, I slipped the gold tooth into my pocket. I could have followed that up by burying my knife in Adam's throat. But while I've been many things, a murderer isn't one of them; even at that lowest moment, with the pile of what used to be my friend in front of me, I didn't have what it took.

The group in front of the fireplace was breaking up, and the masses streamed past the kitchen doorway on their way to the outdoors. Maybe that weakling CEO had climaxed his speech by declaring they needed to plunge into the sea all at once, Jonestown-style. I hadn't heard much over the roaring of blood in my ears.

"I have to go," I said, quietly.

Adam looked up from his blank screen, offering me a little smile. "Anything wrong?"

"No."

"I haven't explained something important," he said. "Things have been a little too chaotic. But I wanted to thank you. For taking a chance on what we're building here. For recognizing that a kinder world stands before us."

"Assume all contact hostile."

His smile twitched. "Excuse me?"

"Nothing. I'll be right back."

Taking the long route through the house, my knife still in my hand, I ducked into the basement. It took me some time to find the gas lines, but only a second to slit open two of them. The basement had a door that led to the outside, and I took care to close it behind me as I headed into the sunlight.

I don't know if the gas reached the fireplace or the pre-heating oven first, but when it went, the explosion was enormous. From my position at the base of the dunes, facing the sea, the black mushroom cloud blotted out the sky. A few minutes later, the bag of grenades in Beau's bathroom cooked off with a stuttering bang, sending another fireball heavenward.

Further down the beach, the merry morons screamed and flailed in the sand, and I gave them a cheerful wave. I felt better than I had in months, maybe years. I had absolutely nothing left, no past and no future; I was a speck of carbon at the edge of the rumbling void.

Under ordinary circumstances, the offseason life is the slow life.

But we left 'ordinary' behind a long time ago.

THE LOYALTY OF HUNGRY DOGS

By S.A. Cosby

Tasha heard them before she saw them.

It was a sound she had become unaccustomed to in the last few years: The metallic roar of a truck's engine. A powerful creature with skin made of steel that bled oil and drank the remains of dinosaurs.

The big truck came bounding over the ruts in their dirt lane like a hungry dog responding to the sound of its food hitting the bottom of the bowl. It came to a halt fifteen feet from her and Luke, her miracle son. Born at home in the bathtub. She and Jimmy waited for him to die for two weeks before they dared to let themselves love him. When everything with the virus had started, they had said babies and young people had nothing to worry about. They'd been wrong.

As the men in the truck climbed out, wearing homemade Hazmat suits and backyard arts-and-crafts gas masks, she thought she and Jimmy had been wrong about a lot of things.

The truck was one of those ridiculous jacked-up monstrosities that would be comical if their owners didn't take it so seriously. Once upon a time, it had been candy-apple red, but now it was just a dull magenta. The color of dried blood.

There were six of them. Four men and two women. She could tell two of them were women by the sway of their hips and their braless breasts that swung like overripe fruit on a dying vine. The men had machine guns, and each had a bandolier across his chest. Some had pistols. The women carried shotguns with extra shells clipped to the stock.

Lucas gripped Tasha's thigh through her house dress.

One of the men dropped to his haunches and removed his mask. "Hey little guy. You ain't gotta be afraid. It's okay. We thought you might sick, but you look like you're right as rain. Just like your mama," he said. The man had the ruddy, shined-leather complexion of someone who called themselves white without looking too closely at their family tree. A mop of shaggy brown hair spilled down to his shoulders. Standing again, he said: "How you doing there miss? My name's Tucker. "

"Mother Tucker," a diminutive Asian man said.

Tucker laughed. "Don't mind Caleb. He's got a weird sense of humor. Now, I know how this question might sound, so don't take it wrong. You here alone...what's your name, darling?" Tucker asked.

Tasha set down her basket of tomatoes. "Tasha."

"Alright, Tasha. You here alone?" Tucker asked again.

"No. My husband is out checking his traps. He should be back by sundown," Tasha said. Tucker glanced behind him. Over the magnolia trees that ran up and down the lane. The amber ball of fire in the sky appeared to be just inches above the horizon.

"Well, he oughta be here any minute. Maybe we can wait for him. Talk some barter," Tucker said, his eyes crinkling at the corners.

"You gonna want to be gone before he get back," Tasha said. She didn't yell or scream. She didn't put any extra sass on it. It was a simple declarative statement.

"Your husband some kind of Billy Badass?" another man asked. He was black but lighter than Tasha. His hair was twisted into loose dreads that threatened to unravel any second.

"No. He's not. I'm just saying you wanna get out of here before he get back. You gonna want to get out of here before dark," Tasha said.

"Now, that's just downright rude. I thought the South was known for its hospitality? We got about fifty gallons of gas at our camp. My girl Mara can sew anything you can think of from scratch. You gonna tell me you can't trade some of those tomatoes or those greens I see back behind that house?" Tucker asked.

A spiky haired blonde wiggled her fingers at Tasha.

Tasha didn't doubt they had the gas. She thought about how all the books and movies had gotten it all wrong. The world didn't end in riots and wars in an endless dystopian wasteland. It didn't end with a whimper like that poet who liked cats had said, either. It ended in increments. It slowed and slowed like the heart of a wounded animal until it just stopped and began to rot. Once the Drip took hold for real, the unbearable weight of reality just ground the gears of existence to powder. Grocery stores fell, of course, but gas stations just stopped operating. Electronics stores became crypts full of useless toys. Jordans sat on the shelves of Foot Lockers, gathering dust. Bookstores became nurseries for silverfish. The Drips was ten times as contagious as measles, with a mortality rate that made Ebola look like an upset stomach. Fear of the outsider had been replaced with fear of the outside.

At first, the Drip had some long scientific name that the President couldn't pronounce so he called it "the Brazilian virus," all because a website with less credibility than your crackhead cousin had postulated it had come from Brazil. But once the first video clips emerged of people in the nation's emergency rooms, laying on stretchers with mucus dripping from all their orifices, well, the name just stuck.

Jimmy had realized how serious it was, even as the president was saying it was all under control. Jimmy had a natural sixth sense. He knew when a cop was going to pull them over for DWB. He could tell when a fight was going to break out in a club. He knew when a waitress was going to be the drizzling shits. He had a gift. Well, Tasha called it a gift.

Its gonna get bad, Tash. Mother Earth has had it with our bullshit, he'd said.

They saying it won't be any worse than the flu, she'd said. Normally she didn't doubt Jimmy's hunches, but this time, she couldn't help but hope he was wrong.

I'm telling you, Tash. It's a reckoning, he'd said.

Two weeks later, the Vice President had issued a national lockdown. The President had died during a press conference—viscous ribbons of mucus pouring out of his eyes, nose and mouth like billowy party streamers.

Jimmy couldn't stay quarantined in their apartment. Half-black, half-Cree and all wild energy, he was designed from birth to run through the woods and swim in rivers. They'd met at American University, where she'd been an art student and Jimmy was majoring in history. His grandparents had lived down here in Virginia in the middle of nowhere for longer than either of them had been alive. When he'd suggested they make a run for it, she'd gone along not just because she loved him, but because she'd had nightmares about marauding gangs breaking into their place and doing what men did when the rules were suspended.

Now the men without rules had found her.

That, Alanis, is irony, she thought.

"I guess the lockdown ain't in effect anymore?" Tasha asked.

Tucker chuckled and said: "Well they say it is, but ain't nobody seen a cop in a coon's age."

The dread-head laughed. It was a braying sound, like a donkey on nitrous oxide.

"Look, little sister, we can just take what we want, but I ain't that kind of man. So why don't you show us what you got in that garden back there. We can give a couple gallons of gas and you can give us these tomatoes, some of them greens, and whatever else you got back there," Tucker said.

"The greens ain't ready yet. All we got now is cucumbers, tomatoes and some cantaloupes," Tasha said.

"Why don't you show me? You guys hang back. Come on Mara," Tucker said. The blonde walked over and stood beside Tucker. She'd unzipped her Hazmat suit to reveal a wifebeater shirt and cutoff jean shorts. Tucker was still wearing his suit, a bulky swatch of heavy-duty blue plastic stitched together like a quilt.

"If I show you, will you leave?" Tasha asked.

"Little sister, I give you my word," Tucker said. Mara snickered. Tucker shot her a look that killed the sound in her throat.

Tasha reached down and picked up Lucas. She gave the darkening sky a glance, then headed for the back of the house. As they passed the well, Tucker touched her on her shoulder.

"How long y'all been out here?"

"Since it first happened. Jimmy's grandparents lived here. They were dead when we got here so we buried them and moved in," Tasha lied.

"Seven hundred thirty-nine days y'all been out here?" Tucker said.

"If that's how long it been, yeah," Tasha said. They came around the corner of the farmhouse. Four steps from the back door, a small garden took up a 30x30 square. Cucumbers, tomato cages and cantaloupes made up the majority of it. Off to the left, a cinderblock building with a heavy wooden door held court.

"Huh, you won't lying. You'd be surprised how many people we've run across who are less than truthful. It's disappointing," Tucker said.

"Life is full of disappointments," Tasha said. She felt a crushing pain in her left arm as Tucker grabbed her. Lucas was huddled in her right.

"Don't get smart with me. I don't like it when people get smart with me. You got pretty eyes. Don't make me take one for souvenir," Tucker said.

Tasha held his gaze longer than he had expected. There was a vacantness in them that made him uneasy. He released her arm and asked: "What's in that building over there?"

"Is it a smokehouse?" Mara asked behind them.

"No. It's nothing," Tasha said.

"Well, I was once from Missouri. Show me," Tucker said. Tasha crossed the yard, slicing through the tall grass like a shark. When she reached the outbuilding, she opened the door.

"Goddamn! What the fuck is that smell?" Tucker asked. Tasha didn't respond. Even in the rapidly dwindling light, Tucker could see there was nothing in the shed except a pair of heavy manacles attached to stout-looking chains attached to the back wall.

"What the hell, you guys into some freak-deaky shit? Like that movie… shit what was it, Mara?"

"'Secretary'?" Mara offered without a trace of confidence.

"No, the other one with the rich dipshit. Never mind. Smells like a… kennel in there. You got a dog? You about to sick ol' spot on me?" Tucker asked. He unzipped his Hazmat suit a few inches. Tasha watched as he slipped his hand inside. She could see it moving under the suit like a pinworm working its way under the skin of a pig. When it emerged, he was holding a chunk of beef jerky.

"A dog is only as loyal as he is hungry," Tucker opined. The self-satisfied look on his face told Tasha he'd used that line more than once before.

"No dog. Just take what you want and go," Tasha said.

Tucker unzipped his Hazmat suit and stepped out of it. He had on a tight black t-shirt and jeans. He had kicked off his boots to get out of the suit. He stepped back into them and rolled his shoulders.

"I don't know, little sister. You got a pretty nice setup here. And to be honest, we been traveling for quite a while. Everything back home is dead and buried. People living like fucking moles. I think I like it here. What you think Mara?" Tucker asked.

"I think we kill this bitch and her brat, then fuck in their bed," Mara said.

Tucker grabbed Mara by the neck and forced her to her knees: "What I done told you about that? We ain't like that unless it's called for. Goddamn it, woman, I'll never understand why that shit gets your pump greased. We ain't like that, little sister. Lots of crazy sons of bitches around these days. When I came out of Jersey, people were getting fat off their loved ones. Ain't that some shit? Everybody so scared of the Drip they wouldn't leave their fucking house, so they started cooking up Nana and shit. When I saw my next-door neighbor tossing out a bucket of femurs, I knew it was time to get out of Dodge. I ain't that kind of person."

Tasha saw Tucker's eyes go wide. She didn't know if he was trying to convince her or himself.

"Just go… please." Tasha said.

Tucker released Mara. "Show us the house," he said.

Before Tasha could respond, they heard a commotion from the front yard.

"Hey, Tucker, Daddy's home!" Caleb yelled.

"Hey, little one, you wanna go see Daddy?" Tucker asked Lucas.

They had Jimmy pressed up against the truck. His long black hair spilled down his back like a waterfall made of shadows. A string of rabbits had been tossed on the hood of the vehicle.

Tucker approached, saying: "You must be the man of the house. I'm Tucker. I was just talking to your lady here about possibly bartering with you. Whew, boy, look at them rabbits. I tell you what: I bet you we can make a deal."

"You don't have anything we need," Jimmy said. His eyes, black as his hair, locked on Tucker. You wouldn't have thought he had an AR-15 pointed at his head and the barrel of a .45 pressed into his stomach.

"I gotta disagree on that one, son. We have your woman and your son. Now, come, don't be like that. Let's talk. Let's parley," Tucker said.

Jimmy glanced at the sky. The blue had given away to black. The moon was a fat onion hanging deliriously close to their heads.

Jimmy grabbed the dread-head's wrist and twisted the .45 out of his grip. It made a dense flat sound as it hit the ground. Spinning away from Caleb and his rifle, he charged at Tucker.

The larger man, seemingly bemused by Jimmy's show of bravado, swung his AR-15 around. "Dumbass," he said.

He pulled the trigger. A volley of bullets slammed into Jimmy's chest and face. He did a lazy pirouette before landing face-first in the dirt.

Lucas screamed in Tasha's arms. Tasha bit her bottom lip so hard she wasn't the least bit shocked when a sharp coppery taste filled her mouth.

"Alright, gang, let's check out our new place," Tucker yelled.

They made Tasha fix them dinner.

She made tomato soup and cucumber salad. Cleaned the rabbits and grilled them in their own fat on the wood stove, making the house so smoky they had to open all the windows and doors. Tucker took this opportunity to strip off his shirt. His chest and arms were littered with jailhouse tattoos, their indistinct blue lines more akin to child-scribbles than art.

After dinner, they raided the liquor cabinet for all of Jimmy's grandfather's moonshine. Most of the crew went outside and hung off the truck as they swallowed the high-test. Tasha washed up the dishes as Lucas sat on the table playing with the wooden action figures Jimmy had carved for him.

Tasha heard the floor creak. She turned to see Tucker standing in the doorway to the kitchen, staring at her.

"You didn't love him? I could have sworn you loved him the way you talked about him. But you ain't shed a tear," Tucker said, moving across the kitchen floor. He ruffled Lucas's hair as he walked past. The boy flinched.

"I love him more than you could ever know," Tasha said.

"You still using present-tense. We gonna have to work that out of you," Tucker said. He was less than a foot away from her. His eyes were red, his chest slick with sweat. He and Mara had retired upstairs after dinner.

"When it's too late, remember I tried to save you," Tasha said as she placed a plate in the drain rack to dry.

"What are you talking about, little sister?"

"You'll see," she said.

Outside, the dread-head, who was named Loomis, said: "Pass the bottle and twist the cap, motherfucker." He held his hand out to Caleb, who took another swig from the mason jar before passing it to his friend.

"This place is nice. I had to get out the city, man. I couldn't take it no more," Chuck said. He barely ever spoke, usually after drinking his weight in alcohol.

"Yeah, yeah, we know," Diane said. She'd taken off her Hazmat suit and was lying on the hood of the truck, her t-shirt pulled up over her breasts. She was fifteen years older than Loomis, Chuck or Caleb, but they didn't seem to mind when it was time to get down to it.

"I think you got a permanent case of claustrophobia." Caleb said.

A loud crack pierced the night. The mason jar froze an inch from Loomis's mouth.

He asked: "What the fuck was that?"

"City kid, it's called a falling branch," Diane said.

"Nah, that wasn't a branch. I don't know what the fuck it was, but it won't no branch," Loomis said. Setting the jar down, he grabbed his rifle. The crickets and katydids had gone silent. The nightbirds ceased singing their songs. A stillness seemed to settle over the whole world.

"You so fucking paranoid. Why don't you put that gun down and come handle these guns?" Diane said as she sat up, running her hands over her breasts.

"D, you got to be the horniest bitch I've ever met," Caleb said as he slipped his shirt over his head.

Another crack, louder than the last, echoed through the air—accompanied by a wet, fleshy ripping sound. It reminded Diane of the sound that meat made when her father had pulled it off the carcass of a deer.

"Was that a fucking branch?" Loomis said. He hopped off the tail gate and scanned the darkness. The magnolia trees swayed like a choir caught up in religious ecstasy. Caleb slid out of the driver's seat of the truck.

"C, where's that old boy? Did you move that body?" Loomis asked.

A series of cracks, pops, and moist tearing sounds bellowed up from under the truck. Diane put her shirt back on and grabbed her shotgun. Just before she hopped down off the hood of the truck, two things happened simultaneously.

Chuck screamed.

Loomis's head went sailing through the air and landed on the hood of the truck, next to Diane. A fine mist of blood splashed her face, warm as fresh piss.

Inside, Tucker, mumbling that he wasn't a bad guy, was just about to stroke Tasha's cheek when he heard Diane's scream. He stopped and looked toward the front door.

The scream was joined by loud voices and gunfire. Then another sound drowned out all others.

When Tucker was a kid, his class had gone to the Brooklyn Zoo. They'd walked by the lion enclosure, which had a thick pane of glass so you could peer at the lions as they did their lion stuff, which Tucker realized mostly consisted of sleeping. Just as bored Tucker was about to yawn, the big male lion had roared, the sound shaking the whole enclosure.

The sound he heard now was that roar—times a thousand. It was a ferocious living thing that crawled out of the deepest pit in whatever your religion called Hell.

Tucker rushed out the door with his backup .357 cocked. As soon as he stepped onto the porch, he realized he'd made a horrible mistake—most likely the last one he'd ever make.

His crew was dead. That was painfully obvious. They hadn't been killed by some deadly Special Ops guy or some crazed hillbilly with improvised traps. They'd been ripped apart. Limbs and viscera littered the front yard. His truck, Big Red, had a fresh new coat of paint, courtesy of the gallons of blood splashed across its rusting exterior.

Standing in the middle of this abattoir was something his mind told him couldn't exist, even as his heart told him it was terrifyingly real: A beast, with what was left of Caleb in its massive jaws. Its shaggy black pelt soaked red. Its nostrils opened and closed spasmodically.

It smells me. Oh my God, it smells me, Tucker thought.

The Beast opened its maw, dropping Caleb's torso to the ground. Shimmering green eyes like emeralds glowed from deep in its enormous skull. The triangular ears atop its head twitched indecently.

Tucker knew he had a gun in his hand. High-velocity hollow points stolen from a gun shop in Philadelphia. He knew the .357 could drop a bison. He knew all this, but he couldn't seem to find the will to raise the pistol.

The Beast dropped to all fours and charged at him. It was his deepest childhood fears brought to life. He fired the .357, all six shots hitting their mark. Tucker was an excellent shot.

It did no good.

Should have had silver, he thought as the Beast sliced open his belly with one swipe of its powerful claw. Tucker felt his guts unspool from his abdomen. It was like the hollow feeling you experienced at the top of a rollercoaster, multiplied by a million.

The Beast gripped Tucker by the throat. It hoisted him off the ground with little effort. Tucker saw the rows of curved teeth inside its gaping maw. Its breath was carrion and corruption. Its howl made the fragile places in his mind shatter like glass.

Tasha had taken Lucas to the basement. It was their backup plan if Jimmy ever got out of the shed.

His grandparents, who had installed a heavy metal door to the basement in event of tornadoes, had welcomed them with open arms when they had arrived from D.C. The first few weeks had been idyllic. After months in their apartment while the world was reduced to putrescence, the fresh air of the Virginia mountains had come as a welcome respite.

Then Jimmy had returned from a night-fishing expedition mangled from head to toe. He survived but seemed… different. Only they didn't realize how different until the next full moon.

After Jimmy went through that first transformation, his grandparents were nothing more than memories and a grease spot on the floor. After that, they fixed up the shed, and Jimmy would go in there during the full moon; for the rest of the month, he was fine.

Tasha heard a woman's high-pitched squeal over the roar of splintering wood and shattering glass. She rocked Lucas back and forth. He was a quiet boy who learned quickly.

"We just gotta wait until Daddy is back. Everything will be okay when Daddy comes back," Tasha said. She figured it was around eleven: Six hours until sunrise. That was fine.

She had a lot of practice when it came to waiting. A lockdown did that to you.

FISH FOOD

By Jen Conley

When I hear the gunshot, I sit up in bed. It's three in the morning. The shot comes from the next block, somewhere on Hemlock Road, so it's okay. Still, my heart bangs and my breath is short. For a moment, I have to talk myself down: *You're okay, you can breathe, you're not sick, you don't have the virus.*

Then there is another shot. In the old days, I would've assumed it was firecrackers. That would be normal, especially if it were summer. But it's not summer. It's early April, more than a year from when the first wave of the virus hit and killed thousands of people. And it's not last August, when two months after the "re-opening," the second wave of the virus emerged and went on to kill millions. So many dead now, it's unfathomable.

My bedroom door opens, and I switch on my light. My niece, Mandy, nineteen, stands in the doorway. "Who do you think it was?" she asks. Her voice rattles.

I shut my eyes. "I don't know… maybe Dan Kolbert over on the next block."

Mandy shakes her head. Her brown hair is long and messy because she won't let me cut it. But it's clean. We ration our shampoo and only wash our hair twice a week. She washed hers yesterday.

"Who?" she asks.

"Dan Kolbert," I say again. "He had his own construction business. He and his wife lost their daughter in the second wave. I think I told you."

Maybe I didn't.

Mandy winces. "How old was their daughter?"

"Sixteen. She had asthma, so that made it worse."

I look at the window. The shades are drawn. I wait. The Kolberts have a son. He's nine, so a third shot should be next.

Then it comes. The final, self-inflected shot. I don't know who did the killing. It could've been Dan or his wife, Erin.

Mandy shivers.

"The Guard will get the bodies," I say. "Eventually."

"I know," she says.

The bodies will be left for days until the suicide is called in.

"You okay?" I ask.

Mandy says she's going to watch *Friends* on her iPad. We downloaded a bunch of shows and movies before everything went super-bad. We get three hours of extra electricity twice a week to charge our devices. Otherwise, the electricity must be saved for essentials: refrigerator, lights, cleaning purposes, laundry use. The Guard monitors how we use our energy allotments.

"Don't fall asleep and waste your battery," I say.

She says she won't.

I lie down and put my hand on my stomach. I'm six months pregnant. My husband is dead.

In the morning, I take a walk to the water, like I always do. It's

Sunday. The day is bright but chilly, and I can feel a cold breeze coming from the river. My neighborhood consists of mostly small houses, and in the old days, there would be kids on bikes, people outside doing yardwork, the usual. But today there is no one outside. There are people inside their homes, and I can feel them watching me through the windows as I walk, but most of the houses are abandoned. The signs are easy to spot: dead leaves bunched up by front doors, yards unattended, vehicles sitting in driveways with flattened tires—not that it matters. They don't let us drive anywhere. Driving is forbidden. Some abandoned houses are still decorated for Halloween—ghosts hanging from trees that are covered in pink blossoms, witches' feet popping up from the lawn near the spring tulips, fake bloody hands stuck to a glass storm door. Sometimes a fake pumpkin will roll around the street, as do random soccer balls and basketballs. The virus nearly wiped out our neighborhood in late October and early November.

The second wave was a death sentence. I was lucky. I had been sick during the first wave, last April. Mandy had it last March. From that, we gained immunity to fight off the second wave, but my husband didn't. He caught the virus in November and died within a week.

The river is brackish and very wide because it spills into the bay, which eventually connects to the Atlantic. Every so often you see a body floating by, on its way to the ocean, where the fish and sharks will eat it. It used to bother me, but I don't think about it now. I only think about the water, how I can smell the salt and that it's good to breathe it in, makes me feel healthy. The baby isn't moving because it likes me to walk—the motion is soothing. When I stop, it sometimes swirls around, bangs against my insides, like it's throwing a fit.

I walk down a pathway next to an abandoned two-story house. One of the windows is open and curtains sway in and out with the breeze. I follow the path until it opens up to a small sandy beach. I make my way down a slight incline to the water's edge and watch two white swans float by. The water laps gently against the shore and I know in the summer there will be crabs and jellyfish.

After my husband died, the Guard moved in quickly and quarantined neighborhoods. In December, they counted who was alive and tested us for immunity. Those without immunity were taken away—to where, I don't know. Word got out that they were rounding up the unimmune, and some choose to run and hide and then run again—they are called "transients."

The government tells us the unimmune put us in danger: scientists believe the virus can mutate into a third wave, and those of us with immunity now might not be immune to a newer mutation. Still, people protect their own. Every so often, the Guard rolls in: A half-dozen officers holding weapons and covered in protective gear leap out of a truck and march down our roads, doing property checks. They rummage through abandoned houses in search of transients. They stomp into occupied houses, looking for the "hidden" cowering in attics and basements, their families and friends banking on what they know from history: All terrible things end. There will be a vaccine.

The baby moves again. I turn around and leave the river, heading back home. It is dangerous to walk alone, out in the open, this I know. A transient can get in, can be waiting in the shadows, ready to grab me to take me hostage… I don't know. Sometimes my mind goes a little squirrely. But transients do get in. They can come along the river by kayak or small craft, quietly moving onshore at night, taking shelter in an abandoned house, hoping there will be something to eat. But those chances are slim. Last fall, when someone would die, the Guard would come, take the dead away, and then send a decontamination crew into a home before they'd let the living return. Anything edible was confiscated and burned in the big pit with the bodies. I never understood the reasoning for this—if we're immune, there is no reason to take our food. And I don't know where the pit is, exactly, but I heard it was an old soccer field across town.

Now the deaths in our neighborhood are just suicides, people who have lost hope. Before the Guard is notified, those of us who are left will go into the suicide house and grab what we can. A transient, driven by hunger, might also risk going into a suicide house, but that would be stupid. Most neighbors are not compassionate. To harbor or abet a transient is to risk being relocated. This is the only crime the Guard cares about. Transients. Anything else is fair game—abuse, theft, rape, murder. I think it's because the Guard doesn't have the manpower to deal with other crimes. They don't have as many officers as they'd like us to think, so they've taken a Darwinian approach, which is why they don't take our guns. Whoever survives will one day be given a vaccination. Whoever doesn't survive, they weren't meant to.

I keep walking, noticing more tulips and daffodils popping up through the grasses of abandoned homes than I did the day before. It makes me think of my mother, who died of cancer years before the virus. She loved to garden, and her flowers were her pride and joy. "Look at these," she'd say to me, pointing to a patch of purple crocus, "aren't they sweet?"

I try not to think of my mother because it makes me sad, and I can't be sad. I only keep walking, suddenly noticing a skeleton with a missing leg hanging from a large tree covered with white blossoms. It makes me shudder. I should keep a gun on me when I walk, but I don't. I leave it hidden in the house. I do not want Mandy knowing I have a gun. She's been depressed.

Until lately.

Maybe I shouldn't walk at all. But this treat I allow myself is the highlight of my day. It keeps me from going insane. It calms me, and that is healthier for the baby.

"We're out of eggs," Mandy says when I return. "Can you add it to the list?"

I nod. We eat sausage links and toast.

Mandy taps her foot on the floor, as if she's nervous or excited. She wants to go outside. She will tell me she's going for a walk, but I suspect she has a particular destination. I suspect there's a reason her depression has faded away. Mandy is my older brother's daughter. Last spring, when the first wave hit, like millions of other college kids, she was sent home to finish the semester online. But she came to my house instead. My brother and his wife lived up north, near the city, where the population was dense, and the number of infected was the highest in the nation. They felt it was safer for her to stay with my husband and me. Then she got sick but recovered easily.

When I got sick, my husband took me to the hospital. My fever was dangerously high, my cough nasty and persistent, and I was unable to breathe. Looking back, it was terrifying, and at the time, especially at the worst point, death seemed inevitable. I would drift in and out of consciousness, alone in a white room because my husband wasn't allowed to visit me. I was contagious. At one point, in a painful delirium, I saw my dead mother. "I miss you," I said to her. "I'm sorry for being a terrible daughter." She only smiled, and said I was just young. Seeing her made me want to go, to leave the pain and move onto another world.

But I didn't die. I recovered and went home. My husband, for some reason, did not test positive for the virus, and although that seemed mysterious to us, we were happy. Still, he wasn't satisfied. "It will be back," he warned.

After the reopening in June, when the government announced that the virus was almost eradicated—that's the phrase they used, "almost eradicated"—Mandy went home for the summer and then returned to college at the end of August. But then, as my husband predicted, the second wave arrived, brutal and ruthless, and it killed my brother and his wife. And then my husband died. The horror was barely manageable, yet being newly pregnant made it a little better for me. I had something to live for. I had hope.

After Christmas, the Guard dropped Mandy at my house. They did that during the holidays—found orphaned children or displaced young adults who tested negative and sent them to live with relatives.

"So," Mandy says, picking up her toast. "When you go to the store tomorrow, can you get those granola bars? The ones with the chocolate chips. We're out."

I had gotten a box of eighteen last week. Eighteen.

After breakfast, she goes to her room. Ten minutes later, she appears, a little makeup on her face, and she announces she's going for a walk. "Do you think they picked up the bodies?" she asks. "From last night?"

"I didn't see the truck this morning."

"Are you going to tell them?"

I say no.

She understands. We're all leaving the Kolbert house open for a day or two so we can go in and take things—food, shampoo, toothpaste, paper products, liquor… whatever we need.

"Okay." She leaves through the front door.

As I do the dishes, I see her walk down the street in the late morning sun. Her hair is flying in the breeze, a backpack hanging on her shoulders. She's wearing her favorite jeans—the tight dark ones that show off her figure. She'll stop at the suicide house first. She'll step over Dan Kolbert, she'll wince at Erin Kolbert's body, and she'll probably cry when she sees the boy. But it won't stop her from taking what she can find. It never stops any of us.

That afternoon, I walk over to Lou Becker's house. He's in the garage, fixing a vacuum cleaner. Lou is about fifty and fixes things for those of us who are still around.

"Who's that for?" I ask.

"Gina Keane. You know what a clean freak she is."

Last fall, Gina lost her husband and two sons. Only she and the cat survived, but her mind is good, and she still smiles and says hello. We sometimes talk about the old days.

Lou stands up and stretches. "You hear about Dan?"

"I heard the shots last night. I figured it was him."

"It was Erin. She came by last week, talking all sorts of crazy. Religious stuff. How we needed to make peace with God. And she was holding the gun."

I frown and the baby moves.

"Hmm," Lou says, licking his lips. His hands are shaking a bit. His skin is thick and worn.

"So, you did go over to Dan's?" I ask.

Lou nods. "They didn't drink. I took a can of chicken soup."

I smile. When we raid a suicide, we're all fair. We only take what we need.

"I'm going to the store tomorrow," I say.

He nods. His eyes are crystal blue. It's unnerving to look at him. I bet he was once a good-looking man, back in the old days.

But he wants alcohol.

"You want vodka or whiskey?" I ask.

His strange eyes drift away before returning to me again. "How are you feeling?"

"Okay," I say.

"That's good," he answers. "Vodka will do."

Even though I am pregnant, Lou will let me use one allotment to buy liquor—that's the deal for his friendship. People his age aren't given many allotments. I'm pregnant so I get more, but the Guard doesn't judge what you buy. They don't care if pregnant women buy liquor.

I hesitate before I leave. "Mandy's stealing from me."

Lou nods. "She brings whatever she's taking from you to the Martin house."

The Martin family died from the virus except for the father. He committed suicide in January.

"But I thought they were..." I trail off.

"Someone is there now. Sean Strout said he noticed a kayak hidden under the Martins' deck." Sean is about twenty-nine, his wife dead and gone. He lives alone in a blue house two blocks away.

Lou continues to speak: "It's a young guy, a boy. Must've come by river, probably a couple weeks ago. He's probably camping out in the basement."

"Did Sean see him?" I ask.

Lou picks up a screwdriver from his work bench. "We know he's there."

The baby moves around and around.

Lou says, "Your niece has formed an attachment." He points to my stomach with the tool. "You need to take care of that baby."

"I know," I say.

"I've got a few extra bullets, if you need them."

My husband left me extra bullets. "I'm fine," I say.

"All right."

I return to my house, understanding fully what I am expected to do, but it's difficult to square with. Mandy is my brother's daughter. Yet, we're loyal to each other in this neighborhood. We have to be to survive.

Mandy is home for dinner. We eat rice and beans because we're out of meat, something else she's stolen from me. I pretend I don't notice. She thinks I'm grief-stricken because my husband died. She thinks I'm too old to catch onto her scheme, even though I'm only thirty-two. She thinks I don't know that a bottle of orange juice went missing the other day, as did some bread, some ham, a few slices of American cheese. In the beginning, she was sneakier, taking just a little bit. In the beginning I thought it was me, that I was the crazy one. But then I caught her wrapping a sandwich in aluminum foil, and I knew. I wanted to follow her, but it's difficult to trail someone on these empty streets without being noticed. But I figured it was a boy, I just didn't know where. Or I didn't want to know where.

But now I've been told.

After dinner, Mandy and I sit on the couch together. She watches Friends on her iPod with her earbuds on. She chuckles and smiles as the episode goes on. She looks like my brother, who was good-looking: pale white skin, dimples when he smiled, large dark eyes.

I read my book. It's something I've read before, back in the old days. It's a silly mystery, but it takes my mind away for a bit. When I get to a part about a missing ring, it makes me think. I get up and go to my room. I open the bottom dresser drawer where my husband kept his t-shirts. Several are gone. I look in another drawer: several jeans are gone. In my husband's small closet, a pair of brown hiking boots are gone. I kept his things because if my child is a boy, I plan to give him his father's clothes.

And Mandy has given them to some boy.

I can feel myself wanting to scream but I don't. I don't know why I am angrier at the stolen clothes than I am the stolen food. I wonder if she understands how much danger she has put us in. I am the "head of household" so if she is caught harboring a transient, I will take the fall. And what about the virus danger? This boy is obviously not immune to the virus. He could be asymptomatic, someone who carries the virus and never gets sick but still doesn't have immunity. If my baby is born without immunity, and Mandy carries the virus home on her clothes, that could kill my child. They promise us that we can keep our babies if they are born without immunity—it's a one saving grace. They are sure a vaccine will be created soon.

The next morning is Shopping Day. The Guard picks me up in a van and I sit quietly near the window as we retrieve the other pregnant women in the area. I am the second to be picked up and there are five in our designated area. During the drive, I get to see other neighborhoods, other roads, other houses. It all looks the same, but it doesn't matter. I love the ride anyway.

The "store" is in a former strip mall. I go through a checkpoint and then enter the supermarket. The shelves are sparse with supplies. I'm allowed fifteen allotments a week. I buy eggs, meat, more ham, bread, cheese, and shampoo. To my surprise, there is a small stand of oranges!

A young Guardsman smiles at me. "It's our turn to get them," he says. "You can take two." He gestures toward my stomach. "It will be good for the baby."

He picks them up and places them in my cart. I thank him.

"You take care," he says, nodding, his smile fading because he's not supposed to show emotion. He's supposed to scare us by his silence.

When I get back into the van, I hold my shopping bags close to me like all the pregnant women do. Two of them chatter happily to each other, excited about the oranges, but I keep my mouth closed. I am the second woman to be dropped off. The Guard is fair. They know our trip in the van is special and the ride makes it even more special, so the first ones picked up are the first ones dropped off.

At home, Mandy isn't there. I put the food away and hide the oranges under my bed. Hours go by and she doesn't return.

In the closet, I see my husband's rain jacket is gone.

I find my gun. It's a small revolver, like a child's toy.

It's dark when I start walking. A bright full moon illuminates my walk. The streetlamps aren't lit anymore—this is to save energy. I hold a small flashlight in one pocket and my gun in the other. I walk and walk, smelling the salty water from the river.

The baby is motionless as I walk and remains motionless as I approach the old Martin house, a narrow two-story structure with long windows and white siding. It has a finished basement and a huge deck in the back that overlooks the river. In the old days, the Martins would throw wonderful parties—Christmas, New Year's, St. Patrick's Day, Fourth of July, Halloween—so I know the house well. Eileen Martin was a natural entertainer, gracious and sweet; a few drinks in, she could have you laughing until your stomach hurt. Her husband, Tom, adored her. He adored his two sons, too. I can imagine how difficult it must've been, sitting in his empty house at Christmas, his wife dead, his sons dead, most of his neighbors dead or rounded up. He had no reason to live anymore.

I am lucky. I have the baby to keep me hopeful.

I make my way to the back of the house, down a path and then quietly up the steps to the deck. I am wearing my old yoga sneakers, flat and smooth, so my footfalls barely register on the wooden planks. The river glows in the light of the moon. The stars are bright, and I can hear the lapping of the water along the shore. I stand near the slider and pull on it gently. It's open—Mandy forgot to lock it. Inside, the kitchen is dark, so I use my flashlight to light my way. I travel down a hall, catching glimpses of family photos: the Martins on a trip to Hawaii; a graduation picture of the older son; a baseball picture of the younger son; a wedding picture of Tom and Eileen. I take the gun out of my pocket.

There is no light along the stairwell as I descend. The basement is large, and I am guessing Mandy and her boy are near the far corner, sitting on the couch. A small camp-light glows, and Mandy has her iPad playing music.

They notice me.

They notice the gun.

"Whoa!" the boy says. I can barely make him out, but I can tell he is tall, lanky, twenty pounds too light, and his messy hair needs a cut.

Mandy stands up. "Wait! He's my friend."

I don't put the gun down. I keep it pointed at them. My husband taught me to use it after the first wave. "You'll need this one day," he said to me. He never thought the reopening was safe. He always told me to stay inside, to stay away from people. And when the second wave emerged, after I told him I was pregnant, he refused to stop working at his job. "We need the money." Within weeks, he was sick and then dead.

The boy holds his hands up, as you would in the old days to the police. "Hey, I don't know who you are…"

I stare at Mandy, her hair wild and her eyes frightened. "He's a good guy."

"You're stealing from me," I say to her.

The boy says, "I'm just trying to get by. Like everyone is."

The Guard has killed transients like him, and they toss them in the river to remind other transients what will become of them. To warn families who are hiding the unimmune what will happen.

I don't know where this boy came from. But he can't stay. And I can tell by his eyes, he'll abandon Mandy if things get dicey—if she gets pregnant, or if I cause trouble. He'll get in his kayak and go down the river. Find a new girl to lie to and get what he needs.

"Don't..." Mandy begs.

But I do. My heart is battering, and my breath is shallow, yet the baby is still. It's my job to rid our neighborhood of this danger. I pull the trigger. I'm close enough to not miss. He seems to die instantly and Mandy screams: "What! Why?"

The baby flips around in my stomach and settles.

I look at her. "You were stealing."

I am supposed to spare her. She's my brother's child, but what will she do to my baby? Girls like her, at this age, lovesick and starry-eyed, are foolish and dumb. When I was nineteen, I also fell hard for a bad boy and nobody could tell me otherwise. I blamed my mother for the breakup. She kicked him out of the house because she caught us smoking weed and he never came around again; he stopped calling, just sent me a text saying he was sorry but it wasn't going to work out. I turned my rage on my mother. I refused to speak to her for weeks and I deliberately pulled out a bunch of tulips and daffodils and ripped them to shreds. It was ridiculous and stupid, but that's what this type of love does to you: It makes you silly and stupid, but more importantly, it makes you untrustworthy and disloyal to the people who care about you the most.

There's too much at stake for me to deal with Mandy. There might not be a vaccine for years. I might fall asleep and then wake up and find my baby dead because she wanted revenge.

Or none of that might happen. It might be all in my mind, which is squirrely at times. It goes straight to the worst possible scenario. But history has proven, at least for me, that the worst possible scenario is always in the cards.

"Please," Mandy begs.

This virus, the roundups, the containment, the Guard, the suicides, the allotments—it all messes with your brain. Makes you crazy, makes you scared, makes you cruel, makes you disloyal to your own family.

"He wasn't going to hurt anyone," Mandy cries. "He was waiting out for the vaccine."

I can take Mandy home, attempt to talk some sense into her, hope that she grows up quickly and will help me raise my baby.

"I loved him," she says, whimpering. "You killed someone I love." She straightens up and pulls her wild hair behind her. "I can tell the Guard what you did. I can tell them you murdered him."

Like the Guard will care. Mandy's boy was a transient. I will have done them a favor.

"I'll tell," she whines. "I will."

I know I can never trust her.

I shoot my niece, killing my brother's child.

I leave the gun in the boy's lap. Like I said, the Guard doesn't solve mysteries. Especially mysteries of dead transients and silly lovesick girls. They only pick up the bodies.

The next morning, I stop over at Lou's. Sean and Gina are there, along with an older couple who live three blocks away, and a mother with two little girls, and a man with his son. We are all in the garage. We listen as Lou calls the Guard about Dan Kolbert and his family, but he doesn't mention the boy and Mandy. Later, after the neighbors leave, he informs me that he and Sean plan to let Mandy and the boy rot in that basement for a while. "We'll get them out of there eventually. Put them in the river."

"Fish food," I say.

He agrees.

I take an orange out my pocket and hand it to him. "Hm," he says, placing it on the floor next to the vodka bottle.

He points to a chair in the corner. "Rest," he orders.

I take a seat and watch Lou work on the vacuum cleaner, my baby swirling around my stomach, reminding me it's unhappy that I'm not moving, but also reminding me it's alive. I wear one of my husband's t-shirts, one that Mandy didn't take for the boy. I left the clothes she stole in the basement with their bodies. They were infected.

My husband's shirt is red. For love. For spilled blood.

I won't wear it again. All of my husband's clothes are for our baby. For my baby.

THE SEAGULL & THE HOG

By Johnny Shaw

She sounded like a seagull. He sounded like a hog.

Seagull.

Hog.

Seagull.

Hog.

Seagull.

Hog.

The seesaw back-and-forth of their barnyard coitus sounded rehearsed, a perfected and practiced predilection. The syncopation was maddening. The two of them went at it for twenty-eight minutes, timed. Three sessions a day. The same starting times, the same ending flourish. Their climax was a haunting cacophony of animal noises. A zoo in an earthquake, finishing with what sounded like Eeyore holding back a sneeze harmonizing with the Doppler screech of a receding French ambulance.

Renato stared at the shared wall and wondered if they had a schedule taped to the fridge: Wake up, breakfast, Seagull-Hog, shower, emails, check the radio for emergency announcements, lunch, Seagull-Hog, three hours of Netflix, Seagull-Hog.

Through the thin walls, Renato heard every movement, thrust, and moan. He could hear the sound of their skin slapping together, disturbingly similar to the taffy machine down at the boardwalk. In a moment of desperation, he had tried to jerk off to the couple's impromptu radio play, but between the taffy sound and the seagull sound, it had reminded Renato too much of the times he spent with his grandfather down by the pier. Any chance of using the neighbors' sex concert for his own personal gratification died on those rocks. Nothing like pleasant memories of dead Grandpa Bill to wilt his celery.

It hadn't bothered him the first week. He could pop on his headphones and drown it out with his own pornography preferences. Renato had been on a retro Christy Canyon film jag lately. But when his phone shit the bed two weeks earlier, he was without any visual aids to offset the thrice-daily audio assault. He could turn on the radio, but there was nothing sexy about the voice of the Emergency Broadcast announcer. Too robotic and the mortality count was a bummer.

Renato was trapped in his apartment, ball-hurtingly horny and anxious about the situation outside. His chest hurt, his stomach was oogy, and he had constant headaches from the stress. A quick hand-shandy would have relieved some of the symptoms, but he was left with the cruelest torture. To stare at the bare wall and listen to the couple next door bang their way through the apocalypse, while he had to rely on his unimaginative imagination and scattered youthful memories to try to get some pants action.

He had no idea how his forefathers had done it before the internet. His imagination had the range of a crayon drawing of boobs compared to the bountiful cornucopia of depravity that was the internet. He knew about magazines, Playboy and Penthouse and Hustler, but they felt quaint. Two-dimensional and paper seemed boring, but compared to his worthless brain, he would have taken anything. The best he could do from the contents of his apartment was the Chicken of the Sea mermaid, but he thought of her more like a sister.

The closest Renato got to any kind of satisfaction was when he thought about Leona Marks, the first boobs he had ever seen up close. He shut his eyes tight. Teenage lust returning to his mind. Leona in the backseat of his Dad's Skylark. Her shirt unbuttoned. He felt a crotch twinge, but it didn't last. It ended up like that magic trick where the magician's wand turned into rope. He yanked on it anyway for due diligence, but when it started to hurt, he gave up. He cried holding his soft dick in his spitty hand.

Then the neighbors started up again.

Seagull.

Hog.

Seagull.

Hog.

Seagull.

Hog.

Renato opened his window and stuck his head outside. Fresh air and the eerie quiet of the city. He could still hear Seagull-Hog, but a slightly more muted version. Some asshole sang "Rocket Man" in the distance. Nobody sang along. The streets sat empty, except for a patrol car cruising slowly through the neighborhood. He was glad he had a view up on the sixth floor, but he would have given anything for a terrace.

All the stores looked closed. The nail parlor, the pizza place, the pawn shop, even the liquor store. And then he spotted it. Why hadn't he thought of it earlier? He didn't know the name of the place. He had been in there a dozen times minimum. The sign just said "Adult" in big block letters, so that's what he had always called it in his head. More important than its name, he could see that the door on the roof of the building was open an inch.

A pornography oasis was only two buildings away. Not just porno, but probably a decent supply of hand sanitizer and toilet paper, as well. If he could make it there, he could ride this thing out without ever having to hear Seagull-Hog ever again, shelter-in-smutty-place.

All he needed was to get from Point A to Point P. The P stood for pornography.

Renato had always believed that he was capable of climbing a drainpipe. So much so that he had never felt the need to test his acumen. It was one of those things that he had seen in a movie and decided that it was in his skill set. Like breaking a brick with his hand and moonwalking. It didn't deter him that he had neither the upper body strength nor grip. It was going to be about technique, everyone knew that. Besides, descending was a cakewalk compared to climbing. Gravity would do most of the work for him.

It was only two stories down to the roof of the abutting apartment building, where the entire surface was covered with discarded trash bags, like a safety net. Once on that roof, it would be a hop, skip, and a literal jump to Adult and paradise. Along the way, he would have to figure out how to overcome the eight-foot alley gap between the two buildings, but that was details. A plan would form between now and then. You didn't need a plan if you had confidence. That was one thing that Renato was confident he knew for sure.

He filled his backpack with Slim Jims, Beefaroni, Chunky soup, Funyuns, Top Ramen, Oreos, and the rest of his emergency food stash. As much as he could fit. It weighed a ton, pulling him backwards, but it was a short jaunt.

With one leg draped over the windowsill, he looked around his apartment one last time to make sure he didn't forget anything. God, his place was depressing. The furniture looked like he had found it in the alley, which he had. He should have put some art on the wall. A couple Nagel prints would have made a hovel a home. Once this thing was over, he was going to get his shit together. He was going to go to Ikea.

Renato reached for the drainpipe.

Renato had definitely dislocated his shoulder. Something poked him in the back. He stared at the scattered clouds above him. One of them was shaped like a dick with one ball.

Phase one was complete. He had made it down onto the neighboring roof, that's all that mattered. It was trivia that he had not been able to descend from the drainpipe, but instead had fallen out the window immediately. He should have worn gloves. That had been the problem.

The plastic sacks of garbage had mostly broken his fall. His left arm dangled in place. It didn't hurt, but he looked like a broken puppet. Luckily, he was right-handed. That fact was going to come into play when he finally reached the pornography. The last thing he wanted was some Burgess Meredith irony bullshit, surrounded by smut with a damaged stroke arm.

He tried to jam his shoulder back into place by lifting his upper body and then falling back down against the roof, but that only made it hurt. He needed to get a running start and slam it against a wall. Once again, it all came down to technique.

Renato tried to forget about his functionless arm and shifted his focus to whatever was stabbing him the back. He tried to reach it with his left arm, but that only made him scream in agony. How could he have forgotten that he had just dislocated his left shoulder ten seconds earlier? He tried again with his other arm, but couldn't quite reach whatever it was.

He sat up and dragged his back against the wall of his building. Something snapped. He still felt the stab—and discovered the culprit. A syringe, minus the needle. The needle which was most definitely still in his back. He hoped his neighbors were junkies, but knew that wasn't the case.

Renato scanned the garbage bags that covered the roof. He couldn't tell what they were from his apartment, but now that he was closer, he saw the symbols and words. "Medical waste," "Toxic," and "Hazardous Materials" were the three phrases that jumped out at him.

That was the luck Renato was having. He had fallen into a medical waste dump during a pandemic, a viral landmine. There was nothing he could do with the needle in his back. It would do one of three things: kill him, give him superpowers, or nothing. Not bad odds.

He couldn't change much now, but if he was going to make it to Adult without getting infected with every disease known to man—and a few only known to animals—he was going to have to find a way to traverse the roof without touching anything else.

The entire roof was covered three bags deep, but the one-foot-wide brick ledge that ran around the perimeter was free of detritus. Renato would have to walk that tight rope. He held his arms out to the side—the wounded one screamed bloody murder at him—and stepped up onto the bricks. He was only four stories up, but the ground looked a hundred feet away. He might be able to roll with it if he fell, but he didn't want to test that theory. It had been nine months since he had fallen off a roof and was hoping to keep that record intact.

Renato took a step. So far, so good. And then another. His backpack shifted, his body leaning over the edge. He adjusted, overcompensating and leaning toward the yellowing sacks of pus or livers or whatever was inside them. Bending his knees, he quickly got a hand on the bricks at his feet. He stopped moving. His heart raced. He gulped in air.

Nobody was looking. He didn't have to be cool. Renato crawled slowly along the ledge on all fours. He kept his eyes on the bricks in front of him and focused on his goals. It took twenty minutes, but he made it to the other side. Adult was just across the alley. However, he had miscalculated the distance. It wasn't eight feet. It was more like fifteen. There might have been a time when he could have made that jump, but even a deluded guy like Renato wasn't that deluded.

He carefully took off his backpack and dug a Slim Jim out of it. While he chewed, he surveyed the situation, using the protein and awesome tastiness to spark the synapses in his brain. He needed something that could serve as a bridge.

Below, a police car cruised into the alley. He didn't bother ducking.

People were dumb. They never looked up. He knew that from staring out the window for the past few weeks. The cops gave their siren a quick blurt.

At the end of the alley, a guy wearing a facemask and gloves carried a four-pack of toilet paper and a bag of groceries. Renato had been relying on the government packages and his paltry stash. The guy must have found a black market to procure the butt wipes. Renato had been using a carton of unlicensed Sponge Rob birthday napkins that he had scored at the dollar store just before everything shut down. They worked okay, but he was nostalgic for a classic wipe.

The two police officers got out of the car and said something to Toilet Paper. The guy shrugged. They approached, hands on the top of their guns. Toilet Paper backed up a step. A baton came out. Toilet Paper turned to run. The baton hit the back of his legs, tripping him. He slid across the concrete. As one cop kicked the guy, the other picked up his baton, the groceries, and the toilet paper. He walked slowly back to the car and put them in the trunk. The two police laughed and drove away.

Renato waited for the man to get to his feet. He didn't know if he would. Finally, after almost a full minute, the guy rose and stumbled out of sight around the corner.

Renato had been pacing the ledge for the better part of a half hour. There were no nearby boards long enough, no extendable ladder, nothing to make a bridge. He wondered if there was a way to construct a makeshift span from medical waste, but knew that was ridiculous. He would need glue.

He considered jumping, but he didn't have a clear enough path to get a running start. Even then, he was pretty sure he would Wile E. Coyote the whole thing and end up getting halfway, stopping in midair, pulling out a tiny umbrella, and plummeting to the earth.

Then Renato remembered the simplest, most basic fact that the cops had reminded him of. People are dumb. People never look up. Including him. And of course, above him was an electricity or telephone line, a thick cable that ran at an angle from his building down to Adult.

He didn't know if it would hold his weight. He didn't know if he could hold himself up for long enough. He didn't even know if he would actually slide all the way.

If he thought about it too long, he would change his mind. Taking off his jean jacket, he secured his backpack tight onto his back and climbed the pole that held the cable.

Renato tied one jacket-sleeve around his left wrist, draped the jacket over the cable, and tied the other sleeve around his other wrist. His left shoulder was still dislocated, dangling strangely and hurting like hell, but his grip was fine. He hoped the skin or muscle or whatever held his arm to his shoulder would hold. Tightening his grip on the sleeves, he took a deep breath.

One last look down at the alley beneath him. A pile of jagged metal sat inexplicably right below him. It might break his fall by impaling him, but that was not optimal. The mystery needle in his back was still enough of a worry that he didn't want to insert any new metal into his body at this juncture.

Maybe he should just go back home.

Then he heard it, faint but distinct. So familiar that it drilled into his brain. From out an open window:

Seagull.

Hog.

Seagull.

Hog.

Seagull.

Hog.

Jumping forward, he slid down the cable toward Adult and an endless heaven of pornography.

He landed hard on his back. Sitting up, he stared for ten straight minutes without moving a muscle, amazed that one of his bonehead plans had actually worked. From his new vantage point, he had a wide view of the roof covered in medical waste. He could now see that many of the bags were stamped TONY'S MEDICAL WASTE REMOVAL. It was funny that he had never noticed that stamp before.

When Renato got a new phone, the first thing he was going to do was write a scathing Yelp review about how Tony had half-assed his responsibilities and just chucked his shit (and some of those bags most certainly had shit in them) on the roof, when he should be burying them in New Jersey with all the other garbage in the world.

The fall had knocked his shoulder joint back in place, which made it hurt ten times more, but now he could move it. The stranger was back in play. Everything was coming up Renato.

The door on the roof was still open. He had made it.

He stood slowly, knocked some of the gravel off his back, and took a few tentative steps toward Oz. The door made no sound when he opened it wider. The staircase was dark, leading sharply down into the store below. He ended up in a storeroom packed so full of dildos that he had to back against one of the shelves just to get the door open. The disturbing feel of the raw rubber gave him chills, like what he imagined alien dong felt like. Depending on the planet, of course.

With the door open, he heard it.

"No, no, no, no, no!" Renato pleaded.

But the sounds grew louder, coming into focus as he walked down the hall to the sales floor of the store.

Cow.

Mouse.

Chimpanzee.

Old-timey car horn.

Twiki from Buck Rogers.

Goat.

As the colorful displays of magazines, videos, lotions, and accoutrements came into view, so did the horror of his reality.

Seven guys sat in the store, strategically spaced about six feet apart from each other. Six of the guys were partaking in the pleasures that the retail outlet provided, facing into corners as they moved like they were trying to start an engine.

The seventh guy ate a Hot Pocket while he did a crossword. He turned to Renato and gave him a head nod. "What's up? Someone should be done soon."

Renato tried to look away, but couldn't. He held his hands over his ears, but the sounds still penetrated.

Cow.

Mouse.

Chimpanzee.

Old-timey car horn.

Twiki from Buck Rogers.

Goat.

Renato fell to his knees and screamed to the heavens. "You maniacs! You blew it up! Damn you! Goddamn you all to hell!"

After a moment, Hot Pockets asked, "So, you want to wait for a spot?"

"Sure," Renato said, standing up. "I'll be in the dildo closet."

POR SI ACASO

By Hector Acosta

Larry died over a plate of Nachos Bell Grande.

"They weren't even Nachos Supreme," Dwayne mutters from his spot by the television. He's splayed on top of the beanbag chair we found a couple of weeks ago, and when he shifts to scratch his balls, little puffs of white dribble out a gash in its side, the bag sagging just a bit more. "If I'm going to die, it better be because of Nachos Supreme," he says, shaking his head. Almost makes you think he cares about poor dead Larry.

"I think technically Nachos Bell Grandes are better than Supreme," Carlos mutters from the sofa. He holds a rectangular controller in both hands and stares intently at the video game he's playing on the television, the colorful pixels reflecting off his dirty glasses. "Supremes are smaller and you get less guac."

Dwayne flicks some of the beanbag's filling in Carlos's direction and says, "Bullshit. Why would they call them Supreme, then? Supreme means, like, super great." He flicks another puff, this one arcing over the living room and hitting Carlos on the nose. I want to tell Dwayne to stop it, but I don't. Besides, Carlos doesn't even flinch, because he's so into the game.

"Grande means big," Carlos says, maneuvering his little green guy around a yellow field. Top-of-the-line speakers (acquired by me when things really took a turn and folks started caring more about medicine than electronics) eke out tiny blips and bloops that, if my ears could squint, I *guess* would sound like music.

"You would know," Dwayne says, picking the filling that's piled on the carpet and trying to cram it back inside the beanbag.

This time Carlos flinches. Dwyane doesn't notice it, but I do.

I watch Carlos play his game for a few more minutes. I try to be sad about Larry, I really do, but all I can think about right now is how much I miss my PlayStation. It still sits on the entertainment unit, alongside all its cords and multiple controllers, covered in a thin layer of dust. Carlos's Nintendo is hooked up next to it, and I think I finally understand the saying about how sad it is for fathers to see their children die before them.

The day Sony shut down their servers and made everyone's downloadable games unplayable was when I knew we were all in trouble. Before that, it was easy for me to ignore everything shouted in social media about the virus. I filed that stuff away in the same part of my brain that I filed my mother's old warnings, about how I should clean all my groceries before putting them up and how if I was going to go out, it better be with a bandolier of disinfectants and a mask. Even the lockdown order wasn't a big deal to me. Work had let me go a few days prior, so I was already spending most of my time indoors watching shit on television and masturbating myself into afternoon naps.

It was a pretty good life, so long as some stuff went unconsidered—like the breakdown in society, the thousands dead and dying, and what ultimately killed our friend Larry: the dwindling fast food supply.

Tired of watching Carlos move around pixels on the screen, I get up from the couch and walk into the kitchen, stepping over a pile of dirty laundry I keep meaning to do.

"Hey, Luis, we got any of those spicy pork rinds left?" Dwayne shouts at me.

"No," I tell him without checking. We probably do, but spicy food and Dwayne go together as well old video games and me, so I try to keep hot stuff away from him when I can. We don't need him to hog the bathroom all night and use up our remaining stock of toilet paper.

The kitchen is the only part of the house that is in pretty good shape, cleanliness-wise. That isn't an easy thing to make happen when you have three 17-year-old guys living together, but I have dear mom to thank for it. See, when I was growing up, she was always a little bit of a neat freak. I say it this way 'cause I loved her and it's not nice to speak bad about the dead and shit. Those who didn't like her called her a nutjob. Those who didn't like her and had a medical degree used the word *hypochondriac,* which I remember looking up in a dictionary when I was ten.

Mom was tuned to the virus way before the news started talking about it nonstop. We already had tons of canned goods in the garage thanks to her belief of being prepared, alongside a bunch of freeze-dried stuff the guys and I still weren't desperate enough to try. When people finally realized how serious the whole thing was and rushed the grocery stores, trying to stock up on bottled water and toilet paper, I was set. Even had a tent, a generator and first aid kits in every room of the house. "I told you this was coming, mijo," she said as she squatted by a box of pasta and wiped it down before bringing it into the kitchen. "I know you laughed at me, but we're going to survive because of me."

I think about her and the brain aneurysm she never had a chance to prepare for as I walk over to the commercial freezer the guys and I dragged into the kitchen when they moved in with me. The padlock hanging from the door's latch is cold to the touch, and I wait a few moments for my hand to warm it up enough to loosen the dials, the numbers to the combination in my head before my finger grazes the first dial.

The inside of the freezer is a foodie's paradise, so long as the foodie in question has lowered their standards to the new reality. One side is lined with Big Macs, the burgers taken out of their cardboard packaging and individually placed inside their own, separate Ziploc bags. Carefully stacked one atop the other, they reach to the top of the freezer, like a wall of heart attacks waiting to happen. We also got burgers from Wendy's, Burger King, and a couple other places, though none sell as good as Mickey D's. Next to the burgers, we have our international section. We're talking cartons of lo mein, orange chicken and honey shrimp from the Panda, two big pans of pasta from Olive Garden, and an assortment of tacos, frozen burritos and plates of nachos from Mexican restaurants. And Taco Bell.

Two tubs, both the size of bowling balls, are stacked atop each other, one filled with frozen special sauce, and the other with spicy ketchup. Even got a couple of frozen Szechuan sauce packets, 'cause it might be the apocalypse, but there are still Rick and Morty fans out there. Everything is carefully labeled, documenting the restaurant it came from and when it was bought. Best way to piss off a customer is to bring them the wrong order. Most of them are already angry at us for the prices charged, so you want to make sure you get their order right. Especially 'cause by this point, we're pretty much their only option.

It's how I figured things would go. When the guys moved in, I told them my plan, and we spent the next few weeks going to all the fast food places and restaurants we could think of, buying up as much of their inventory as possible. Afterwards, we just sat on the stuff, waiting for the gold arches to fall down and the Taco Bell to stop ringing. When that happened, we put the word out that you could still get your artery-clogging fix through us.

I finish taking stock of the contents of the fridge and make a mental note to move some stuff over from the other freezer we have running in the garage. Locking the freezer, I grab a bag of regular pork rinds from the pantry, along with two bottles of water, and head back to the living room. The pork rinds I toss to Dwayne, who catches them with both hands and tears the bag open. Taking a seat on the sofa next to Carlos, I drink from the water bottle and watch him.

His eyes are glued to the television, tracking the little green guy as he moves through a pixelated maze, occasionally swatting at enemies with what I imagine is meant to be a sword. Either that or the game is a lot more interesting than I gave it credit for. Carlos sits on the edge of the sofa, hunched over like he's on the toilet squeezing a big one out, holding the controller tightly in both hands. His right foot taps a tempo on the carpet, and when I glance down, I note the red stains on his tennis shoes.

"We need to talk about what happened," I tell Carlos, reaching for the controller.

"Yeah," Dwayne adds, his mouth full of pork rinds. "Tell us how you offed the dude."

I shoot him a look. I had hoped the pork rinds would keep him from talking. Then I turn back to Carlos and put my hand on the controller. "Come on, Chuck, talk to us."

Chuck. His old nickname, the one he decided on when he got really into X-Men comics. Why he'd pick a bald dude who couldn't walk as his role model I'll never quite get, but that was Carlos for you, then and now.

Carlos doesn't look at me, just keeps on playing.

"Fuck this," Dwayne says. Rolling off the bean bag chair, he crawls on all fours to the entertainment unit, and before Carlos or I can stop him, reaches behind the Nintendo console and rips out the power cord. The little green dude, who I think Carlos managed to get all the way to the end boss, is instantly swallowed up by gray static. Carlos blinks once, then twice, but otherwise continues to stare at the television, and I wonder if, like my PlayStation, he's beyond bringing back.

Tossing the power cord against the wall, Dwayne walks over to Carlos and swats the controller from his hands. "Stop acting like a retard and tell us what happened."

I'm in Dwayne's face in an instant. "Watch it," I tell him. Funny how fast I slip into my old playground role again.

The smell of pork rinds and built-up tension wedges between Dwayne and me as we stare each other down. It's a dumb thing to do, I know, both of us jockeying for a position that no longer matters, but it's hard to let go of all the high school crap, you know? I look at Dwayne and think of all the times he acted like he was better than Carlos and me, or made a crack about Carlos's weight or my mom, always followed by *Shit, you guys can't take a joke* when one of us would get butthurt over his comments and call him on it.

"Move," Dwayne says, his face set with the same determined look he used to get on the track field as he waited for the starting gun to go off.

"Nuh-uh." I think about telling him he has pork-rind dust all over his upper lip, a mustache of fried pig particles.

"He," Dwayne points at Carlos, and damn it, I flinch when he moves his hand to do so, "needs to talk, and you," he pokes me with his other hand, "need to stop babysitting him. The guy just goes off and kills our best client and then comes back and parks his gigantic ass on the sofa to play his stupid game and we're supposed to just be all, 'Well, that's okay, little buddy, you'll talk to us when you're ready.'" He shakes his head and looks at Carlos. "Fuck. That."

I've fought Dwayne three times in the eight years we've known each other. First time happened in fifth grade, when Dwayne found out I liked wrestling and called it, and by extension me, gay. Second time happened four years later, when we found out we both liked Becky Rogers and he went behind my back and asked her out, even though he 100 percent said he wouldn't and I'd called dibs. Third time was right before the virus made everything to go in lockdown, when, drunk off some beers he'd taken from his dad's stash, he asked me if I ever worry that my brain was as fucked as my mom's. I lost all three fights, the first one ending with me on the ground and my Mankind figure broken in half. Second time, I had a bloody nose and no date for the dance. Last time, he gave me a black eye and a mumbled apology the day after.

I think about this because I'm pretty sure we're seconds away from our fourth fight, and if I'm being honest, I think my chances to win are about the same as all the other times. My hand is balled into a fist, nails digging into my skin, and I'm considering kneeing him in the groin to give me better odds when Carlos speaks up:

"I'll tell you."

Carlos tells us the story in a rapid, hushed voice, having to stop several times to catch his breath. He remains seated on the edge of the sofa, his right foot tapping up a beat while he rubs his hands on his jeans and makes me wish I could hand him the controller just so he has something else to do with them.

"It was, you know, it was a big order, right? One of our biggest ones, I think." He stops and looks at me for confirmation, and I nod. Because yeah, when Larry called me up the other day, I had to get a pen and paper to write down what he wanted. Usually, when folks reach out to us, it's for a burger, two maybe. But Larry was ordering like he'd just taken a really good hit of weed and was at the drive-thru line of Taco Bell.

I reminded Larry that, unlike Taco Bell, we didn't have no ninety-cent menu. The stuff he was rattling off would cost him. Just the In-and-Out Burger alone would set him back a couple of presidents. Larry just laughed that long, wheezy laugh of his, the one that made you want to put a hand over his mouth and have him swallow whatever he thought was funny. "Amigo, when have I not been good for it?"

God, Larry was such an asshole. Then again, if I was the hometown football hero, prom king and the one and only cum stain of Ted Drake, owner of a bunch of drive-thru Daiquiri stands across Houston, I might be an asshole, too. It was Larry's lineage, and nothing else, that kept me on the phone with him. Everyone knew Mr. Drake was loaded, thanks to his stands using Mad Dog for the drinks and having a rep for not checking IDs too carefully, making them popular with everyone in our school. I didn't even think the lockdown stuff affected them. In fact, it probably helped them. What else was there to do at home than get drunk off cheap, super-sweet, route 44-size drinks? And the drive-thru meant you were still doing the whole social distancing thing.

"Man, remember when we couldn't get near Larry's bougie

neighborhood without that security guard threatening to call the cops?" Dwayne asks me, already forgetting how close we came to fighting. "Anyone watching the place nowadays?" He asks Carlos.

Carlos shakes his head. "I don't think so. No one stopped me when I drove in."

Dwayne's eyes glimmered with a stupidity I knew was coming. "We should go and get one of those houses. Eminem Domain the living shit out of it, yeah?"

"Eminent," Carlos mutters, before continuing. "I get to his place and after I get the stuff unloaded, I ring the doorbell and wait." Carlos is back to staring at the television, and I feel bad. He and Dwayne both pushed for me to accept the PayPal, but I convinced them cash was the way to go. "We want to have cash on hand," I believe were my—or if we want to be honest here—my mom's exact words.

"The door opens, and I'm expecting Larry—"

"So you could fuck him up for all the times he shoved you in the hall!" Dwayne walks up to Carlos and places two of his fingers on his temple, as if they were the barrel of a gun. "BLAM," he says, using the fingers of his other hand to mime blood spurting from the side of his head.

Carlos ignores him. "But it's a girl. I think maybe she went to our school?"

"Was she hot?" Dwayne wants to know.

Blushing, Carlos looks down and nods. "She was pretty. Nice too, asked me how I was doing and saying how I, I mean, we were providing a cool service to folks. She takes the food to kitchen, and it takes her a couple of trips, cause there's a lot. After the last one, she comes back with her purse, and I have my Ziploc bag ready to have her put the cash in, just like you told me, Luis, when we hear yelling coming from the kitchen. It's Larry, he's calling the girl—he called her Kristin—over. And Kristin, she kinda freezes for a second before turning around and heading to the kitchen."

"Shit, what you do?" Dwayne asks.

Carlo's lips tremble, and I hate Dwayne for asking the question. But I hate myself more, because now I'm thinking about the gun that my mom kept by her bed and showed me how to fire. "Por si acaso," she said that first time at the range, the smell of gunpowder burning my nostrils and my ears ringing.

Just in case, I'd told Carlos, showing him how to switch the safety off before sticking it in his waistband. We'd been hearing helicopters overhead nightly for the past week, and supposedly stuff was getting even worse out there.

"What you do?" Dwayne asks again, jabbing Carlos in the shoulder.

"She hadn't paid me." His eyes flick to the controller a few feet away. "I followed her inside. Called out, too, but she ignored me. I find them in the kitchen, arguing." Carlos takes off his glasses and starts to clean them. "That's not right, 'cause it's just Larry shouting and Kristin taking it all. He's super-pissed, pacing back and forth and screaming about how useless Kristin is, and how she can't get anything right. The food—our food—is on the table, some of it anyways. A bunch of it is on the floor or splattered against the walls of the kitchen. I don't think either of them notice me watching them."

"What was Larry mad about?" I ask.

"The order. How Kristin got it wrong. He kept pointing to the nachos and saying they're the wrong ones. How there's not enough guacamole and beans."

Dwayne, maybe for the first time in his life, stays quiet here.

"Which is dumb, right?" Carlos pauses and looks from Dwayne to me. "It was Larry who placed the order, so if anyone made a mistake, it was him. But Kristin doesn't say that. She just stays quiet."

"And you spoke up," I say. Because of course Carlos would.

He nods. "Larry turns and looks at me. I don't think he recognizes me, even though we were in the same group in Spanish class, freshman year. He points at me and asks if I'm the one who ate his nachos. And, I don't know, I guess I didn't like that. Cause he wasn't just asking randomly. You could hear it in his voice, the way he looked at me. It was—"

Here Carlos pauses, and I notice the way his eyes glance at Dwayne for just an instant. "It sucked," he says. "I guess I got mad or something."

"You got more than mad," Dwayne mutters, and I wonder if he gets it at all.

Carlos doesn't respond, and we sit in silence for the next few minutes, the sound of the motor from the freezer scratching my right ear. I think about the story Carlos told us and wonder if this is the end of our business.

"There's something else," Carlos says, so quietly I almost don't hear the next part. "Larry, he doesn't look good, afterwards, lying on the floor. He's a lot skinnier than in the ads he used to run on TV. And then I remember how he kept coughing in between yelling at Kristin. I think, I think that's why she didn't really shout back or anything and just took it."

I want to jump off the sofa. I want to burn the sofa. And the living room. And maybe Carlos? Every tidbit, every rumor, every tweet about the virus fills my head. Contagious. Transmittable. In the air. Through contact only. Maybe. Probably. We don't know.

"Yeah," Carlos says, putting his glasses back on. "When I sho— when I did what I did, I got blood and stuff on her and me. But she didn't even freak out at me. Just said something like, 'At least I can stop wondering if I have it or not.'"

I'm staring at Carlos's shoe, the one with the red stain. I'm thinking of how he came into the house with those shoes on and how we've been sitting feet away from each other all day. Then I think about my mom again, about her need to be prepared. For anything.

"Carlos," I say. "What did you do with the gun?"

HERD IMMUNITY

By Eryk Pruitt

You carry shoes with you. Some in better shape than others, some brand new. Some are a bit worn and tattered, but still, they would be better than trucking about the dirt roads to and from the ragtag campsite in bare feet, like the Calebites are known to do. You've never seen them up close, only from a distance, and have been warned to stay away from them.

"Those dirty hippies up there are dangerous," your mother used to tell you. "They're a cult. They do drugs and have unprotected sex, then sell their babies to young mothers with barren wombs."

Mom also used to tell you to turn the other cheek and do unto others. Dad, on the other hand, never cottoned to that kind of talk.

"They locked themselves away during the outbreak, all those years ago. Most folks had the good sense to get back to work and rejoin society." Dad would then spit on the ground. "Not the Calebites. They never again stepped foot off that property."

Their camp is down at the end of a long dirt path that cut through the backwoods, down near the river. You always heard there were nearly twenty of them. Used to be, you and your buddies would dare each other to breach the campsite, just touch the bumper of the busted RV, first person to make it to the rusted-out station wagon… each time, a little further. Each time, a little deeper in.

You've been by three times over the past two weeks. You've carried with you sacks of old clothes, some cough syrup, cans of food.

You've never seen so much as a soul.

"You ought to steer clear of those Calebites," said your buddy Gregson. You suppose you've known him long as anyone. Most of your other classmates graduated high school and sloughed off to college. Not Gregson. He stayed behind with you to man the counter at the Dairy Mart. "They're not like you and me. They got themselves a God who says it's okay to do wrong by other people who don't believe the way they do."

"Doesn't everybody?"

"Their God is different." Gregson spoke in high pitches, but not when he talked about the Calebites. His voice sunk to near-whispers: "Those ones will make short work of you."

"They're people. Just like you and me, I reckon."

Lately, you have begun to grow into yourself. A small town can fold in on a fella. It can make him do things and think ways he might not, if left alone. There is a common ideal to which all must subscribe and, as of late, you have begun to fill out your shirts, your britches, the shoes on your feet. The words sent forth from your mother, your teachers, the preacher at your church, have all begun to ring hollow. They are keeping something from you. They don't want you to know everything just yet. You send out for books not kept at the town's library. You study subjects nobody has ever taught you. Your hometown grows smaller and smaller and you fear that one day you might pop it at the seams and they will have to rend you limb-by-limb, lest you tear the entire place to smithereens.

You start by loading up your old clothes into trash bags and hauling them down to the camp where live the Calebites.

Again, like last time, there is no one at the camp when you arrive. The smell of fire lingers fresh, but there is no flame. Forgotten automobiles ring the perimeter like rusted sentries. A station wagon, half a pickup truck, an old RV, the other half of the pickup…

The grass reaches to your waist here, and this time of year you must mind for snakes. Never once in all your childhood dares had you made it this far, but you're not a child anymore. You say it over and over:

I am not a child.

Where the woods break, there is an old tobacco barn. There's been no tobacco out this way since long before the pandemic, but the air still tinges sweet like peppered honey as you near it. Someone is inside. You can hear nothing, but still you know it.

"I carry with me shoes," you call out. Your words drop like anchors, so you call them again. "I carry with me shoes."

You could turn and run. You should turn and run.

But you don't.

Instead, with a shaky hand, you creak open the door.

She is naked by firelight. A single candle burning in the corner of the room. There is no furniture—nearly a dozen neatly bundled bed rolls—except for the ornate vanity before which she sits, gazing at her nakedness in a mirror as she brushes slowly her long, blonde hair. She is a perfect human being, of a perfect shape, with skin untouched by time or the elements. She is a vision. You have seen naked women before, but only Heather Tidwell or Candace Swanson or women on

TV, no one quite so fetching or dangerous as the one before you. You can tell by her eyes, which cut sideways at you, that she sees things no one has ever known or will ever see.

You could fall to your knees.

She gives you hardly a second thought. She returns her attention to the mirror and continues stroking the brush through that long, lustrous hair.

"They will send one to destroy us," she says in a sweet murmur. "He will claim to be our friend."

"Beg pardon?"

"Do you claim to be our friend?"

You hold the trash bags about hip-high. "I carry with me shoes."

She smiles. She half-turns in her high-backed chair. The cushion gives a little squeak, rubbing against the flesh of her buttock. She faces you. You fight to keep your eyes off her breasts, focus instead on her soft-spreading smile. Her eyes, which pool and sparkle.

"So, you are our friend?"

I return the smile. "I'm not the enemy, that's for sure."

She tells you: "One time, I heard music. Do you listen much to music? Sure, you do. You probably listen to it all the time. We're not supposed to enjoy it, not what you call music anyway. The stuff that's been recorded and mixed and played through speakers. We find music in other places. Have you ever lay down on the grass and turned your face up to the moon and closed your eyes? You should do it sometime. You should do it *all the time*. The trees creak and sway in a strong breeze. The bullfrogs scream with glee. There will be shrieking in the night and it is both melodious and terrible. The cycles of life happen after dark. There is death and rebirth and consumption. There is *reproduction*."

She stands. Her every curve is a symphony. Her hair drapes behind her shoulders. Her eyes…

"When I heard it, my entire world stopped turning on its axis. What is this? What is that sound? Why had I not been told of it before? I still hear it—over and over and over—but not half as clear as I did that day in the woods. Listen..."

Her voice cracks only slightly as she sings the first lines of "When a Man Loves a Woman." Maybe she is off-key and perhaps she's remembered the notes wrong; that sound is from another world than you. You never want it to end. You want her to sing for you the rest of your days, even a song as cliché as "When a Man Loves a Woman," just so long as she never stops.

Eventually she does. And when she does, she speaks as if something has taken hold in her throat.

"The human memory is a funny thing," she says. "I remember the words to the song. I remembered following the music through the forest until I came upon the campsite. Everything else—the two campers and what they were wearing and the bitter taste of the coffee they brewed 'fore me—I remember it all. What I don't remember—"

"I can play you that song."

"My father—you can what?"

"I said, I can play you that song."

You can. You reach into your pocket and pull out your cellphone. You thumb the screen alive. The room lights up as if on fire. Her skin takes a florescent tint. Her eyes are alive.

"You keep a radio in your pocket?"

"No, no." You try not to laugh. "This is a phone. A telephone."

She cocks her precious head to the side.

"It does a lot of things," you tell her. "It can do anything. Watch."

You're all thumbs. You can't type fast enough. It auto-fills and you select the first video. But first, a fifteen-second advertisement for car insurance.

"It's just like I remembered." She sways to the rollick of the organ. "It's *better* than I remember."

You can honestly say you've never heard this song in such a way, either. It's been on the radio hundreds of times, or in a movie, elevators, or even commercials, but your entire life it has been only background. You've never heard the lyrics in such a way. Standing in that old tobacco barn with that pretty girl rocking naked to the smooth, soulful moans of Percy Sledge, you think perhaps you have become someone new. For the first time, your eyes and ears have opened.

"And you say you can listen to this anytime you want?"

Your mouth hangs open, and the weight of your jaw bears heavy. "I can listen to anything, anytime I want."

"Oh, that must be wonderful."

"You are very beautiful."

"How many songs are there?"

"More than the stars," you tell her. "There are all the songs you could ever wish for."

"How do you choose which ones to hear?"

You've never thought about that before. You don't know how to answer, so instead, you take a step closer to her. Then another.

She asks, "How do you know when it's time to make it stop?"

You take her face with both hands and bring it to yours. The smell from her mouth shocks you at first, but soon you've covered it with your own and your tongue is inside her. She does not struggle, and in fact, for a moment, she does not move. Not her hands, not her mouth, not her tongue. But only for a moment, for soon she is alive and the two of you are lips and hands and hips grinding into hips. Your mouth moves with the beat of the song. You can't get enough of her into your arms. This is not her first kiss, not by any means, but that is not your concern. Nothing, for that matter, is your concern, until finally she pulls her mouth free of yours and, amid mad gasps for air, pants:

"My father…"

"He won't find out," you say. "I'll never breathe a word."

"No," she tells you. "My father…"

She's no longer looking at you. She looks behind you. You turn and see, only in a flash, the little man leaping across the darkness. The scream by which he fills the air. The glint of the knife from the candlelight.

He's spry. You've just enough time to shield your face with one hand and strike out with the other. You don't care where your fist lands, so long as it lands at all. If you can find something to hit, your plan is to hit it again.

Then again.

And again, so many times that hopefully somebody will tell you when it's time to stop. But that first parry does not strike gold or, for all you know, anywhere near it. Your blow flies wild, which furthers the advantage for your attacker.

Your face meets the hay-strewn floor of the tobacco barn. You suck motes into your lungs. Mites. Fistfuls of dirt.

You wait for the black.

"Daddy! Please!"

It's her. You'd recognize that voice anywhere, even without the sing-song joy of your previous and only interaction. Even behind the curtains of fear and outrage and—

It comes: *The black.*

You come to, you think, in a cave. At one end is light, but that end is far, far from where you are. The sounds you collect: water that drips…drips…driiiiips. A mourning dove when it is light; the hoot of an owl in the black. The throbbing in your bandaged head.

Your hands: also bandaged. Someone changes them. You never remember it happening, but you are in a constant state of finding yourself with fresh dressings.

The feel of the rough and splintered wood that forms the bars all around you.

The ever-present smell of a recent campfire and… *sulfur?*

And as always, the return to the black.

"I am not like my sister."

He speaks in silhouette against the bright of the faraway day that ends the tunnel of black. It takes time for you to make sense of his words. Your head is thick.

Thick.

"I used to live among you," he says. "Like my father, I am immune to it. We are no longer carriers. Not like her. Not like the others."

His silhouette bends into the black. You hear the sound of tin scraping against the smooth cave floor. It stops at your feet. Your nostrils fill with the unctuous smells of meat and dairy.

"Back when I lived amongst you, people would forever say that breakfast was the most important meal of the day. Do you agree with that?"

You fight the urge to fall upon that smell and devour it.

The shadow asks, "Do you agree with that?"

Your mouth is too dry to answer.

"I don't," he says. "I think that's another thing your people got wrong. Do you know which meal we believe should be the most important?"

He gives you time to answer. When you don't, he kicks the plate. You hear it rattle against the far wall.

"The next one."

Later that night, you hear her sing again. How long have you waited? Did you think it would ever again happen?

It's the same song—"When a Man Loves a Woman"—but this time it sounds like it's being sung underwater.

It takes time for your words to form in the canyon that is your throat. "Where are you?" you ask the darkness.

The singing does not stop.

"How long have I been here?"

Still, there is no answer. Instead, the cave is filled with the off-key warbling of the Percy Sledge classic. It does not take long for you to become grateful. You close your eyes and tell yourself that if the rest of your days are spent with that voice in your ears and the memory of her vision in your brain, then—

"Stop that racket!"

The voice comes from the black. It's gruff and deeper than the one who brought food. This voice carries weight and when he commands the music to stop, it comes as no surprise that only silence would follow.

As does the flame.

Your eyes take time to adjust to the low light of the fire. It's lit in what appears to be the center of the cave. As suspected, you are trapped inside a wooden cage. Across the room is another one, similar to your own.

Between them stands a man.

"Where is she?" you ask him. You squint deeper into the shadows but still come up empty.

"The child has been quarantined," comes the answer, "just like you."

The man is smaller than his voice might suggest. Even in darkness you can feel the rage behind his eyes.

"Your people had a choice," he says. "You could have made a difference, but instead you chose to make a dollar."

"I don't know what you're tal—"

"We have no idea what you brought with you."

"I brought with me shoes."

The little man picks up something black and bulky. You recognize it as the garbage bag you slogged to the camp of the Calebites. It is quickly thrown into the fire.

"Why?" you ask. "Why all this?"

The man narrows the distance between you. He twists both hands around the wooden slats that form the bars of your cage. He brings his face close enough for you to smell the rot in his breath.

He growls, "We do it for survival."

"Survival? From what?"

Overhead, the sound of helicopters. This means it would be six o'clock, time for the evening disinfectant. The noise of it whips to a crescendo, then—just as quick as it started—dissolves behind a curtain of cicadas.

The small man twists his lips into a grin.

"We will talk again in the morning."

It is sometime in the night when next you call out to her. At first, she does not answer. However, upon the second calling...

"Daddy won't let me talk to you."

You inhale deeply, as if you might possibly savor the scent of her voice. Instead, all you can taste is the burnt rubber of the shoes.

"Why not?"

You are greeted only with silence.

"What happened to those campers?" you ask.

"We better go to sleep," she murmurs. "We've caused enough trouble."

Those words echo off the cave walls. You try to suss out something to say that might restore the connection you possibly imagined earlier. Had you, in fact, imagined it? This moment did indeed exist, didn't it?

"How long is the quarantine?" you finally manage to ask.

"Forty days."

"What happens at the end of forty days?"

"If we have not caught the sickness, then we shall be released."

"What sickness?"

The only answer is the faraway dripping of water to the puddle in the cave floor. You think about the tickle forming at the back of your throat and suppress the urge to cough.

"What happens if we get it? The sickness?"

She takes a breath. "They will do anything to stop it from spreading among us."

"How?"

The remnants of the earlier fire pop and crackle.

You ask again. "How will they stop it from spreading?"

"It's time to go to sleep."

You have no idea if she does or not. All you know is that she says not another word until morning.

That night you don't sleep so much as you drop into depths upon depths of the black until you lay broken at the bottom of it. You can't find a single use for your senses, nor any of your limbs, nor a simple thought in your head. You are empty, yet at the same time you are awake and aware of every whisper of wind that filters through that cave, every drop of blood that oozes through your bloodstream. None of it matters. Nothing matters. Nothing save the solitary thought that, somewhere at the end of this darkness, she lies in a cage much as you.

You are not alone.

Your memory of your small town is but a tiny pinhole, a light only as large as the afternoon sky at the long end of the tunnel of black. You are no longer formed by the opinions and morals of your father, your mother, your priest, those around you, but instead by your solitary mission in life which is that young woman in the cave with you. To show her how much bigger is the world, which you'd previously believed to be so small. There should be a claxon to signal this realization, this transformation, but there is not. Instead, there is a thin veil of frost that dusts the limits of this confident serenity.

No sooner had this fragility touched your bones than it sank into the marrow of it. The pain in your head. The dry misery scratching your throat. The damp sauna in your lungs. The raging of fire through your veins, the thick scent of the burning shoes. You'd brought them. This was your fault. This was all your doing.

You'd crash your own head against the bars, but for the energy it would require for self-loathing.

The next time they approach you, they protect themselves. They wear masks that cover their nose and face. Plastic shields their heads like halos. Rubber gloves. Her brother and the little man are joined by another. Their every set of eyes is a bastion of curiosity.

"It's remarkable," says the third man.

"It is hardly remarkable," says the smaller one from before. "It's a *mutation*."

"Regardless."

You open your mouth to speak, but all you can manage is to choke on your own phlegm.

The smaller man lowers himself to his knees. His eyes swim with an emotion you don't recognize. If you had anything resembling energy, you might reach out to touch him, for fear you might never touch another living thing.

When finally he speaks, he says, "I hate your people."

"Daddy, please."

It's her. Still, she speaks from the distance, only this time it sounds as if she—

"I hate what your people have done." The small man runs his gloved hand along the smooth cave floor. "This planet is strong, and it was healing. It had erased centuries of harm caused by your people. But you had other priorities."

"I didn't—" Your tongue is thick inside your mouth. You can hardly speak around it.

The little man rises to his feet. He shuffles to the cage door and opens it.

"It's your world out there," he says, as he steps aside. "It is where you belong."

"I'm taking her with me."

You're surprised. Not only by the authority in your voice, but the fact that you were able to speak at all. You've never felt like this. You feel like you are still falling. You feel as though there is no bottom to which you might sink.

Still, you say it again:

"I'm taking her with me."

The little man considers this. He turns to the others. They shrug their shoulders.

"She has served her purpose," he tells you. "Now she may serve another."

You use her as you might a crutch. It takes near an hour to reach the old tobacco barn. It takes another to maneuver to the end of the skinny dirt road that delivered you into the camp. However, once you are free from the confines of her childhood, she lets fly a delightful squeal. She drops to her knees at the road which will take you to town. She scoops handfuls of gravel and showers them down atop her head.

"All the world is a wonder," she tells you. "All the world is a mystery."

You are too weak to walk on your own. You see before you two roads where previously there had only been one. You see above you two firmaments and two skies. Two earths below your feet.

"I want to see everything," she says.

You drape your arm around her shoulders and slouch toward home.

"I want to touch it all."

You watch her with abject sadness. You hallucinate the sound of laughter at the juxtaposition that now separates you both.

"What if I've made a mistake?" you ask her.

She answers with a sneeze.

UNSCATHED

By Michelle Garza and Melissa Lason

His corpse sat in the recliner. His eyes were closed, and if it wasn't for the pallor of his skin, he might have looked as if he was only sleeping. Mark liked to do that, fall asleep in odd places, in strange positions, especially after he had his nightly round of drinks. Marnie's mother used to say drunks and cats could sleep anywhere and she believed the old woman. He wasn't asleep, though. Marnie knew better. If she pulled aside the plush throw blanket she would see the wounds she left in his chest. She already removed the steak knife, but she didn't have the emotional strength to clean up the bloody pool that gathered on his chest and soaked into his shirt.

If the world hadn't come to a halt, she would have already found herself in a jail cell. Her husband's partner, Allan, would have certainly come to check in on the man who never missed a day of work in their real estate office, even when everyone knew he was an alcoholic and came to the office half-hung over.

Allan never spoke of it. He had no need to address it when they were still raking in mountains of cash. The second secret Allan concealed was the fact that Mark abused his wife, but Allan never lifted a finger to help Marnie. Doing so would have threatened his paychecks, so he chose to pretend like he never saw anything.

Marnie could smell him. It would be impossible to just leave him to rot in the living room. She wondered if she could toss him in the trash can, which was in the garage, out of sight of anyone in the neighborhood, if anyone was still alive. He was a large man, tall and barrel-chested, and she wasn't sure if she could fit him inside doubled over… but she could cut him into pieces, then shove him down inside. She could even throw the kitchen trash on top of him, to cover him if anyone opened the lid.

The plan was coming together in her mind. The can would become a stinking green tomb, a fitting end to trash like him. It might work, but she worried someone might see her as she struggled to haul him to the curb, a nosy neighbor who was still well enough to tell the police when someone reported him missing. If they discovered she murdered him, she would be dragged away in handcuffs, even after she proved she was only defending herself after twelve tiring years of being his punching bag.

She imagined the scandalous trial as she sat down at her kitchen table. Her face would be all over television, the mere sight of her eliciting cries of anger from droves of strange men who also believed a woman should obey their husbands even at the cost of their souls. And somewhere in the crowds and lights there would be other women, standing silently, watching her as she was burned at the stake for salvaging her own life. They would know their voices, and their suffering, would always remain meaningless.

The microwave beeped, loud enough to rattle her from her daydream. Her dog, Sparky, barked at the sudden beeping and then at her. He pawed at her ankle and ran to the kitchen door and back.

Marnie bent down to stroke the Pomeranian's red fur. "He deserved it. If he had just stopped coughing, or slept downstairs, then you wouldn't have barked at him. And he wouldn't have kicked you, and I wouldn't have…"

She sighed, then went to retrieve her mug from the microwave and filled the dog's bowl with food.

"He was sick anyway. I did him a favor."

She let her husband slip to the back of her mind once more as she went to open the door to the yard, a soothing numbness settling in on her. There would be no calling the police, there would be no scandalous trial, there would be no howling hordes of red-faced men to point their fingers at her. Most of them were dead by now. In a way, the virus was a blessing to her.

She slid the door open to be greeted by the scent of summer lawn. She felt strangely content even with the threat of a deadly virus beyond her house, because the worst nightmare she could ever imagine was finally dead. She was finally free of him and his humiliation. If she would live long enough to enjoy her new sense of freedom, she wasn't sure, but she would make the most of what she had left.

The garbage men had either retreated or perished. A green trash bin sat on the roadside, full and stinking, claimed by insects and maggots weeks prior when those last great bastions of society ceased making their rounds. Carlos marked their disappearance on his desk calendar, mourning their loss more than the silencing of the neighborhood streets in the evening. He didn't particularly like most of his neighbors, but the memory of their incessant noise was a sad ghost of the way life was before the world shut down. There were no more conversations around the community mailboxes, no children riding their bikes around the cul-de-sac, no gatherings on front lawns to discuss homeowners' association policies. There was no one around.

Most of them were dead, and those who weren't soon would be.

But the pests were alive and thriving within the sixty-four gallon roll-away can, flies and cockroaches, all caring only to reproduce and live out their lifecycles in the small utopia of rotting food and dirty paper towels in the splitting trash bags cradled within the sunbaked bin before it could no longer house them or their young. Summer had come and dried up the once-sticky rivers of garbage juices running down the side of it. The garbage can was no different than the rest of the neighborhood; things were left untouched, abandoned in the hysteria of quarantine. Yards were overgrown with dried weeds, cars sat in driveways unmoved in months, their gasoline slowly turning to turpentine in their tanks. The remnants of civilization would still be around for many years if mankind lost this battle, thousands upon thousands of lifecycles of flies and maggots could pass by and there would still be empty houses, cars, and shopping centers, eons to the short-lived buzzing and writhing masses who sought to claim dominion over the earth as its apex predator languished and died.

Carlos sat in his office chair, looking out his bedroom window on the second floor of his house. He hadn't stepped outside in months, and didn't plan on it unless his house suddenly caught fire, and even then he would consider trying to put it out with sink water before emerging from his sanctuary. The virus was out there. It was known to strike swiftly, devouring nearly everyone who came in contact with it, leaving hospitals overcrowded and morgues overflowing with corpses within a matter of months. A plague of nightmares, a sickness the likes of which mankind had never imagined took hold of entire countries and left them nearly void of life, frail bodies of what they once were, losing hope of ever returning to their former states, but Carlos had escaped unscathed. He had taken heed at the virus's arrival. While many people scoffed at rumors of its destruction, he stockpiled a mountain of supplies. He sat and watched from his bedroom window as his neighborhood became a ghost town, each house a crypt for the families inside. The end of the world was a worm swallowing each city one by one, and though the orange-skinned leader on TV claimed his armies would soon rescue everyone, it looked as if they would never come—not to Acacia Hills, anyway.

The area was left ravaged by the virus after neighbors held a block party instead of participating in the recommended social distancing. Nearly every man, woman, and child were in attendance, and all but one carried the virus back to their family members who didn't attend, all but Carlos. It wasn't like he was a social butterfly before the virus emerged. He was an outsider among them. They had abided by the herd mentality, and often conducted what they referred to as "good neighbor checks." They had a Facebook group called "Acacia family." He perused it just to make fun of the posts.

He saw it all as them being nosy assholes, and never opened his door when they came knocking. Never responded to any group posts when someone asked his opinion on homeowners' association matters. Even after the news warned of the spreading virus, he saw his neighbors attempting to band together, and he gave them a little credit for trying, but when Kelly Hutchins went around the cul-de-sac with her young granddaughter handing out homemade bread, he cringed and caught himself calling her a *fucking idiot* from behind the safety of his locked door.

"We're all in this together, Carl," she'd huffed, as if saying his name properly was just too complicated for her tongue, and then exited his yard with her granddaughter close behind her, carrying the basket of bread.

His neighbors could never conceal their fake smiles, their eyes searching him, noting the differences in *him* and *them*. The stupid questions always came about his name and where he was from. There was always the look of surprise and disbelief when they learned he wasn't a mechanic or gardener. It was an experience he only endured once, when he first moved in, and swore to himself he never would again. That was a year before the virus erupted, twelve months before the small neighborhood became a graveyard.

From his vantage point, he could see into many of the backyards around him. He liked to watch his neighbor, Marnie, as she stood on her back porch every morning and let her little dog out to do its business on the dying grass. Seeing Marnie meant at least she was still alive, her house had yet to be visited by the invisible predator. She didn't really attend the neighborhood party—her asshole husband got drunk way too early and she had to drag him home, but Carlos knew he was probably already trashed before heading to the doomed get-together. Carlos had watched the embarrassing spectacle from his living room window and was grateful she hadn't stayed longer. She wasn't overly exposed, and he hoped it meant she would make it through.

Carlos admired more than her looks; he admired her bravery for standing outside and refusing to let her life be halted completely. The news broadcast nearly all day, and every report agreed that even stepping beyond the front door could be dangerous. Their words constricted his lungs with anxiety, but watching Marnie's dark hair in the breeze could almost get him to take the risk. Almost. She was like a siren calling sailors to their doom, dressed in a purple bathrobe and drinking from a mug of the same color. This was the time he usually daydreamed of her, of smelling her neck and feeling her inhale deeply as he wrapped his arms around her—but since the virus, he could only daydream of surviving, of remaining alive.

Marnie whistled softly to her dog and it ran to her, scratching at her ankles with its tiny paws, excited to have its breakfast. She stepped back into her house, sliding the glass door closed behind her. Her show of bravery was brief, seven minutes in total, but it stayed with Carlos. It somehow kept the tiny spark within him burning.

Sparky bounded through the living room and jumped up on the couch. His constant barking was what led to the final fight between Marnie and Mark; one last grim battle she always knew in her heart would come. She counted herself lucky to be the victor after years of having nightmares about being the corpse in the recliner. She retrieved the shower curtain from the guest bathroom upstairs and placed it on the floor before looking at his body, heavy and leaking, stinking more by the hour. Marnie gathered her courage up to grab his wrists. Then she held her breath and tugged him. The weight of him was almost too much for her, and for a moment she contemplated cutting him into pieces right there, but she knew the mess left behind would be too much to handle. She strained, her face turning red, but she managed to drag the corpse down onto the shower curtain.

She stepped back and took a break, breathing heavily but she wiped sweat from her brow in satisfaction. It was a little easier to drag him across the tile floor wrapped in a shower curtain than it was to get him out of the chair. The garage door was close, so Marnie made it with only one break to rest her arms. Sparky stood on the arm of the couch, supervising as she got rid of the bastard who'd kicked him against the bedroom wall.

She barely managed to pull Mark into the garage before she collapsed into a dusty lawn chair. There was tightness in her chest, and she wondered if Mark hadn't brought home the virus after all.

She felt a pang of fear in her gut as bitter tears threatened to fall. He would get what he always wanted: to kill her. She pounded her fists on the aluminum chair-arms and focused once more. Her eyes searched the wall where her husband had hung a multitude of yard tools—like the bastard ever used them—and located what she needed to dispose of him completely: the axe.

Carlos sat at his computer and began working on lessons for his students. Being an online educator didn't change when the world shut down, but it gave him a frightening idea of the destruction wrought by the virus beyond his neighborhood and city. Each week, he had fewer and fewer students signed in and returning work.

This morning, there were only four students checking in. His throat tightened as he looked over their work. Four souls he once connected to, four souls he led and instructed, but the other eighteen were nowhere to be seen.

Carlos pulled his phone from his pocket and checked his call log. He hadn't heard from his parents or brother in two weeks. They lived in a virus-ravaged neighborhood in California. They were all he had left. He felt his heart growing heavier by the day, an emptiness devouring his insides. It scared him to think of what would even be left once the virus was gone. How many would survive, and what would life be like?

He pulled out a navy-blue envelope from a mound of mail piled on the edge of his desk. He didn't know why he hadn't thrown it away yet. The mail service had already shut down. He guessed he kept it just to remember, to hold in his hands a memory from life before. He opened it and pulled out the red, white, and blue invitation, another block party planned for the Fourth of July weekend, a party he wouldn't have to think up excuses to not attend. There was a promise of barbecue, coolers full of beverages for both adults and children, and a grand finale of fireworks.

He smiled sadly at the invitation, realizing the party would have been that very night if the virus hadn't hit. He slid it back into the envelope and tossed it on the mail pile, then opened his desk drawer and grabbed a bottle of whiskey. He was apprehensive about day-drinking when the isolation first started—he had a stubborn sense of responsibility he clung to in those early days—but that faded as the days passed. Now he drank when he felt his anxiety climbing up his back. He didn't bother pouring it in a cup. He drank it straight from the bottle in an attempt to kill the sadness welling up inside of him like sudden storm. He gazed out the window, his mind lost in imagining the racket outside of children screeching in delight while they ran down the sidewalks with sparklers in their little hands, music pumping from a nearby stereo, and the thundering of fireworks in the sky. It would have annoyed him, he would have complained to himself about the noise, but the silence of the real world was now more deafening.

He recalled sitting here just last Christmas, drunkenly scheming up ways of ruining the neighborhood holiday caroling, like an inebriated Grinch who stole Christmas, as their voices grated at him like every other thing they did.

"Those days are gone."

The thought of no longer being just an introvert, but possibly a lone survivor when it was all said and done, chilled him. He turned the bottle up and felt his insides burning, but his heart still felt cold. He got out of his chair and turned on his stereo. He blasted music as loud as he could stand and sang along as he slowly emptied the entire bottle down his throat. From his bedroom window he watched the sunset staining the horizon red as the day died, bringing the darkness of night and the crushing loneliness he had failed to drown.

A loud thud echoed in the distance. The neighborhood was so silent now, the racket startled him. He lurched forward in his seat, groggily wiping drool from the corner of his mouth. A muffled voice filled up the quiet vacuum of silence beyond the wall of his house. It was faint, but as he stood up and exited his bedroom it grew a little louder. He walked to a decorative window in the stairwell leading to the bottom floor of his house and squinted through it.

Outside, a figure was struggling on the curb. He saw the fluttering of a purple robe in the breeze. Carlos trotted down his stairs and watched her from the peephole in his front door. He couldn't see Marnie very well, but he knew she was struggling with her trash can, which had tipped over on its side. Her tiny dog was hopping about at her feet.

He smiled for a moment. The comical scene made his heart race. He knew it would replay in his mind for the eternity of his quarantine, a beautiful thing amidst the living nightmare. Even though his eyes couldn't quite see clearly through the tiny peephole, his imagination would fill in the blanks, and paint her as an angel in purple.

Then his grin faded and he felt a stab of fear in his gut. She was being careless. Marnie was putting herself in danger. How could she not have realized the trash stopped running? He guessed she had been too busy taking care of her asshole husband to notice. It made him angry to think of Mark, the prick, making his wife haul a heavy trash can to the sidewalk in the middle of a pandemic, he must have been real piece of shit to treat her so terribly, as if she didn't matter.

He gripped the doorknob. His internal alarms went off, the screaming anxiety that had kept him alive wailing in his brain. He knew he should just leave her alone; if she was going to ignore the reports of how easily the virus was spreading, then there was nothing he could do. He unlocked to door and pulled it open, even as the alarms continued to blare in his mind, louder than his own voice as he attempted to get her attention.

She either ignored or couldn't hear him as she struggled with the can and the yapping dog, so he tried again:

"Hey, Marnie!"

Marnie jumped and spun, frightened.

"I'm so sorry," he yelled across his yard, "but the trash hasn't been running in over a week."

She stood completely still. The look on her face was a mixture of fear and confusion.

"Really?" she finally answered.

"Yeah, but I guess you could leave it there. The news said sooner or later the trash company would be back in business… even if it takes a few more weeks."

She nodded and bent down to grab her dog. Sparky wouldn't stop barking at the fallen can. Carlos felt as if he was bothering Marnie. The times of spontaneous social interaction were gone; what replaced them were weary stand-offs of quickly spoken words at six feet apart. It was the new way of interacting in the plague-ravaged world. Her eyes were filled with worry, so he just smiled and started to pull his door shut.

"Wait!" Marnie yelled over the yapping.

Carlos felt himself tense up. He knew she was going to ask for help, and he really didn't want to refuse her.

"Can you please help me stand it back up?"

He glanced over his shoulder, searching for the face mask and gloves he kept by the door.

"I know, this is a terrible time to ask you that," she said, "but I can't,

I'm not strong enough."

"Sure. Hold on just a second."

Carlos closed the door and began putting on his protective equipment. Something inside of him begged him just to leave the door closed, to abandon Marnie to her fate. He berated himself for being a coward. He wasn't raised to leave a woman in need all by herself, what would his father say? He felt his lungs constricting as he opened the door once more. The mask felt as if it was suffocating him. His mind already imagining the scenario of him lying in his bed, drowning in his own blood, all alone.

"Step back a bit more and I'll get that can back up."

Marnie nodded, a nervous smile on her uncovered face. The sight of her grin was both welcoming and concerning, because she was unprotected.

Carlos kicked the trash can lid closed. She didn't appear to have much trash but when he bent over and grabbed the handle, he struggled to get it standing.

"Dang, what do you got in there, a dead body?" he teased.

They usually made small talk at the mailbox and joked back and forth before the virus came. She shared his dark sense of humor, but he never guessed his joke would miss the mark so horribly. Marnie stumbled back, unable to talk, and stared at him until his awkward laughter ceased.

"Oh, oh, I'm sorry. This isn't the time to joke like that. I'm so sorry." He felt his face burning behind his mask.

"Oh, no," she laughed and ran her hand through her dark hair, "it's OK."

"How's your husband?" Carlos asked in an attempt to divert her attention to another topic.

"He's sleeping," she stuttered.

After a long moment of silence, Carlos decided it wasn't time for chit-chat and started to hurry back up the sidewalk to his house, "Well, take care. Stay inside, stay safe."

"Yes, you too," she said, "and thank you."

A sudden burst of light exploded in the street, a flash of red flames, accompanied by a deafening sound that caused Marnie to jump and scream. Sparky scrambled from her arms and ran down the sidewalk, yelping. Carlos, frightened and confused, needed a second register the cause of the explosion: a firework.

Marnie chased after her dog, and Carlos followed. He wanted to help, it was in his nature, but the farther he got from his house, the tighter his lungs constricted and the feeling of germs crawling over his skin slowed him. He halted next to the community mailbox and squinted to watch Marnie cursing Sparky as she chased him.

The dim yellow glow of the streetlights revealed his neighbor's houses, front porches and shrubbery, the windows filled with faces. He froze, glancing around as they filled with glaring eyes and frowns. He began backing away, uneasy at disturbing so many suffering people. The dog's yelps went silent and so did Marnie's cursing. Carlos felt his fight-or-flight response kick in. He turned to run back to his house, only to be met by a group of his neighbors stumbling from their houses. He saw Joanna and Ted, Gabby and Steve, little Roxanna and her grandma Kelly. They lived the closest to him; he recognized them easily despite how the virus had ravaged them: Their skin too pale and thin, like crepe paper, fragile and ready to split. Their hair tangled with knots, their eyes deep-set and bloodshot.

The fabric mask covering his mouth and nose was far too thin. So were his latex gloves. The virus would find its way inside of him and make a home in his cells. He was easy prey.

He panicked and held his hands out before him. "Stay back. Six feet, remember?"

The group grew larger. They acted as if they didn't even hear him; instead they just kept coming closer, their limbs stiff with the atrophy of being confined to their beds.

"I said stay back!"

"We're all in this together," Kelly gurgled, sounding as if her throat was clogged with phlegm.

Carlos heard Marnie scream from somewhere in the darkness of a neighbor's yard. He spun around and ran, slapping away the groping hands of an elderly man who had just moved in three months prior.

The touch of old George made Carlos's skin crawl. He held his breath as much as he could as he ran for his front door. He hadn't locked it when he left, thinking he'd only be outside for a couple minutes helping Marnie.

These neighbors… hadn't the neighborhood Facebook group said they were dead?

He ran down the sidewalk, eyes fixed on his front door. A group of bloody-eyed children tried to pounce on him from behind Marnie's trash can. He stumbled on the wheel of it, falling to the concrete. The bin tipped over again, this time spilling most of its contents into the street. Carlos felt a shock of pain in his wrist as he impacted the sidewalk, and something snapped.

He knew in an instant it was broken, but he was still too terrified to care. The moans of his neighbors were getting closer, and the undead kids were already reaching out to grab him. He got to his feet, hesitating at the mound of garbage spilling from Marnie's can.

Within that trash, there was something huge wrapped in a purple shower curtain, held together somewhat by strips of duct tape. It wiggled, and the head of Marnie's husband inch-wormed its way out of its tacky purple cocoon, followed by the torso. He was missing his arms and legs, yet dragged himself along in the same fashion a caterpillar would. His mouth opened and closed like a fish suffocating on dry land.

Mark's corpse struggled and rolled over, revealing deep stab wounds in his chest. Carlos remembered Marnie's reaction when he interrupted her. She hadn't been afraid of him passing the virus to her; she didn't want him to discover what was hidden in the filthy trash can.

Carlos screamed. He turned to his front door, but a group of men already stood in front of it. He spun in a frantic circle, crying. They were all dead yet alive. Scott Matheson walked stiff-legged, closing in, and his rigid blue hand held a lit sparkler that popped and sent tiny red sparks out before his haggard face; a ghoulish grin split in two. A radio turned on, a patriotic tune filled the night, and a few women began to dance, their bodies leaking fluids down their bare legs. He heard Marnie weeping. He was almost too terrified to look at her. Almost.

When he did, he saw she was being forced to kneel before Karen Sanderson, the housewife who held the party that infected everyone in attendance.

Karen began vomiting bloody mucus into Marnie's face.

Carlos knew he would not make it out of this block party unscathed. No, he would be joining his neighbors in this macabre new form of existence. He would be forced to join the herd at last.

They came for him, bony fingers digging into his skin, twisting his already-broken wrist. They held him in place. From beyond his neighborhood came a cacophony of sirens, more than he had heard during the whole horrific ordeal of the virus taking over the world, an explosion of noise in an otherwise dead and silent world. Carlos knew the plague was mutating into something unstoppable. Something with a new way of finding hosts. Forced to his knees, he prayed as they baptized him in their infectious fluids.

"Join the party, Carl," Kelly said.

ASYLUM

By V. Castro

The corpses are a bloated, stinking reminder of my station in life. That's how it is in The Asylum, this new demilitarized zone that separates the living from the dead. When you're an asylum-seeker, you take what you get, and we've got border duty. What was once America is now a wasteland of disease, hunger, feral animals, and things that were once human.

I think I heard the siren. You ready for lunch? C'mon, we can sit in the communal gardens. It smells of oranges and lemons this time of year. I know you're scared, but you don't need to be. You are too young to remember most of it. Even now it remains a surreal dream in my mind. Every day like another page being turned in some cosmic comic book.

You see, a long time ago a wall had been partially built between the two countries. Miles and miles of camps held the line between us and them. Once the virus mutated, the cartels threw all their resources into finishing the wall to keep the Americans out—unless you possessed a useful skill, had enough melanin in your skin to take the harsh sun increasing in intensity year after year, or were a citizen from any country south of the border. When the time came for Mexico and the Cartel of Central and South American Countries to decide which asylum-seekers they would allow in, all the built-up resentment and frustration between the divided countries foamed like poison from a dying man's mouth.

As you have seen, when the mutants clamor for a way in, they eventually die. Oof, it's fucking gross up close. The smell is worse with that first blast from a flamethrower, both with the power to knock you off your feet. The stink rises with the smoke, sticks to your hair like cooking fat. Mexico remained unscathed from that damn wall and the heat. We owe our gratitude to the blistering sun.

By the time most of the virus-infected bodies made it to the border, they shuffled half-decomposed and slow as hell. The mutants are only as strong as the sloughing muscle left clinging to their bones. An armadillo could out-run them. Those things weren't the threat; it was the tiny creature that could not be seen until it was too late. Entire reservoirs of water left no good from decomposing flesh seeping into the ground.

To stave off the infection from spreading, the cartel ordered the bodies collected and burned before whatever's left of the stray animals had a chance to feast on the decaying flesh and make their way into Mexico. There are men whose sole duty is to shoot down buzzards. The crack of high-powered rifles is almost like a call to prayer here. Animal traps lay in wait like IEDs. The rat poison so strong it stings your nostrils when the wind kicks up. That's why we all wear bandanas over our noses and mouths. I already know I'm probably in for an early death. Same for you.

Thank Dios for Felicia Garcia, narco queen turned leader of a Mexico that has never done better for this part of the world. When the Mexican government couldn't pull enough resources together, they reached out to the cartels for help enforcing the closed border. Felicia took this opportunity to strong-arm her way into government with the finesse and sense only a woman could bring to a situation that teetered towards disaster. Like a virus, she took control when the elected officials failed in their political cowardice to make big decisions. Didn't even see her coming as they squabbled over petty shit to stroke their male egos. It was a bloodless coup that happened before anyone could stop it. With a swift declaration of power, she separated Mexico before the infection had a chance to take root like in America. Locked and loaded, she ordered a complete lockdown.

Maybe I should rewind a bit. I think I'm making it sound too simple. Before you even reached the border, a line of military trucks and SUVs with armed soldiers waited for you to pull some shit so they could shoot. If you looked healthy enough to get past the men in tanks, you would be directed to the doctors in hazmat suits. A simple jab to your palm alerted them to foreign bodies your system. Any traces in your blood, and you were taken to the far side of the desert to be put to sleep on the spot. No questions, no tears. Nada. To be fair, many people accepted this. Nobody wanted to wander around in a stupor, covered in black spots with little things swimming beneath their skin, crushing their veins. The mutants embodied the merciless rot the world had become.

The infection begins like a cluster of blackheads on your face. This is viral waste. It then painfully pushes through the pores and spreads like mold. The waste contains more virus that spreads through coughs, sneezes, bodily fluids or touch. Eventually the creature takes over the brain and gives only one directive to the body: infect others, spread. Within a few weeks the body decomposes as you're eaten from the inside-out. After a while, you are walking around with half your skin hanging off and insides oozing from your ass. You are a walking virus particle, a mutant.

Mutant bodies and infected animals burn day and night in an area called The Pits. The flames and smoke remind us of the light Felicia has returned to our great nation. Don't look at me like that. The tales are true. Seen it with my own eyes, with googles of course. Not even the scavengers, human or animal, dare to go to The Pits. You have to piss someone off real bad to be assigned to The Pits. A great number of politicians who didn't leave the U.S. in time or make it as far as Canada tried to bribe their way into Mexico. Felicia was having none of it. But like a glamorous telenovela villain, she had a plan. Make no mistake, she is no villain; she is a savior queen. These enemies who sauntered in were sent to The Pits for work as payback. Those who opposed her, dictators south of Mexico who refused to cooperate because they cared more for their own pockets instead of their people—pobrecitos in The Pits. Video from the drone over The Pits played in every football stadium for us to watch the worst of the worst get marched to hell. People need entertainment. And the Gods need their sacrifices.

My job these days is to stand in a turret along the wall, looking at far distances with drones. If we spot packs of mutants or the barely living, we alert guards on the ground who ensure whoever approaches doesn't get too close. If they appear to be living, we meet them and see if they are of any value. You must have value. No family names, bank accounts, companies, business cards matter here. There is nothing but what you can do for the survival of the Cartel of South and Central American States and Mexico. The new superpower of the world I am proud to call home.

I remember the first time I genuinely felt sorry for some of them. The Others.

As I passed through the safe zone, a family begged the guards to be let in. Their pale white skin blistered from waiting for days to get this far into processing. The asshole guards toyed with them. The family had two small children who looked malnourished and dehydrated. One of the guards I knew, Francisco, called me over and stuck an elbow in my rib as he asked: "What you think, mujer? Should we let them in?"

I couldn't look into their pleading blue eyes. Instead I stared at the scruffy shoes of the children. "Let them in, cabron," I said. "They have kids. You got kids? Plus, it's almost harvest time. We will need more workers." My job wasn't easy standing in the elements all day, but I did not want to get transferred to harvest.

Francisco sucked his teeth and narrowed his eyes as he scanned the family. "What do you have to trade?"

The little girl (she couldn't have been more than five or six) reached beneath her sock to unlatch a watch wrapped around her scrawny ankle. As she did, the family tightened closer around her. Her father squeezed her bony shoulder. The guard bent down to look into her eyes, trying to appear friendly (and he mostly is), but I know what sits behind his resentment. He was only a kid when he was separated from his parents. He sat in a camp for weeks watching other kids from all parts of Central and South America die from a flu outbreak. Yea, the fucking flu. Tax breaks before outbreaks in those days. Anyway, a riot broke out and he escaped. Been with the cartel ever since. Helped me get fluent in Spanish. So, he was still kinda angry.

He said: "Mija, this is all you have for me? Nothing else?"

She began to cry like children do when they have been scolded, even though Francisco spoke in a quiet and calm tone. "Yes. I'm hungry." It was the voice of a little mouse.

"You aren't lying to me? I get very angry when people lie."

Her bottom lip quivered. I could tell she was trying to be a big girl. Save her family. It rested on her ability to convince us they were worthy. "No, sir. Nothing."

The guard inspected the watch, then faced the parents. "You're lucky this is a Rolex. Follow the signs for water and processing. The cartel is gonna put you all to work. It's harvest time soon. Our great nation needs feeding. ¡Ándale! Before I change my fuckin' mind."

"Ay, be nice, Francisco," I scolded him. "Felicia does not approve of children being treated like that."

He shrugged his shoulders. "You are right. But some things I will never forget, and we shouldn't forget them." I stood there, watching them all wait in line, not knowing how to feel. The family scurried past me in a hurry. The woman turned and mouthed "Thank you" to me. I'm not sure I deserved a thanks, because getting into Mexico is just the beginning, you must learn to survive living here. Registration begins your journey. You will be assigned work immediately and found refugee accommodation. Felicia cares for all.

I'm a single woman so I need very little. I have a comfortable room with a bed and small kitchenette in an apartment complex. The toilets and showers are communal. It isn't Trump Tower, but I'm alive. No rent due, no grocery bills because we are all fed enough, no cost for my education if I decide to start classes again. Felicia is very clear on her protection of women and children. For her, it's personal. The consequences of abuse are fatal. The Pits, in fact.

How did it all start? Might want to take that last bite of flauta. It's going to sound like a cliché, but it all started with the poorest of the poor. Ain't that always the way? You wanna know how to take the temperature of a nation? Check on the ones left at the bottom. They will let you know if you have motherfucking fever or not. That's why no one bothered to notice or take action until it was too late. That would have never happened with Felicia. U.S. government-sponsored food was cheap, processed crap that looked barely edible, but governments around the world took the hard line that beggars couldn't be choosers. Same went for healthcare and education available to a majority of the populations. All these kids around the globe fell ill. Most of them died. Protests and outrage dominated the news coverage, and committees looked for the source of the problem. Suits with red ties blamed it on the same reasons there were all those e-coli outbreaks with lettuce and spinach years past. The world called it a bunch of poor people getting sick and spreading their sickness to others.

All it took was one elite boarding school and a shipment of organic milk and vegan sausages to change the tune of those in charge. Seventy-five kids, all sick, and taken to the best hospitals. Whatever was in that milk mutated since it killed those on government cheese.

We now know the free-range, super-cared-for special cows giving the one percent milk, were drinking infected water from a pond located on their idyllic home. The same company also ran a beef processing plant with less-than-hygienic practices that hired illegals at an alarming rate. Turns out, whatever they used to process the beef and their vegan sausages was not fit for human handling. They were bringing in illegal immigrants because the desperate are considered expendable, and the company covered it up. Just like a damn conspiracy film. What did they play last month in the stadium? Some old-time one: "Erin Brockovich." Yea, it was some Erin Brockovich shit going down. I shit you not.

Mija, sometimes when your skin is closer to the color of shadow, that is exactly how you are treated.

For days I lay in bed sweating, scared as hell to eat or drink anything. The situation worsened by the day and my anxiety threatened to take control over my every thought and movement. I didn't want to shower for fear there was something in the water and it would inadvertently splash into my mouth. That is when I decided to get out. My parents passed, and no siblings made the choice easy for me. Life inside my home and mind was unbearable. I packed quickly and set off for Mexico because none of this was happening south of the border, or remote places that didn't take part in the food scheme. I'd rather die on a beach in Mexico in a tequila and lime stupor, getting laid every night, or in Guadalajara at the feet of María Natividad Venegas de la Torre, a saint my Catholic father said we are related to. Anything besides a crowd of virus-carrying people fighting over a pack of toilet paper. Don't they know that, by the time you shit your liver, you lose the ability to know how to use it?

I made it just in time. The day I left, I took only what I could carry on my back. I knew my car would eventually have to be sold, or I'd have to sell the remaining gas in my tank. I needed to be swift on my feet so I could hide or run at a moment's notice. The cartels took control of the camps at the border because the Americans were losing control everywhere else. Focus shifted to closing the cities. The cartels patrolled the area while those things were on the loose; infected animals also ran wild, biting and spreading death. People wanted to take whatever they had of value as rationing became difficult to enforce. Half the rich fucks fled to Europe, but many didn't make it out once the rest of the world closed their borders. Even private planes had to turn back or be shot down before reaching foreign airspace.

When I reached Mexico, I gave up my car, what little jewellery I had on me, showed a guard my family photo album to prove my ancestry, plus a printout of my DNA from a service that was popular at that time. Second-generation on my pop's side and fourth on my mom's side. After all this, I was free to cross into Mexico. They processed me and gave me the job of drone lookout. Mexican American by birth raised in a country that never made me forget I was Mexican first. My skin just a shade too dark to pass for anything but an invader, an inconvenience, like a cold sore, even though I was born there. Felicia welcomed me like a prodigal daughter.

After Mexico sealed off its borders, so did everywhere else. The Americans left on their own with no allies. If not for Mexico or Canada, all would be lost on this continent. Without the cartels led by our narco queen, chaos would rule. She has brought the underworld to our world, which has made the difference to millions of people. The developing worlds have been given the space to truly develop. All of Felicia's guns, goons and money created a well-oiled machine made for a part of the world on the brink of collapse.

Mexico, and South America on a whole, have never been more at peace or successful. Bounty abounds. Fun Fact: Central America is home to one of the largest pharmaceutical companies in the world. Production rivals India. They have plants all over. No, not recreational drugs, but shit for the shits, headaches, antibiotics, to name a few. All in our brown hands, including the priceless drug to kill those silent virus motherfuckers. Believe that. A teacher from Guatemala sick of seeing her children suffer created a test and a cure. Felicia wasted no time bringing this woman to the border and giving her a blank check to recreate her discovery. All the foreign-owned maquiladoras were seized and repurposed to bring hope to the world.

Felicia Garcia brokered deals with the rest of the world to maintain the balance between life and death. Sure, it is a ruthless rule of law that will pluck your heart out with bare fingers, but the rules are very clear. You work, you pay your dues, you don't fuck with anyone's shit, you're all good. Stealing, rape, murder (unless sanctioned by a Jefa) is strictly forbidden. When the shortages hit, the cartels set up a food-for-weapons trade. A dead man doesn't need a weapon, and a weapon can't grow maize. Hunger won in the end. Felicia has created a space where only she has the firepower.

But there is a freedom in this. I feel safe. It's far from perfect, but it's all we have: A dystopian tale of rotting flesh, heat and salvation in an unlikely place. The cartel goes for the better-feared-than-loved philosophy. Snitches don't get stitches. They are rewarded, so keep your eyes open and your hands to yourself.

We love Felicia because she has reinvested everything back into the country. Look to the sky, that building over there. A banner with her dark brown eyes looking down upon her flock like the blessed La Virgen, but with gold earrings and red lipstick, hair long and blowing in the wind. One hand carries a torch. Its flames burn bright with small viruses dying as they touch the flames. In the other a banner with the image of La Virgen de Guadalupe. Thick vertical scars on her exposed wrists show us that she, too, is a survivor who has bled. She knows sorrow—can't you see it in her eyes? She is one of us. If only Diego Rivera were alive to paint a great mural in her honor. She is the Miguel Hidalgo of our time.

North. What about up North? Canada shut its border, but had a harder time fighting the mutants with no wall. The cold months kept them somewhat safe, as the mutants couldn't withstand the volatile storms of winter. Hell returned with spring. The warmer weather brought animals out to feast on the decomposing bodies until they fell. When the liquid rot seeped into the ground, or washed away with the melting snow, who knew where the virus would find sanctuary? What is laughable is some of the American politicians actually thought the Canadians would allow them to run The States from within their country, not that there was anything to run. America itself was a living dead thing.

I don't know how many are left in what used to be the U.S. The flow of healthy humans has slowed in recent months—lucky for you. I've heard rumors there are some who live in remote areas like the mountains, living off the land and what healthy animals are left. We had a few enter, stating the Native American reservations are boltholes that remain safe; everyone who isn't a member of a tribe is turned away, good for them. Maybe the land will heal itself and they can reclaim it. I'm not too smart, no fancy degree yet, but I think it belongs to them anyway.

The virus spread exponentially through the U.S. until nothing remained. We watched from the outside, thanking the Gods and Felicia for taking us into their bosom for protection. That is why we owe Felicia our loyalty. Respect her claws as sharp as those of the eagle perched on a nopal cactus. While we work, we recite her Mantra: *Love the Cartel and the Cartel will love you back. ¡ Viva La Raza!*

Let's get back to work. We have a world to fix.

OUTPOST

By Alex DiFrancesco

There are times that it still flickers out of control. I have a certain way of dressing—jeans not sagging but not tight, loose black t-shirt, black cycle boots—that serves as a kind of camouflage particular to the Outpost. There's no way to pin those things down, not out here, not where every other person in these dark saloons with the puke and piss gutters under the bar looks the same way. It softens the uncertainty of not always being sure when the change will come on.

I've mostly been able to feel it coming on. If my limbic brain has ever done anything for me, it's that. In the dimness of the Outpost, with my knowledge and my camouflage, there's time for me to get out when I have to, to be just another anonymous face.

The times it surprises me don't come frequently. They're not so seldom that I think they've ceased, but rare enough that I am sometimes imprudent. Like that night in The Sputter. Keegan was drunk and drooling, and his lack of control made me feel strong. In no time I would have him handing over the keys to his ship, which could travel longer distances than my old cycle, and his transit papers, and

I would be piloting out of this pisshole of an outpost. There might be some theft reports, but more than likely no one would believe that it wasn't the sorry drunk's own fault he'd been robbed. The fangs probably wouldn't follow up, and, anyway, I'd be long gone. But there were too many people in The Sputter. I should have known. Good as I am at controlling the change, there are still times it flickers out of control.

For me, the initial sensation is a feeling like static electricity at my edges. My skin suddenly feels like it doesn't have a distinct end point—I am all possibility. I feel blurred, like someone who has moved too soon in one of these old photographs you still see sometimes in junk shops down on Patterson Row. I can feel my body strain and push in different spots, mostly my chest and between my legs, but also the bones of my hands and jaw. Things that would move me to tears are suddenly less oppressive. A shift comes into my brain like a gentle wave. Suddenly, the way people speak, the way their hands and eyes move have subtle yet greater meaning to me. Or less. The tide brings words to me, or takes them away as if caught in an undertow.

"Whassa matter, sweetie?" Keegan said, leaning towards me. The smell of the booze on his breath mixed up with the smell from his rotted-out teeth was too much to bear. Without waiting for an answer, he leaned in for a kiss. No segue, nothing. A classy guy. I leaned back and he fell forward, his face colliding with my left shoulder, just as his hand reached up for my left breast.

"Bathroom," I managed, pushing away and sliding off of my barstool. My change takes fifteen minutes at most. It was better to be long out of there when it happened.

I headed towards the bathrooms, figuring I'd fake that way, then turn and sneak out the front when Keegan wasn't expecting me to. I suppose it was curiosity that made me linger, looking about. I was searching for whoever had precipitated the change. Whoever had overridden my years of careful training with biological frequencies they probably didn't even understand they were putting out. Sometimes my change is sexual (and often appallingly heterosexual), so I looked for the sort of woman I'd be attracted to. Unsurprisingly, there wasn't a single female in The Sputter that I'd want to take home with me. Who could it be, then?

I had just about given up on the search when two burly men who had been part-hugging and part-wrestling each other broke apart, and I glimpsed a face: smooth, tan skin and delicate features—a small, celestial nose, two perfectly symmetrical almond-shaped eyes, slightly downturned lips. The person's hair was short and spiky and a light brown that was almost blond. Not the sort of face you'd expect in that kind of place, ordinarily, but even more so when it was a face you recognized the way I did. And the way those almond-shaped eyes were trained on me, I knew that ey hadn't forgotten me, either.

A blurred feeling began to pulse along my edges. My breasts became tight; I felt the tingle of thickening hairs in my pores. I had to get out of there.

Breaking the gaze between us, I made for the door, the heels of my boots striking the floor beneath me.

Ducking down the alley behind The Sputter, I paused to catch my breath and collect myself. This was not going to be a normal change, I knew already. Part of it was seeing em. Ey'd been in the state that ey only used to reserve for private moments, moments when we were alone together. Or perhaps it was eir form when ey were there alone with others, and I thought ey only trusted me enough to be that way. Maybe having me think that form was reserved for the times we were alone was just as much of a con as the rest of it had been, like the con I'd just been running on Keegan. It was certainly easier to think of it that way now, after all that had happened.

As these thoughts ran through my head, I felt the usual pain as my breasts receded into the flat, taut chest muscles they'd been long before I hit puberty, before my body began to shift like a dying supernova giving birth to a wealth of new elements. But the muscles never tightened and rose the way they did in the typical change. I felt my chest become a flat plane with a slight depression in the middle.

The stomach muscles never came, either, that hyper-masculine washboard that draws lingering stares and invites fingers to trace over it. The bones of my hands were aching and stretching, but not devolving into the painful elongations they were capable of. My fear, the fear I had felt so often when I first met em, when this third change began to present itself in moments of closeness, began to dissipate as I thought of the change as what it had come to represent for me. *My form, my true form.*

The buzz and haze at the edges of my skin became full-fledged electricity. I could feel myself losing tone, my body elongating into that beautiful midway place that was somehow the point where I had always longed to arrive. The pleasure sensations began to pop in my brain left and right, and I knew I had to get back to my cycle before I became drunk on them, and it was unsafe for me to pilot the back roads.

I straightened and tossed my hair out of my eyes. Dark brown and curled, I kept it a messy shoulder-length appropriate for a man or a woman. I felt that shorter was too male and longer was too female. Certainly that was a generalization, but there in Hezama Outpost, where I didn't have the luxury of leaving, my shaggy curls were another layer of protection like my loose jeans, t-shirt, and cycle boots. They might buy me an extra thirty seconds in any given situation that could mean life or death.

Life or death. Sounds pretty dramatic. But imagine a place like the Outpost, if you haven't already been in one. Imagine a saloon like The Sputter. Imagine a guy like Keegan. And then you imagine the big-breasted woman who's wooing him and reaching for his keys turning into a washboard-stomached man. And you think that all the way through to see how good it goes over. Or imagine another kind of person we get in the Outpost, the kind of person who would love nothing more than for all of this to transpire, but would never admit it to themselves or anyone else. And then maybe you'll realize why I was out there in that alley trying to get it together enough to get on my cycle and get the hell out.

Someone started stumbling towards me then, a burly man dressed much the same as me and everybody else in that filthy saloon. The pleasant static of my transformation jolted into a shock of electricity as my fight-or-flight instincts kicked in. He was coming straight for me. Keegan? Some other guy who had seen too much of what was happening? I tried to steady myself internally despite being torn inside and out in fifteen directions, despite the heady buzz that was flooding my mind as I shifted to my favorite and least easily achieved state. I rooted my boots in the ground, ready to kick out at the first opportunity.

Then he leaned to the side and started puking his guts out. Some kind of prima donna too good for the puke gutter, it seemed. *Fight* became *flight,* and I pushed around him and out to the front of The Sputter, where my cycle was parked in a row of others in various states of disrepair.

I kicked it into gear and pulled away from the saloon. The only danger now was that I might get too spun out on the good feelings in my brain and have an accident. But I felt back in control. And as I cruised just above the ground, the sounds of my old cycle rumbling beneath me helped put me in the mindset that I was exactly where I should be. That I was reaching a state of exactly who I was. The wind blew back my hair (I never did get used to wearing a helmet) and I felt my body's stretchings and achings become gentle shiftings, motions towards a blissful center. I almost forgot about those almond-shaped eyes peering at me through the dim light in The Sputter.

Fai.

I felt a twinge in a part of me that the changes didn't usually effect.

I left home when I was fourteen by the grace of stolen travel papers, and it wasn't until I was twenty-two that the official letter caught up to tell me my parents were dead and the shack on the wild edge of the Hezama Outpost was mine now. Who knows how long that letter had been floating out there, lost between all my moves and all the shambles of official channels. I never got the details of what took both of them out at once, and considering what they put me through before I left, I never did care. I assumed it was the lingering Illness, that they were some of its last casualties. I still shudder when I think of the shack full of the faith-healers and demon drivers that were meant to "cure" me from whatever spirits they claimed had hold of me when the shifts began. And those are only the tip-of-the-iceberg memories.

Sometimes the harder, deeper ones come back at me too thick to fight off, and I have to get out of the little plywood structure and out of the Outpost. That's what happened earlier that night, before I found Keegan. One minute I was sitting in the shack, having just sprayed a dose of Alkohol in my mouth. I wasn't in the mood to be social; I just wanted to sleep through the night. The smallish dose of Alkohol had barely kicked in when I spied the moon rising just above the lone window of the shack.

The mild blur at the edges caused by the Alkohol put me in mind of the blur in light caused by eyes full of tears. And that put me in mind of a night long ago. A night when I was twelve. Though I'd been designated female when I was a child, I had just a few months before begun to shift in little ways. My voice grew deeper or higher, my lips filled out or thinned, my chest rose or fell. At first no one noticed. I had kept it hidden like I suppose a child going through a more accepted form of puberty might if they were very shy or uninformed. But before long, it became apparent. Words like *freak* and *devil* were first used in whispers that I wasn't supposed to hear, then directed at me.

Sitting alone in the shack, remembering that time, I began to tremble. That was when I went to The Sputter, looking for a way out.

But by the time I got back to the shack, all the bad memories had been pushed out and all that was in my mind was Fai. Where had ey come from? What had happened to make em leave in the first place? Was eir relationship to me a con after all, even if that had always been more my M.O. than Fai's? And if it was, for what? What did I have that anyone would want?

There were bad memories in with these thoughts, too. I had

thought, after all that I'd been through, that nothing would ever be able to touch me again. But the days after Fai's departure had been days of sorrow and searching. I had spent days lying in a pile of blankets and sheets in the shack in the Outpost, only getting up to spray more Alkohol into my mouth. After those days passed, I went all the places I could conceive of finding em. All to no avail.

As I paced the shack, these bad thoughts were mollified by the warmth of the transformation I had not achieved since Fai's departure glowing in me, like just enough sips of wine. I thought quite suddenly of the good days. The first time we had been alone together, in the empty fields of Terra Thia. As if we were children cutting classes and causing trouble, Fai had set fire to several of the veins of strontium chloride that ran through the ground. We were alone there, watching the bright flames snake across the earth, crackling and fizzing apple red. I felt Fai's hand tremble slightly in mine, and my hand respond with its own tremors, the likes of which I had never felt before. I was barely twenty then, the whole of my being honed for survival, unable to recognize when someone wanted to give me love, only able to find what people wanted and how to make it into what I needed.

Back in the shack on the edges of Hezama Outpost, I laughed to myself. Love did not take you to a state of physical and mental bliss and understanding only to pull that state out from under you. And love sure as hell didn't come back and force that state on you right when it was most likely to get you killed. There was no question about love. The only question was, what was the con?

I kicked one of the shack's already questionably sturdy walls with the steel toe of my boot, but not with the force I would have, had the transformation taken me into my male state. My body as it stood now, fully transformed, was lithe and smooth and strong, but didn't have the brute force that my male incarnation did. I called him Nik. The name was short and abrupt, aggressive and fitting. I had no name for the person I was now. This smooth person full with the certainty of self-knowledge I thought I had lost so many years before. This person who felt like an epiphany.

I tried to reconcile the deep, satisfied, indisputably correct feeling coursing through me with the thoughts racing through my head. The state Fai brought me to dulled my survival instincts, made me feel like I could get through life just by being. But I knew I had to control myself and focus on the important questions buzzing through my brain. Where had Fai come from? What did ey want? Fai had never been able to make me change so easily in the past—what had made it happen so quickly and effortlessly this time? What was more, I had hidden from Fai where I came from; the dark pit of Hezama Outpost was something I never shared with em, even when the state had me feeling as little need for self-defense as a cub born to the fiercest of wild animals. The mystery remained of how ey found me at all.

I had piloted down back alleys through twists and turns, so I was fairly sure I hadn't been followed. That left me at least one advantage in whatever game was at hand. I focused hard on the muscles of my chest and stomach, visualizing them, willing them to be. It was a technique I had perfected over the years, long years in which I had first been tortured by the change, then gradually learned to control it. Years in which I had practiced little actions—swinging a leg over a bar stool to sit instead of perching on the side, for example—that helped along the change, that helped me perform states until I could push them all the way into reality. As I stood in the shack, I pictured my body changing, a centimeter at a time, a muscle here, a hair there. I felt my skin tighten, roughen, and my bliss begin to subside.

I had the upper hand for the moment, I decided as I began to shift again. I had to capitalize on it and find Fai before ey could find me. I kicked the wall again, and the shack shook. Good. I was going to need my strength for whatever lay ahead.

"What can I do to convince you?" Fai had said, the first time. "What will it take for you to allow yourself absolute happiness?"

A million thoughts ran through my mind. *A different life. A better world. A cycle so fast that I can outrun anything.* But what came out of my mouth was, "I'm always happy. Everything I want, I can get—from anyone I want. What is there to be unhappy about?"

Fai sighed; I was fooling no one but myself. "Picture one person—or a place even, a place—and with this person or place, you can be exactly whom you want."

I exhaled through my nose, a cynical snort that fell short of laughter. "No such person. No such place."

Fai had a rare moment of consternation. Fai came from a different place than me entirely, from an enclave called Campelli, which was home to most of the dissidents left over after the Final Illness and The Last War. Most of them were rich enough to access the proper means to travel wherever they chose. They did not understand Fai, but eir parents and the people around em had been tolerant. They had taught Fai to talk things through, not to lash out, to keep a level head when angry. All the things I had never learned.

But right then, a moment of consternation lowered Fai's brow and darkened eir eyes. Eir hands clenched together, and for a minute I wondered if ey would completely lose it—grab me, hit me, engage in some sort of violent action. I tensed up, ready to run, ready to get out.

Maybe Fai saw this; quicker than a summer thundershower, the moment passed. Fai's slim hands moved together. It was like watching a graceful bird's wings fold. Fai's left hand moved away from eir right, then raised up, holding a dark circle that shone with the most impossible colors. A sly smile flickered across eir face.

"What if I gave you a magic ring? And even if none of those people existed, even if there was never a place like that, this magic ring, just for the time you wore it, made me a person like that and this a place?"

"Magic ring..." I began, derisively. Then I looked at it more closely. It was black opal, and one of the most beautiful things I had ever seen. I wanted it. I would con em, I thought. No harm in letting someone think you're playing along.

"Okay, hand over this magic ring."

Of course, there was never any magic in the ring. But sometimes believing, or in my case, pretending to believe, is enough to open a door just a crack. That was how I got conned into changing into that blissful state of liminality that first time.

After Fai disappeared and I came back here, I threw the black opal ring into one of the most foul-smelling pits in Hezama Outpost.

I was the first that Fai found. The only, as far as I knew. There was just us, piloting through the black opal pits of the Cerbeus enclave where the stone eir magic ring had been fashioned from was found, though the vast expanse of dust fields mid-land mass where stars as bright as supernovas shone in the distance. There were their highly coveted travel papers that took us anywhere, even me when I was with 'em. There was only us, and I couldn't imagine there ever being anyone else.

But Fai could. Alone back in Campelli, ey had poured through what books had been saved by the once-rebels, looking for any hint of something mirroring eir own existence. And ey had found it, one day in a dusty vault lined with shelves of books. A book of myths that spoke of people like us, and a place where real supernovas shone but never burned out. Fai had clung to it like the Micantologists in the Selva enclave hold onto their dogma. Here was proof, ey thought, secreting away to that vault and reading that book again and again, that ey was not alone.

At the time ey told me, alone in eir ship, with both of us in our true states, I held back tears. Even in my state of bliss and perfection, I could not allow myself to cry, had not since I was a child.

"If only you'd known about these myths," ey said, sensing my emotion.

"Myths never would have helped," I said, the edge of Hezama Outpost and my bad history still there with me.

"One day, I will find that place," Fai said with a determination that I never heard. "I will take you there, and we'll never leave for anything."

I had smiled, a tear finally slipping down my face that I had found this person who seemed not to want my body, my money, my strange abilities—only my joy.

"Magic rings," I muttered. But even as I hastily wiped the tear trail off my face, the slightest of smiles had begun to turn my lips up.

The aloneness had never been so vast as it was after ey left me in one of the enclaves we'd been traveling through. At first I waited for em to come back, even though ey'd left without a word. When it became apparent that ey was gone for good, I began walking and hitching back to the Outpost, back to the evil I knew rather than the vast landmass I was no longer up for wandering in solitude, to the search for the papers or money that would allow me out. Myths were myths and facts were facts. At least in the Outpost, I knew how to survive.

What had ey wanted from me after all? I wondered even now. As I paced the shack, a resolve formed inside me to find out. To find em.

I searched through the Outpost's feral night. I ran a race over the edge of a cliff at Giant's look, just above the tar pits, surrounded by people with hard eyes filled with fury or perhaps some sort of insanity—the poverty, violence, and short, hard lives of people in the Outpost filled many of us with the same look. I passed saloons, cruised through ditches, circled pits. I even went to Old Rena's shack and let her throw some runes over a cloth that was the cleanest thing in the whole place. She spoke of the undercurrents and overtones, the center of the pattern. She agreed that something was coming.

Early in the dark morning hours, I found myself in Maswit Forest. I rode my cycle into the woods a bit, but then the trees became too thick and the paths too indistinct. I rested it by the side of a tree so thick that three of me—even the burly, strong me that was Nik—could have fit easily in the trunk if it were hollowed out.

There was a motion off in the distance. I could see darkness and shadows sliding about between the trees. I kicked at the ground and pulled out the gutting knife I'd slipped into my pocket before leaving the shack. I didn't know what I would find, and it was best to be prepared.

The closer I got, the more I could see a figure that hulked in the pre-dawn darkness. The person was pitching and heaving towards the ground, then coming back up again in a regular rhythm. It looked like they were digging. Not good news. I crept closer, willing my massive form to be quiet and lithe. As a twig snapped beneath my boot and sounded like a gunshot, I was reminded that dexterity was not one of Nik's qualities.

The person ahead of me in the trees threw their shovel to the ground and ducked down. I stood frozen for a moment. Slowly, the shadowy figure came back up and ran right at me.

I hit the ground hard as the person tackled me. I heard a familiar-sounding grunt and smelled familiar-smelling rotten breath. Who did I stumble across but Keegan. I saw a something human-shaped in a blanket lying on the ground. Out burying a body, from the looks of it. Like catching a bear at a kill site. Actually, almost exactly like that.

And then I was down on my back and there was a red light shining into my eye that I knew, at the lightest touch of a button, could lobotomize me permanently. I've been in life-threatening situations more than once in my time, and the thing my brain always screams out before sending a jolt of energy and intelligence into the rest of my body is *survive*. But this time was different. This time, as my body prepared, my mind sent out a cry that was plaintive—*Fai*. If I didn't make it through this, I was never going to know why ey had come back, what ey wanted with me. And that I had to know.

I kicked up with my heavy boots, catching Keegan in the balls. He grunted, and the light went out of my eyes. He didn't nurse his injury long before he lunged back at me. His weapon lost, he grabbed for my throat.

I tried to break the hold he had on me, but he was strong. Before a minute had passed, I began to feel a tingling mix with the panic in my head. My head grew fuzzy—I was not going to make it out of this if I didn't do something soon. I was grappling and I was fighting, but the truth was that I was fading.

Then the feeling spread through my arms and legs. Something was not right. And then, though the panic, a warm feeling like being buzzed up on too much of the sun at midday began to pulse through me. I opened my eyes as the tightness of Keegan's hands fell away from my neck. Suddenly his entire weight was on me. I caught his body with my arms even as they began to shift and elongate, to lose their strength and gain grace. Overwhelmed with an emotion like empathy, I cradled his body, thinking of all I had been through, and all he, too, must have faced to become the crude, vile, person he was. As my body shifted, I felt tears sting my eyes.

"Come on!" I heard. And someone was pushing his body and pulling my hand. And I knew who that someone was, the someone who had made me shift again, so against my consciousness will, but not against my desires. Fai.

"What did you do to him?" I asked as we ran through the forest. Around us, animal noises were stirring in a cacophony.

"He'll wake up in a few hours," Fai said. "He'll have a hell of a headache. But he'll be fine as long as he doesn't run into any cretins as big as himself."

Fai's hand was in mine, and the pleasure from it and from the change I was going through was so great that I wanted to stop, to climb to the tops of the trees and sing to the moon. But in the center of all of that bliss, the reality of the situation came crashing through. I pulled my hand away from Fai's.

"Why?" I demanded.

Fai stopped and stared at me as if I were insane. Eir almond-shaped eyes flashed.

"He was about to kill you!"

"Why save me? Do you know how many times since you were gone I came close to death? Do you know how close you put me to death the other night in that shitty saloon?"

Animal eyes flashed here and there in the darkness between the trees as the forest sang with sounds. We had to get out of there. And there I stood, defying all the danger.

"I know."

Fai grabbed my hand again. I felt something hard there on eir fingers, and I looked down to see the ring, the magic ring, the one I had thrown deep into some foul-smelling pit, there on eir hand. I pulled eir hand up to look closer.

"There will be time to tell you all of it when we get out of here."

The bliss came back, but not so greatly that I did not feel the danger. We ran through the woods, to my cycle. We coasted through the trees, out into Hezama Outpost proper, down dirt roads, past twists and turns, to where Fai's ship sat glinting in the far-off lights of what little town the Outpost had to speak of. I wasn't sure why I was getting into that ship. The ring glinted on Fai's hand, beckoning me. Keegan was out there somewhere, and so were the people who wanted people like us dead, or slaves to their fantasies. They all rose up together and spun in the darkness, and there was this person who knew what it was like to change, and ey was offering me a door out of that darkness.

And then all the bad things of the Outpost—Keegan, the Sputter, the shack where the faith healers had pressed hot stones to my skin and worse—all began to fade until they were specks beneath us.

"Myths are myths," Fai said, as the dark earth shrunk beneath us. Even eir ship couldn't get us away from this dying landmass, but ey could get us far enough away from the Outpost so that it felt like nothing more than a bad dream. "And the truth is the truth. The truth is that there never was that place with the supernovas. Or, if there was, I was never able to find it."

"That's why you left me?" I said. "To look for a place that you read about in a storybook?"

"I had to find it," ey said. "It tortured me thinking I'd be able to take you there if only I could find it. I had to go."

"But you never found it," I said.

Ey smiled on one side of eir mo

"Why do you look happy?"

"I made it."

"What?"

"I found us. Others. Just like I k

it. We made it. And I'm taking you

For a moment I didn't know w

and out, amazed I was able to do e

Fai went on. "It's not a utopia.

there's a foundation."

The earth flashed by beneath

landmass, the great expanses of n

we used to go and dream of this p

I looked up. The stars were

bright. But they were blaring ou

heading towards what awaited us

COME AWAY, COME AWAY

By Cynthia Pelayo

"Of course the Neverland had been make-believe in those days, but it was real now, and there were no night-lights, and it was getting darker every moment..." - J.M. Barrie

Before Mother and Father went to sleep, they made sure that the nightlights above their children's beds burned brightly, just in case.

"Just in case," Mother whispered softly to Daughter shortly before the fall. "Turn these nightlights on every night. Just in case."

Daughter believed that Just In Case was meant to happen someday, any day soon. She just did not know when. Because those are the things that are kept secret from children like her, like why do we wish upon a star, and why do witches live in dark woods full of strange creatures, and why in fairy tales we never know what time exactly, and in what world those 'Once upon a times' take place. Yet, we just assume they are so, and just like that Daughter believed, she knew, that one day Just In Case would happen. So, each night she made sure to tell her two little brothers a story, to fill their heads with wonder.

In the large room they shared on the top floor of their house, Daughter would make sure each night to tell her little brothers a story, tuck them into their beds, give them a kiss on their foreheads and then turn on their nightlights. Just In Case. Daughter would then walk to that large bay window overlooking the once-busy street below and search the empty sidewalks, scanning across the street and beyond into the darkened windows of apartment buildings and houses as far back as she could see. She listened for once-familiar noises; a car horn, music playing from a house nearby, a baby crying, or even the long dreaded mourn of ambulance sirens, but there was nothing. Just stillness.

Daughter realized it had been just as long as she had not seen Mother and Father as she had not seen the stars. So, on this night, for the first time since the nightlights had gone up, she walked over to the twinkling strings above the beds of her brothers and above her own bed and turned them off. Daughter did not like the feel of darkness. Yet, within the darkness she hoped to find a comforting light. She moved to the window seat at the large bay window and looked out and above searching for the moon. Yet, there was no moon this night. A new moon lay above the folds of black sky. The new moon, so black that it was not visible to the eye—yet it symbolized renewal and new beginnings.

Nothing about any of this felt new. There were the long empty bags of potato chips scattered across the floor of the room. Empty plates, and crusted forks and spoons stacked against the wall. Along the floorboards she felt the sticky remnants of stale marshmallows caked into the wood. Empty cans of spaghetti and meatballs, beans and canned pineapple sat stacked in the center of the room, holding worn pencils and broken crayons. All along the room hung pictures and paintings of what their life once was. There wasn't much paper left to draw. There wasn't much food left to eat except one last case of water and a bottle of apple juice beneath her bed and a box of crackers and canned cheese. There was one candy bar left. She stored it safely in her pillowcase for a day like today. In the morning she would split the candy bar and give half to each of her brothers—anything to just see them smile once more.

It was then that Daughter spotted the star, brighter than any she had ever seen, lingering just above. Daughter closed her eyes and just like in the song from her favorite movie about a puppet brought to life by a blue fairy, *Pinocchio,* she sang:

When you wish upon a star, your dreams come true...

Daughter then searched once more in the apartment buildings, houses and streets, desperately scanning the sidewalks still illuminated by streetlights for any movement, but there was nothing. There was no one. Daughter opened the window just a crack, allowing for some fresh air to comfort them in the night. Then, she moved away from the window and turned the nightlights above her brothers' beds on again, and then the nightlights above her bed. She turned her head back to the large window overlooking her silent city and whispered "Just In Case" before falling away to sleep.

The boy entered the same way he entered on many nights, through the large bay window. Most nights he would just rest behind the window, listening to her voice and the delicate perfection with which she weaved every story. At first, the girl told fantastic tales of shipwrecks, witches, knights, trolls, and queens. Soon however, the girl's stories turned tragic, but even though her tales now bore such heaviness and sorrow, the way her voice wrapped around each word sounded so beautiful and soft, like the lapping of a crystal-clear ocean wave along a deserted coastline.

The boy looked to the shimmering spot in his left palm and said, "I'm going to do it today," and with that, the shimmering spot blasted through the cracked-open window. The shock shook him so much that his insides rattled so forcefully a piece of him split away. His shadow dashed inside the room after the shimmering light.

Once inside, he was struck with various smells. The smell of wet clothes that had been left to dry in piles. The smell of tear-soaked pillowcases. And the smell of something so sad, so sickly sweet he brushed it away quickly from his mind.

He knew this room very well, the paintings and colorings on the wall of Mother and Father and of their loving dog. The dog so loved by the children, until one day someone crawled into the backyard and took the dog away. It was that day that the children did what they could do with the wood and nails and boards they had gathered in Father's shed. The windows on the first floor were boarded up, as were the front and back doors. All throughout the house the children scattered coffee mugs, glasses and mother's crystal bowls, in hopes that, if an intruder tried to sneak in, they would strike one of the objects and the children would have time to react. Just outside their bedroom door the children had strung up plastic water bottles filled with pennies, a final booby trap to warn them if someone had gotten too close. The boy wondered what the children planned to do if such a thing should happen, but that no longer mattered.

The life they lived before no longer mattered because he was here now. He sat on the floor just beneath the girl's face and watched her sleep, closing his eyes and breathing in the scent of gummy bears on her breath. He took her thin hand in his and it was then that he heard a soft rumble from a nearby dresser. It was then that he remembered his Fairy.

The boy scanned his flashlight across the room, settling on the two boys in their beds for a moment. They lay still in their sleep. The dresser in between their beds shook. The boy rushed to it, opening drawers, shaking out socks and shirts and turning every pocket he found inside-out.

"Fairy, where is my shadow?" He loudly whispered.

The loveliest sound of bells heard by him and only him answered, telling him that his shadow was in the large chest at the foot of the girl's bed. He turned and saw the dark figure, blacker than any black hole, but full of as much mystery. The figure, exactly his size, stood on top of the chest at the foot of the girl's bed, hands on its hips, mocking him. The boy dashed after his shadow, grasping it by its hands. As soon as he took hold of it, the black mass collapsed in his hold into a fine gauzy dark fabric. Then the boy, frustrated and exhausted on this adventure, fell to his knees and began to cry.

"Boy," there was that small voice that had taken him to fantastic realms so many times. "Why are you crying?"

He looked at the girl in awe. The reflection of the sparkling nightlights around her bed danced in her eyes like fireflies on a cool summer's night. Her face bright with wonder. He wanted to tell her why he was really crying, because now that he was finally so close to her he could feel her heavy, strained breath. He could feel every tear that rolled down her cheeks across so many weeks. He could hear clearly each and every one of her cries and pleas for the sickness to please go away, and for her world to return to how it once was. Nothing, he knew, would ever be the same again for her.

He did not know how to answer her, and so he asked, "What is your name?"

"I'm certainly not going to tell you that," she said. "Who are you? How did you get in our room?" She looked at the closed door.

"I did not come that way." He turned to the open window. The night breeze shook the nightlights, casting golden shadows across the wall.

She kicked off her bedsheets and rushed to the window, looking down and to the sides, knowing there was no way the boy could have climbed this way up. There was nothing to hold onto. The wind tossed her hair, and she closed the window.

"I don't want them to get sick," she cried, thinking of her brothers as she turned to face the strange boy in her room.

"What is your name?" She asked him.

"I'm certainly not going to tell you that," he mimicked her with a smile.

"Well, then..." she noticed now his dark clothes were covered in dust and leaves. "Where do you live?"

"Second star to the right," he said. "And straight on until morning."

"First you lie to me about how you got in my room and now you're lying to me about where you live."

"No," he shook his head. "I'm not lying. That's where I live."

"You're not supposed to leave your house," she almost shouted. "None of us are supposed to leave our houses. Wouldn't your parents be upset that you're not home?"

"I don't have parents," he said.

The girl took a deep breath and then sat down on her bed. "No parents? Is that why you were crying? Did the sickness get them?"

"No," he raised the dark fabric in his hand up to her. "I was crying because I can't get my shadow to stick on."

Before the girl could say anything, he lifted the brilliant black material closer to the light. In that moment, she saw for just a brief second how the fabric escaped his hold and floated in the air on its own before he grasped it tightly again.

"It does that sometimes," he said. "It breaks away when I am afraid."

"Why are you afraid? I'm the one who should be afraid. You're a stranger, after all, and we're not allowed..."

"But I am not a stranger," he interrupted. "I know you very well."

"You don't even know my name."

He nodded. "That's the only thing about you that I don't know, and I would very much like to know it."

She sat in silence, searching his face for a lie, like the lie her mother told her—that one day the scientists would find a cure for the sickness. No matter how hard she searched his face she could not find a trace of a lie, those lines of worry. The girl then reached into the top drawer of her nightstand. "I have tape," she said.

The boy smiled and reached his shadow out to her, knowing that if anyone would handle it with good care, it would be her.

Before the girl took it in her hands, she hesitated. "How can you trust that I am not sick?"

"That's simple," he said. "because I cannot ever get sick. Ever." He turned his back to her, and just like that he felt her press his shadow to his arms, and he heard the peel of the tape and felt each piece sticking to him, and when the last piece of tape was finished attaching his shadow back onto him, he felt whole again. And in that moment, and in this place full of misery and disease and destruction, he knew that if anyone could put him back together, it would be her.

"Thank you," he smiled. "That feels much better."

"How old are you?" She asked him, and she could immediately see that he did not like that question.

"I don't know, and it does not matter because I am very young. When I was born I ran away. I ran away as soon as I heard my mother and father talking about the things of this world, of panic, of desperation. I did not want to live in a world with endless sirens and flashing blue and red lights that signaled so much pain. I will always be young. I will never grow old."

"If you do not want to handle anything from this world, then why are you here?"

"Because I heard you telling your stories of enchanted castles and forests, of ogres and beasts, giants and beanstalks, and of such fierce princesses who fought and defeated death, and then one night I heard you laughing in your sleep. I thought only fairies could laugh like that."

She had not heard of fairies in such a long time. Her mother had read to her stories about fairies, of their magical dust. She tried to hold on to those memories, of sweet stories told to her by her mother, but as the sun rose and set each day over and over, she grew to forget about fairy dust, and could only think of the ash and smoke outside her window.

"I don't believe in fairies, or anything anymore."

"You believe in me, and I am here, and so is my fairy."

"There's a fairy? In this room?"

He pressed a finger to his lips and pointed to one of the empty cans on the floor.

"Listen."

The girl did not hear anything.

He reached into a can and pulled out a gold bracelet.

"That's Mother's," she said. "She fell in the kitchen, and the snap must have broken. I helped her to bed where Father had already been for some days. Her cough was just awful, and she kept trying to sit up, but I told her I would dash back down to the kitchen and find her bracelet. I found it under the table, but by the time I got back to her room she was asleep. I told her I would hold onto it until she woke up."

He reached into the same can again and this time produced a small shimmering bit of light. It was like a speck of sunlight in his hand. He placed it in her palm and watched as golden light filled in the dark shadows around her eyes and her sunken cheeks.

"We all grow old," she said, "and die."

"Not me, and now not you. Come away with me."

"Where?"

"Where we will live forever, you and me and all my Lost Children."

"Who are they?"

"They are the children who were left behind. They are the children who did not stop laughing. You need someone to tell your wonderful stories to. I need you to tell me your stories."

She looked to her brothers who had been asleep far too long. She moved over to their beds and sat on the floor in between them.

"Once upon a time, there was a little girl who lived in a house all alone, in a city all alone because one day the sickness came and took everyone whom she loved. Then one night, she made a wish, a simple wish, a Just In Case wish to be taken away to someplace happy, where there was no more sadness, no more loneliness, no more sickness and no more death. And then, her Just In Case came."

She stood up and pulled down the bedsheet on one of the beds, revealing the long-desiccated corpse of her brother. She gave him a kiss on his forehead and turned to the next bed and did the same, whispering, "I love you."

"They are no longer sick," the boy said. "They are sleeping and forever alive in one of your stories."

He took her hand and led her to the window. "And now we fly."

"Fly?"

"I will teach you how to jump on the back of the wind and then away we will go. Just think of something happy, think of the time before the sickness when you could feel the sun on your skin. When you could hold your brother's hands and spin and laugh in your backyard as your dog ran around your feet."

"What do you think of when you fly?" She asked him. "I only ever think of you."

"But you don't even know my name..."

"I'm Peter," he finally said.

"I'm Wendy," she finally offered.

And just then the window blew open and the stars burst in the heavens and like birds they flew.

ABOUT THE AUTHORS

Hector Acosta is an Edgar-and ITW-nominated writer. His work has been featured in Shotgun Honey, Thuglit, *¡Pa'Que Tu Lo Sepas!* and more. He's also the author of *Hardway*, a wrestling inspired novella and continues to work on a novel. He currently resides in Houston with his wife, dog, and cats.

Scott Adlerberg is the author of four books. They include *Graveyard Love* (2016), a psychological thriller that takes place in the dead of winter in upstate New York, and *Jack Waters* (2018), a story of revenge and revolution on a Caribbean island in the early twentieth century. He contributes pieces regularly to Criminal Element, Crime Reads, and Mystery Tribune, and every summer he hosts the Word for Word Reel Talks film series in Bryant Park in Manhattan. Most recently, his essay on Chester Himes had a place in the book *Sticking It to the Man: Revolution and Counterculture in Pulp and Popular Fiction from 1950 to 1980*. He lives in Brooklyn.

Gemma Amor is the Bram Stoker Award-nominated author of *Dear Laura, Cruel Works of Nature, Til the Score is Paid*, and *White Pines*. She is also a podcaster, illustrator and voice actor, and is based in Bristol, in the U.K. Many of her stories have been adapted into audio dramas and live performances by the wildly popular NoSleep Podcast, and her work also features on shows like Shadows at the Door, Creepy, and The Grey Rooms. She is the co-creator, writer and voice actor for horror-comedy podcast 'Calling Darkness', which also features TV and film star Kate Siegel. Heavily influenced by classical literature, Gothic romance, tragedy and heroism, she is most at home in front of a fire with a single malt and a dog-eared copy of anything by Angela Carter.

Ann Dávila Cardinal is a novelist and director of student recruitment for Vermont College of Fine Arts, where she earned her MFA in Writing. Her novels *Five Midnights* (2019) and the sequel, *Category Five* (2020), are published by Tor Teen. Ann lives north of Stowe, Vermont with her husband Doug and son Carlos, and likes to spend her free time cycling, doing fiber arts, and preparing for the zombie apocalypse. Though a work of fiction, "Misery Loves Company" was based on the actual ghost that haunts College Hall at VCFA. However, Anna has not infiltrated the college's Zoom meetings. Yet.

V. Castro is a Mexican-American writer from San Antonio, Texas now residing in the UK. As a full-time mother she dedicates her time to her family and writing Latinx narratives in horror, erotic horror and science fiction. Connect with Violet via Instagram and Twitter @vlatinalondon or www.vvcastro.com. She can also be found on Goodreads and Amazon.

Jen Conley is the author of the Anthony Award-nominated short story collection, "Cannibals: Stories from the Edge of the Pine Barrens" and the YA novel, "Seven Ways to Get Rid of Harry." She lives in Brick, New Jersey.

Terri Lynn Coop is a recovering lawyer and author. Her superpower is teaching high school. She and her sidekick, Foxy, are currently self-quarantined in St. Pete, Florida and both are thrilled to not be in Kansas anymore. Check out her award-winning mystery series featuring disgraced lawyer Juliana Martin wherever fine books are sold. She's also been known to blog and hang out at www.terrilynncoop.com.

S.A. Cosby is an award-winning writer from southeastern Virginia. He is the author of the hardboiled southern mystery *My Darkest Prayer* and the rural neo-noir novel *Blacktop Wasteland.*

Alex DiFrancesco is a multi-genre writer whose work has appeared in The Washington Post, Tin House, Vol. 1 Brooklyn, The New Ohio Review, Brevity, and more. Their essay collection *Psychopomps* (Civil Coping Mechanisms Press) and their novel *All City* (Seven Stories Press) were both released in 2019, and their short story collection *Transmutation* (Seven Stories Press) is forthcoming in 2021.

Michelle Garza and Melissa Lason have been dubbed the Sisters of Slaughter for their work in the horror and dark fantasy genres. Their work has been published by Thunderstorm Books, Sinister Grin Press, Bloodshot Books, and Death's Head Press. Their debut novel, *Mayan Blue*, was nominated for a Bram Stoker award.

Rob Hart is the author of *The Warehouse*, which was translated into more than 20 languages. His next novel, *Paradox Hotel*, is coming soon from Ballantine. He's also the author of the Ash McKenna crime series, the food-noir short story collection *Take-Out*, and *Scott Free* with James Patterson. Find more at www.robwhart.com.

Gabino Iglesias is a writer, teacher, editor, and book reviewer living Austin, TX. His reviews appear in places such as NPR and the Los Angeles Review of Books. He's the author of *Zero Saints* and *Coyote Songs*, which won the Wonderland Book Award for Best Novel. His work has been published in five languages, optioned for film, and nominated to the Bram Stoker Award and the Locus Award. He recently edited *Both Sides: Stories from the Border* for Agora. He teaches creative writing at Southern New Hampshire University's online MFA program. You can find him on Twitter at @Gabino_Iglesias.

Nick Kolakowski is the Derringer Award-nominated author of *Maxine Unleashes Doomsday* and *Boise Longpig Hunting Club*, as well as the *Love & Bullets* trilogy of novellas. He lives and writes in New York City. Visit him virtually at nickkolakowski.com.

Angel Luis Colón is the Derringer- and Anthony Award-nominated writer of five books, including his latest novel *Hell Chose Me.* In his down time, he edits anthologies and produces the writer interview podcast, the bastard title.

Richie Narvaez is the award-winning, frequently hand-washing author of *Roachkiller and Other Stories.* His debut novel *Hipster Death Rattle* was published in 2019. His newest novel is the YA thriller *Holly Hernandez and the Death of Disco.*

Cynthia (Cina) Pelayo is an International Latino Book Award winning author. She has written *Loteria*, *Santa Muerte*, *Poems of My Night*, and multiple short stories, poems and articles. Her upcoming novel, *Children of Chicago*, will be published by Agora.

Renee Asher Pickup is a writer living in Joshua Tree, California. She's a USMC Veteran, a mellowed-out punk, and loves writing about bad things happening to flawed people. Find more at: reneeasherpickup.com.

Eryk Pruitt is a screenwriter, author, and filmmaker. He is the author of the Southern crime novels *Dirtbags, Hashtag,* and *What We Reckon,* which was nominated for the 2018 Anthony Award. His short fiction is collected in *Townies and Other Stories of Southern Mischief* by Polis Books . He is the writer and co-host of the popular true crime podcast *The Long Dance.* He lives in Durham, North Carolina, with his wife Lana and cat Busey. A full list of credits can be found at erykpruitt.com.

Johnny Shaw is the author of a whole mess of novels, including *Dove Season, Big Maria*, and the upcoming *The Southland.* He has also been known to write under a few pseudonyms to keep the completists on their toes. Johnny is currently in lockdown in Portugal.

Steve Weddle is best known for his novel *Country Hardball*, which The New York Times called "downright dazzling." The follow-up story, "South of Bradley," appeared in Playboy magazine. He is the co-founder of the crime fiction collective Do Some Damage, the co-creator of the noir magazine Needle, and a regular instructor at LitReactor.

CPSIA information can be obtained
at www.ICGtesting.com
Printed in the USA
BVHW031758080920
588374BV00001B/7

9 781951 709174